AS THEY ROUNDED THE TURN, they saw a creature made entirely of fire standing against the far wall. Blue flames dripped from his extremities as though they were melting, dropping flaming gobbets on the floor.

The horrible spectre stood at least thirty feet tall and lit up the entire cavern with the sickly glow of dead meat fluorescing in darkness.

The evil spectre roared with laughter and the waves of heat singed their skin and shriveled the beards of the army of deep-dwelling dwarves.

It bent forward, a single blazing hand on its fiery hips and pointed at the dwarves. The point-man of the formation began to scream, grabbed his helmet and ripped it off his head. His hair was on fire and his scalp could be seen to bubble with the intense heat. His face and arms were covered with blisters that sloughed off, revealing the cooked flesh beneath them. His screams turned to a sickening gurgle and the unfortunate dwarf dropped to the ground, dead.

This awful sight was viewed with horror by all those who stood behind him, awaiting their turn.

GREYHAWK™
ADVENTURES

Book 5

THE DEMON HAND

by Rose Estes

A journey to a land of wizards, demons and magical gems

Cover art by Clyde Caldwell
Interior art by John and Laura Lakey

TSR, Inc.

GREYHAWK ADVENTURES

Book 5

THE DEMON HAND

©Copyright 1988 TSR, Inc. All Rights Reserved.

Al characters and names in this book are fictitious. Any resemblance to actual persons, living or dead, or to actual places or events, is purely coincidental.

Distributed to the book trade in the United States by Random House, Inc., and in Canada by Random House of Canada, Ltd.

Distributed in the United Kingdom by TSR UK Ltd.

Distributed to the toy and hobby trade by regional distributors.

ADVANCED DUNGEONS & DRAGONS, AD&D, DRAGONLANCE, and ENDLESS QUEST are registered trademarks owned by TSR, Inc. PRODUCTS OF YOUR IMAGINATION, GREYHAWK, and the TSR logo are trademarks owned by TSR, Inc.

First Printing, February, 1988
Printed in the United States of America.
Library of Congress Catalog Card Number: 87-51253

9 8 7 6 5 4 3 2 1

ISBN: 0-88038-542-1

TSR, Inc.
P.O. Box 756
Lake Geneva, WI
53147 U.S.A.

TSR UK Ltd.
The Mill, Rathmore Road
Cambridge CB1 4AD
United Kingdom

This book is dedicated to
Lyn, Lael and Linda Buchanan,
old and best friends, without whom
this book could not have been written.

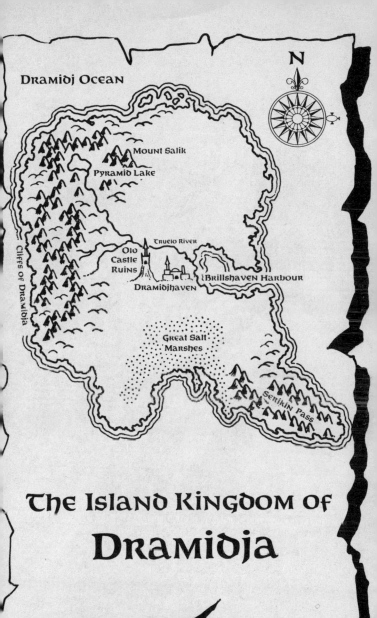

Dramidj Ocean

Mount Salik

Pyramid Lake

Trueio River

Old Castle Ruins

Dramidjhaven

Brillshaven Harbour

Cliffs of Dramidja

Great Salt Marshes

Serikin Pass

The Island Kingdom of
Dramidja

Chapter 1

THE DEMON MAELFESH was restless; even worse, he was bored. Life, or what passed for it, on the abysmal plane of existence inhabited by demons, was pretty dull after the first few thousand years.

Maelfesh shifted on his throne, and even the constantly shifting panorama of lost souls, pressing their agonized faces against the clear crystal sides of the throne, begging wordlessly for release, somehow failed to cheer him.

Maelfesh drummed his fingers against the armrest, sending several hundred poor souls writhing away in torment as he sighed, and wondered what there was left to do.

In his younger days, as a lesser demon, he had done all the usual things as he worked his way up the ladder; creating mischief and bringing havoc to humanity at the chaotic behest of the more powerful demons whom he had been forced to serve.

Eventually, however, creating two-headed calves for superstitious farmers and levying lifelong curses began to pall, and he began looking for a way to advance more quickly.

His opportunity came sooner than he expected when he cleverly came into possession of the magic amulet of the demon prince who commanded his services. This magic amulet held all of his vital essences, his soul as it were, and in its absence, the demon prince became extremely vulnerable. It was with almost real regret that Maelfesh banished his boss to a truly abysmal plane, where he would languish forever.

With the magic amulet's help, Maelfesh filled his former employer's shoes, or flaming footsteps if you will, with new zeal. No war was too petty, no plague too minor, that Maelfesh could not be counted on to lend a fiery hand.

But, in time, even major wars and wholesale slaughter began to lose their appeal and Maelfesh looked about for blacker pastures. With the help of several other demon princes (who between them foolishly thought they could control Maelfesh) he challenged a great and even more powerful demon lord.

When all was said and done, there were four more demons on the abysmal plane and Maelfesh took on all their combined nastiness himself. It was a tough job, but someone had to do it.

With the demons' passing, Maelfesh inherited a number of useful trinkets. Among them was a gemstone, blue in color, fashioned into a necklet that acted as a window onto the world and allowed Maelfesh to watch the goings on of whomever wore the necklet.

Power attracts power and in the eons that followed,

Maelfesh grew more and more powerful, clashing with and ultimately subjugating all those who dared to challenge him. Eventually, there were no more challengers and once again, life became dull.

Out of boredom, Maelfesh allowed himself to be drawn back into the game, toying with the minor politics of a mildly interesting race on the prime material plane, a race that called itself human.

Out of that same ennui, Maelfesh had loaned the blue stone amulet to a king on a small island called Dramidja. The king had used the amulet to retain power and in return had sent his only daughter as payment to a lesser demon (toward whom Maelfesh felt kindly disposed.) The demon wished to drink her virginal blood, or some such nonsense, in an effort to renew himself.

Maelfesh had viewed this hackneyed plot out of sheer boredom. But the plot became suddenly interesting with the advent of a player from a primitive subculture called Wolf Nomads, who driveled on endlessly about loyalty and honor and other such noble creeds that gave Maelfesh heartburn.

This Wolf Nomad, one Mika-oba by name, had been thrust against his will into the position of escorting the princess, who conveniently lay in a deep enchanted sleep, to the demon who awaited her.

Maelfesh had watched with interest as Mika-oba acted in a most decidedly unwolf nomadly manner, protecting himself first and foremost. This Mika-oba was a man after Maelfesh's own black heart.

In spite of all obstacles, Mika, the princess, Mika's companion, a great muscular oaf named Hornsbuck, and their two wolves, succeeded in reaching the lair of the demon.

And it was there that Maelfesh watched with glee and admiration as Mika, with the aid of the magic stone whose true use he did not suspect, dispatched the unfortunate demon to that same abysmal plane that was undoubtedly beginning to grow crowded.

Just to keep things interesting, Maelfesh, who hadn't had so much fun in centuries, actually made a real appearance, exhibiting one of his many manifestations to the Wolf Nomad. He wondered briefly if the man realized the honor bestowed upon him.

Out of sheer beneficence, Maelfesh had helped the nomad heal his wolf, who was bleeding to death, and gave him a new mission—that of taking the princess, whom the nomad had cleverly turned into a wolf, Hornsbuck and their companion wolves, on a journey to the walled city of Exag.

To make certain that Mika took his mission seriously, Maelfesh gave him a demon finger and promised him that with each and every transgression, the hand would gain another demon digit.

Exag was a most amusing spot, one of Maelfesh's favorites, a city run by religious fanatics who believed that the sun would not rise each day unless it were greeted with a blood sacrifice, preferably a heart ripped from a living body.

Maelfesh was proud to think that he'd had a lot to do with fostering that particular notion, and he liked to check in now and then just to see how the Exagian fanatics were getting along.

They had always gotten along well, until Mika arrived. Maelfesh scowled and thumped on the armrest of his throne with a massive fiery fist, giving several thousand imprisoned souls a howling headache.

Against all odds, Mika had managed to reduce the entire city of Exag to ruins, destroying the empire Maelfesh had so lovingly nurtured.

There was little pleasure to be gained from the fact that the princess had been made pregnant by Mika's own wolf and that Mika's entire hand had become that of a demon.

Maelfesh had even been cheated out of the pleasure of banishing Mika to some dreadful plane where he would spend thousands of years dying in torment, for the stupid man had managed to get himself killed.

Maelfesh had watched in glee as the high priest prepared to cut Mika's heart out, when, out of nowhere (the sky actually), there appeared a harpy who snatched Mika off the stone altar and carried him away in her talons.

Maelfesh received a certain amount of vicarious pleasure via the magic stone, as the harpy bore Mika aloft and then coupled with him against his will. He was only slightly cheered when, her needs sated, the harpy discarded Mika and allowed him to plummet to his death.

But there the story had ended for the harpy, stupid creature that she was, had snatched the necklet from Mika's neck and thence discarded it where it lay forgotten among the gnawed bones and scraps of fur that littered her aerie. There was no pleasure in watching the horrible creature's dreary life and Maelfesh had turned away in disgust.

He had been extremely irritable since Mika's death and whole worlds had felt his wrath. He consoled himself by tumbling several kingdoms and reversing the weather, flooding a desert nation and drying up a jungle, but nothing helped.

The sheer truth of it was that he had become fond of Mika, had actually looked forward to his exploits and wondered what he would do next. Mika was the one truly imaginative individual Maelfesh had encountered in eons and he missed him.

Lately, a niggling thought had come to mind. Was it possible that Mika had survived the fall? Could he still be alive? Maelfesh burned bright at the very thought, searing those unfortunate souls pressed against the surface of the throne, causing them untold further agony.

Maelfesh leaped to his feet, a cascade of sparks trailing behind him, as he determined to search out the Wolf Nomad wherever he might be.

If he were still alive, Maelfesh would find him and then put an end to him as truly befit one of his caliber.

Humming happily, some mournful dirge written back in the depths of the plague years, his humor fully restored, Maelfesh set off on his quest.

Chapter 2

MIKA HUNG ONTO THE RAIL of the sailing ship that carried them to the island of Dramidja and was heartily sick, wishing for the millionth time that he had never left land. He watched the heaving waves through slitted, jaundiced eyes and wondered how he could have ever thought the ocean beautiful.

"Cheer up, lad, we'll be there in two days' time." barked a gruff cheery voice as an immense hand thumped Mika on the back.

Mika clung to the rail, looked up at Hornsbuck, who stood easily on the swaying deck, his green eyes sparkling and long red-blond hair and beard flowing in the stiff breeze. Mika snarled, wishing he had the strength to kill him.

"The lad seems a bit under the weather, my beauty," said Hornsbuck as Lotus Blossom, his massive consort, joined him at the rail, her arms filled with a blanketed bundle.

"And how are the little devils today?" Hornsbuck asked as he parted the blanket and looked down on the peacefully sleeping forms, noting the soft down that covered their limbs and the long, wolflike ears that peeked above their otherwise human faces.

"Quiet for once," said Lotus Blossom. "But I'll be glad when Mika turns the princess back from a wolf to a woman so's she can take care of 'em herself."

Hornsbuck poked the blanket aside still further and examined them carefully.

"Hard to tell what the little critters will look like as they get older. Not having fur proper, just this downy stuff all over, they could almost get away as bein' human. Specially since they don't have no tails, just these little nubs."

"Aye," agreed Lotus Blossom, "But you be overlooking something. Aside of these here ears," she said, gently flicking a delicate pink-lined wolf ear that peeked up out of the blanket, "they've got these dark pink snuffly noses. They're cute, I grant you, but they'd be kinda hard to pass off as human."

"They could comb their hair over their ears an' maybe nobody'll notice their noses, just think they have a cold, like," Hornsbuck said hopefully. Lotus Blossom just screwed her face up in disgust and tucked the blanket around the two sleeping infants.

"Be there soon," said Hornsbuck, turning his gaze back to the ocean. "Wonder what it'll be like. Wonder if we'll be able to find any of those magic stones."

"We'll find them," gasped Mika. "I don't care what I have to do, I'll find them. I'm not going through the rest of my life with this!" He tried to lift his gauntleted hand, but it clenched the rail stubbornly and refused to let go. Mika snarled at it in fury and beat on it, trying to wrench it free.

It was becoming an all too common happening. More and more often the damned demon hand refused to do his bidding, obeying its own strange desires.

Mika never knew when it would happen, sometimes it was merely irritating. But the time it reached out in a crowded tavern and tweaked a tavern maid on a portion of her anatomy not normally tweaked in public, it was downright dangerous.

At times, he was glad for the hand. He had won several arm wrestling matches in Ekbir that helped keep them alive through the long cold winter. The hand had saved his life as well, when it reached out and grabbed the branch of the pine tree after the harpy had had her way with him. But still, it would be nice to have a human hand instead of the green monstrosity with its ugly yellow talons. Just then, another fit of nausea took him and his hand was all but forgotten.

The wolves, indifferent to his suffering, lay sleeping atop a warm hatch cover, undisturbed by the motion of the swaying ship. TamTur, Mika's wolf and the largest of the three, was dark gray in color, tipped with silver on ears, throat, tail and belly.

RedTail, Hornsbuck's wolf, a stocky, square-muzzled male, was the eldest of the wolves. His coat was an odd reddish-blond, like that of Hornsbuck's beard, and his eyes were amber.

The princess rounded out the trio, small, slender and dark. She lay curled in the hollow of Tam's belly, her mismatched eyes, one blue, one green, opening periodically to check on the human who held her cubs.

It was she who had the most to win or lose, for it was her kingdom the ship was carrying them toward. None of them knew what they would find when they landed, for the kingdom had been leaderless since the king had forfeited his crown to Maelfesh. That was the price of losing his power.

Mika, Hornsbuck and Lotus Blossom had discussed the issue at length during the long winter and had decided that it was best for the princess to remain in wolfen form until after they landed on the island. If the kingdom had been seized by factions other than those loyal to the throne, she would be far safer as a wolf than as a princess. Not to mention that Mika still had not the slightest idea how to change her back, though he felt certain the answer lay somewhere in his trusty spell book.

Their fears were ill-founded, for as soon as they sighted land, it was clear that the family banner still flew from the ramparts.

The island appeared out of the sea mists like a story out of a fairy tale, the land lush and green, rising steeply out of the sapphire sea with its lofty peaks lost in the clouds.

"Well, princess, it seems you might have a throne to claim after all," said Mika as he stepped shakily off the ship onto the stone quay and felt his legs buckle and sway beneath him.

"Aye," said Hornsbuck as he cupped his huge hand beneath Mika's elbow, helping him along until he regained his land legs. "Tis a grand sight, all these flags an' such waving in the wind. So let's stop all this yappin' and get on to the castle!"

"Not yet!" Mika said unexpectedly. "We should

stop for the night and make ourselves ready. It would be wise to learn what has happened here since the king and the princess disappeared. We don't want to blunder into some sort of trap."

"Aye, you have a point there!" mused Hornsbuck, as he twirled a bit of beard between his massive fingers, always a sure sign that he was thinking.

"I could do with a bit of ale myself," said Lotus Blossom. With all in agreement, save the princess, who stared after them angrily, they set off in search of a friendly tavern.

They ended their quest beneath the swinging sign of the Sea Serpent Inn, deftly portrayed by a flagon of ale surrounded by the coils of the sea beast.

Rooms were quickly arranged through the landlord, a portly gentleman of middle years who was foolish enough to say that the wolves would be required to stay in the stables.

The sudden silence that followed this statement, as well as the hands that crept toward their swords, quickly induced him to change his mind.

The rooms were bright and airy and the beds, while intended for smaller folk, were clean and almost comfortable.

The travelers used the day to their advantage, strolling through the town, which was mainly composed of shops that catered to the needs of sailing men and their ships. The streets were neat and clean and paved with crushed white shell that had been dredged from the harbor.

Shopkeepers with sharp eyes, quick to judge the weight of their purses, took note of their passage as they perused the narrow winding streets. The shops were a hodgepodge, unlike those of Eru-Tovar, the capital of the Wolf Nomads, where every guild had its own street. Here, wine shops rubbed shoulders with green grocers, which stood next to rope chandlers, which in turn shared window fronts with swordsmiths'.

The citizens were no less a mixture, betraying the many cultures whose ships had called at their port. There, a long, hooked beak of a nose testified to the presence of pirate ancestry. Here was the swarthy dark skin of the Blackmoorians. And that one there, surely that was the short, broad swagger of a dwarf.

Clothing was also a strange admixture of burnooses and tunics, sashes and hoods, leather and embroidery. This was truly a meeting place of the worlds.

Leaving the broadly accented, multiple-tongued throngs behind them, the travelers wandered into what was clearly the heart of the city, where the townsfolk and their families lived. This section reflected the obvious prosperity of the kingdom.

Homes were constructed not of wood or clay, but of brick and limestone, and were thickly thatched, bordered with flower-lined walks and dense vegetable beds. Despite the trauma that had affected the ruling family, it was apparent that the residents of the kingdom had not suffered.

The castle, which was the travelers' real goal, lay high above them on the highest peak of the island. The only access was a single road carved into the mountain in a series of steep switchbacks. Admittance to this road was gained only after passing through a heavily guarded checkpoint.

They did not attempt to pass the guards but merely eyed them curiously as though they were out for a casual stroll. The guards, however, numbering ten strong, watched them closely, their hands never leaving the hilts of their swords. Evidently they did not view three such well-armed individuals, accompanied by a pack of wolves, as the normal run-of-the-mill tourists.

Whatever the status of its rulers, the kingdom had all the appearances of being well-run and in a state of military preparedness. There were more than the usual number of guards stationed at all the likely places and several that were unlikely. The more Mika and Hornsbuck saw of them, the more uncomfortable they became.

They received another nasty jolt that evening as they took their evening meal in the common dining hall of the Sea Serpent Inn.

"A toast to the king!" cried one of the diners and everyone in the hall lifted their mugs on high and toasted the king's health.

The color drained from Mika's face as he turned to his neighbor and said, "The . . . king? Is the king feeling, uh, hale and hearty?"

"Why, of course!" the fellow replied cheerfully.

Mika felt his knees quiver, for Mika had last seen the princess's father imprisoned in Exag, awaiting his death.

This same king had given the princess to the demon in return for the power to keep his throne. He had not realized that the wolf at Mika's side was his daughter, the princess, until the moment she leapt for his throat. And by then, it was too late to explain.

"I heard that he was away," Mika said carefully.

"Aye, that he was," replied the man, taking a long draft of the foamy brew. "But he's returned, back where he belongs."

Stunned by the unexpected and unlikely news, Mika hurried his equally astonished companions and the snarling princess away from the table, barely allowing Lotus Blossom time to pocket four chickens for a late snack before he led them to their rooms.

"How can he be alive?" hissed Mika. "There's no way! She killed him, I saw it myself! What are we going to do? This ruins everything!"

"Why? Because we can't just waltz past the guards, march up to the castle, invite ourselves in and ask the king to turn the kingdom over to his daughter?" said Hornsbuck.

"Let's just kill him again," Lotus Blossom said with a shrug. "He's a rat. I know it. You know it. Hornsbuck knows it and the princess here knows it, too. Kill him again and be done with it. You make everything too complicated, Mika."

Mika turned and looked at the princess, thinking that perhaps she would object to having her father killed, now that her anger had cooled. But she stared back at him, her odd blue and green eyes burning brightly. He shuddered, vowing never, ever to have daughters.

"I think we've got to get in that castle and see what's going on," said Mika. "See this king in person and find out if he's really the princess's father. Maybe he's an imposter."

They discussed many plans during the course of the evening, and just as Lotus Blossom finished the last of the chickens, splitting their bones and sucking out the marrow before tossing the remains to the wolves, they came up with a plan that satisfied them all.

"All right, then," said Mika. "We're decided. I'll use some simple magic and change myself into an old man, present myself to the guards and tell them that I'm an emmissary from Perrenland and must speak to the king right away on business of great importance."

"Why Perrenland?" Lotus Blossom asked, accompanying her question with a great belch. "I never knowed anyone who come from there."

"Precisely," replied Mika, who had learned to ignore some of her less ladylike habits. "That's why. Maybe they haven't either. All right. Now once I'm inside the castle, I can meet with the king and see if he's real or an imposter. Frankly, I don't see how he could be alive. The princess here ripped out his throat."

Mika could not stop himself from looking at the princess, and saw a bright, cheerful light fill her eyes. He shuddered and turned his eyes away.

"So what will we do if he's an imposter?" rumbled Hornsbuck. "Or even worse, what will we do if he's not?"

Neither Mika nor Lotus Blossom had any answers and, deciding to think on it further on the morrow, they bid each other good night. Hornsbuck and Lotus Blossom took one room and Mika and the wolves took the other.

Mika tucked the pillow beneath his head and settled himself for the night. He saw no real difficulty in getting into the castle. In fact, it seemed that his only real problem lay in convincing Tam, the princess and the cubs to give him a fair share of the bed. In this he was sadly mistaken.

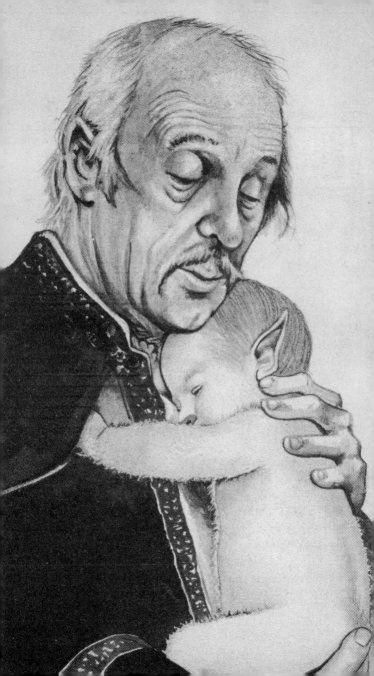

Chapter 3

MIKA DREAMT THAT HE WAS MAKING LOVE to a beautiful woman. She gripped him tightly and he could feel the weight of her on his body. She was a hefty lass, he could barely move beneath her. He smiled as he tried to raise his hands to stroke her satiny skin, but felt himself restrained. Ahh, so she wanted to play that game, did she?

He felt her teeth nibble on his throat; her very sharp teeth. In fact, it almost hurt. Damn it, it DID hurt! He heard Tam growl and the sound of it brought him out of his dream. The growl was harsh and gutteral, indicating danger.

His eyes opened. He blinked, thinking that perhaps it was really a nightmare. Unfortunately, the armed, uniformed figures before him did not waver and disappear, indicating to his sleep-befuddled mind that they were all too real.

"Rise and shine, Wolf Man," said a hard voice, "and none of your magical tricks. The king wants to see you!"

The spear point pricking Mika's throat convinced him that it was in his own best interests to cooperate. After all, he had wanted to see the king, hadn't he?

Graciously overlooking the fact that the guards were shoving him before them, and none too gently at that, Mika stumbled out into the corridor, the wolves growling and snarling at his heels.

One of the guards held the two squirming infants in his large hands, examining them with a curious expression. To Mika's intense pleasure, one of the small creatures, the female, he thought, growled in a fierce parody of her parents and seized the man's finger, her sharp little milk teeth breaking the skin and drawing blood as well as an angry exclamation.

The guard fell back and dropped the infants as though he had suddenly discovered that he held an armload of vipers. Mika leaped forward and grabbed the babes in midair, his heart pounding in his chest.

"Down, Tam! Stop!" he cried, commanding Tam and the princess to heed his warning, for thick, menacing growls poured from their throats and slaver dripped from their snarling jaws.

"NO!" barked Mika, as the wolves crouched to spring, their muscles quivering with tension, at the guard who had hidden himself behind a wall of spear points.

Thankfully, the wolves obeyed his command, yet circled away and watched still. Mika knew that they would not forget. He shivered, even as he held the squirming, down-covered infants safe against his chest, grateful that he was not the guard. But then a thought struck him and he wondered if he would not rather be the guard than himself. At the moment, his own future did not look too promising.

The female stretched in his arms and yawned, ending in a high-pitched little squeal. She found his finger with her tiny, pink, pawlike fingers and gripped it tightly, her clear blue-green eyes looking up at him through slitted lids. His heart gave a lurch and he hugged them to him. The male, round tummy plumped between front and hind limbs, had slept undisturbed through the entire event.

The guards, their initial fear turning to anger, prodded Mika with their spears again and waited until the wolves slunk in front of them, snarling still, before they proceeded.

"Here, here! This ain't no way to treat a lady!" rumbled a loud, angry voice, and Mika saw Lotus Blossom, her more than ample charms threatening to escape the confines of the blanket she held around her, struggling in the grip of two massive guards.

Hornsbuck was lost beneath a heaving mantle of guards, clinging desperately to whatever bits of him they could hold.

"Tell him to leave off," said the captain of the guards as he pointed the tip of his sword at the pups. "And don't even think to set the wolves on me, I'll get at least one of these mongrels before they reach me and cleave you in half as well."

"Hornsbuck! Lotus!" Mika said quickly, noting the steely look in the guard's eye. "Leave off. This gentleman and his associates have come to escort us to the king."

The bucking mass of men slowly stilled as Hornsbuck stood upright. Men dropped off his arms, back and neck, and let go their grip on his hair and ears, more than willing to escape without permanent personal damage.

"They have a funny way of announcing themselves," growled Hornsbuck. "Whyn't they say so? Come on, Lotus, us'll get dressed." And if the guards had any objections, they did not voice them, stepping aside hastily as the huge couple returned to their room to dress.

Night was still evident as they stepped outside the tavern. The dawn star had not yet risen and the "*skree, skree, skree*" of bats, wheeling and dipping above the harbor as they fed on small insects, was clearly heard.

"Strange time for visiting," muttered Lotus Blossom.

"The king don't sleep no more," volunteered the captain as he prodded Mika forward while maintaining a safe distance. Mika wondered at that, a nasty suspicion coming to mind, but he thrust it away and saved his energy for the climb ahead.

The sky was paling over the water to the east as they turned the final curve and presented themselves before the palace guard.

They were ushered into the palace without a word being spoken, the guard standing back against the huge oaken doors as though afraid of coming into contact with them. Mika noticed that the guards would not meet his eyes, directing their gazes elsewhere as he stared at them, trying to discern just what it was that felt so peculiar.

Torches were lit in the sconces beside the wide entrance, but beyond that point all was dark.

"Are you sure we're expected?" muttered Hornsbuck, his voice echoing around them as they slowly advanced down the dark corridor.

The guards did not reply but the feeling of unease lay heavily on the air and Mika sensed that the guards were as nervous as they.

RedTail and TamTur hung back around their legs and only the princess seemed unafraid, in fact even eager to venture ahead. She strode forward boldly, at times lost to their vision, obviously no stranger to the dark corridors.

"Turn here," growled one of the guards, poking Mika with the point of his spear, and Mika had the distinct impression that the man was afraid. It was at that exact moment that Mika really began to worry.

They were momentarily halted by a pair of crossed swords and then there was the sound of a bar being withdrawn, the squeak of hinges and the flow of air, heavy, dank, musty air on their faces.

And there was something else, some other smell that Mika could not quite put his finger on, something that caused the hair on the back of his neck to prickle. It was evident that the wolves felt it too, for all three of them were growling low in their throats and the princess had dropped back and crouched between the two males.

The haft of a spear rested across Mika's back, pressing him forward. Communicated through its length was the guard's fear, as tangible as a lump of rock. All of Mika's senses were alert now as he cast about him, searching for the first sign of danger.

There was a shower of sparks, bright blue and white, directly ahead of them. The darkness lightened with a soft, pale glow that illuminated rather than lit the room. As their eyes grew accustomed to the light, shapes appeared in the murky gloom.

"Come forward," breathed a cold, imperious voice, and shivers broke out on Mika's spine, for undoubtedly this was the voice of the king, as cold and uncaring as the last time he had heard it.

The guards pushed them forward and the haft of the spear cut deep into Mika's back before he could make himself move. How could the king be alive? He himself had seen the princess rip the man's throat out. Now that was a wound you didn't recover from by a mere heal spell!

They moved closer and closer to the pale light which cast no warmth and burned without the brilliance of fire. A shadowy figure appeared before them, seated on a tall throne literally covered with precious gems that sparkled and shone even in that strange light.

So closely was Mika watching the mysterious shadowy figure, ready to fling himself to one side or the other should danger appear, that it took a while before he realized that the guard had gone.

There was a muffled curse behind him, indicating that Hornsbuck had tripped on the paving stones.

"What's going on here?" roared the big nomad. "Light some torches! Show yourself! What kinda' place is this, anyhow?"

"Spoken with all the diplomacy one has come to expect from a Wolf Nomad," the king said with a dry chuckle and instantly, with the snap of his fingers, a multitude of the strange cold lights appeared, hovering in midair all around the room.

The small party stopped in midstride and stared in

disbelief at the figure on the throne. It was the king, of that there was no doubt, but it was also not the king.

When last Mika saw the princess's father, save for the state of his throat, he was a hale, hearty man of middle years. His flesh was ruddy with good health, his blue eyes were bright and alert, and his hair was blond, thick and plentiful. He had been a full hand-span taller than Mika and a good deal heavier, evidence of ample meals and copious flagons of wine.

The man on the throne bore little resemblance to that earlier figure; had it not been for his voice which remained the same, Mika might not have known him.

The figure that sat slumped on the throne, a bony hand propping up his fragile skull, was but a skeletal caricature of the king. Tufts of thin, white hair had been combed over the mottled skin. The flesh was pale and sickly looking beneath the large brown blotches one normally associated with great age.

The skin hung in wrinkled pouches beneath the eyes which had once sparkled as brightly as the jewels on the throne; now they were dull and lackluster with only the barest trace of their former power.

The nose had collapsed upon itself like a blob of melted candlewax and hung beaked over the querulous, trembling mouth. The skeletal fingers fluttered over its throat, in a futile attempt to conceal the damage of the awful wound, but there was no hiding it. The flesh was twisted and mangled and still bore the marks of the fangs that had ripped and torn.

Magic had been at work here, performed by magic-user or healer, Mika could not say. Magic enough to keep the man alive, but at what cost?

The king moved restlessly, dull eyes gleaming balefully, his spindly shanks all but lost on the hard seat of the throne that had been built to accommodate his larger self.

"Do you like what you see?" he asked coldly. "Do you gain pleasure from my present state? Know you that you are responsible, all of you. Especially Julia, my precious pet."

It had been such a long time since Mika had heard the princess's name that it took him a while to figure out just who the king was talking about.

"Here! Who you calling names?" demanded Lotus Blossom, being unfamiliar with the princess's name and suspecting some sort of insult. She strode forward, hands on her hips, chin outthrust, not the least bit intimidated by this shrunken figure whom she could easily break with one hand.

"Now, Lotus," murmured Hornsbuck as he pulled Lotus Blossom back beside him. "Mayhaps we should let Mika and the princess handle this. It's their quarrel and they'll let us know if they need us."

"He can address me proper if he wants to talk to me," murmured Lotus, her anger fading quickly.

Mika closed his mind to Lotus and Hornsbuck, all of his attention focused on the king. His body had undergone a great transformation but it would be foolish as well as dangerous to assume that his mind and powers had suffered as well. The princess evidently agreed with him for once, for she was watchful, a low growl continuing to rumble from her throat.

"How are you enjoying being a wolf, my dear?" the king asked solicitously, allowing only the tiniest touch of malice to creep into his voice. "You always were a snarling wench, as was your mother before you. This persona befits you more than your human form, it is more true to your nature."

The princess's eyes glittered brightly in the cold light, and Mika watched carefully as she glared at the king. Mika hoped that she would not be drawn into attacking her father a second time.

There was some evil at work here that was not clear to him, but Mika felt that were the princess to attack the king again, it would be her last act. Knowing her as he did, he was not certain that she would not attack, even if she knew the consequences, so great was her hatred.

It was obvious that Tam shared some of Mika's thoughts, for he leaned over and took the back of the princess's neck in his jaws, gently, yet firmly. She trembled in his grasp yet quieted visibly, contenting herself with sinking to the floor and watching the man who was her father with a steady, unblinking gaze.

"I see you've found someone who can control you. By all the demons, it's certain that I never could. Was I so terrible?" the old man asked suddenly, sitting upright and staring down at the princess, oblivious to her glaring, hate-filled eyes.

"If you had only once done as I asked. A husband, children, heirs, no more than any father wishes for his daughter, yet you would not obey me in anything. No man was good enough for you and I watched my hopes for the kingdom die!

"And look what it's come to! All my plans gone now, gone because of you!" The king's voice rose to a shriek and he rose from his seat and staggered down the steps toward the princess who jumped to her feet and bared her fangs despite Tam's warning growl.

"Heirs! Did you say heirs?" Mika said, rushing forward and placing himself between the king and the princess. "You have heirs, sir, both a boy and a girl! Look! Here! Come look at them!" he babbled, thrusting the pups toward the king, hoping to draw his attention away from the princess before blood was shed once again and the rest of them paid for it with their lives.

The king swayed off balance, confusion fogging his eyes. Then, curiosity tugged at him, pulling him toward Mika and the blanket-swathed bundle. He tottered over to Mika and with trembling fingers drew back the blanket and looked inside.

"Why, they're not human, they're, they're," and words seemed to desert him as he stared down at the sleeping pups.

"They're your heirs," Mika said firmly, holding out the tiny female to the old man, hoping he would take her.

The old man took the infant gingerly, holding her awkwardly in the manner of men everywhere, whether king or commoner. Against all expectations, his manner softened. He stared down at the small female, his eyes moist, his hands gentle. Even the princess was disconcerted by the change in the man and watched the king to see what he might do next.

In that brief unguarded moment, Mika saw the man as he had once been before power warped him. He turned and slowly made his way back to the throne, still holding the infant in his arms.

"What will they look like when they grow up?" he

asked softly. "Will they be human or wolf?"

"Do it matter?" queried Lotus Blossom. "They be your kin, your grandchildren, heirs to the throne. If such as you can sit on it, they can scarce do worse."

A hard light came back into the king's eyes at her words and Mika felt like throttling her. Damn! Just as the man was mellowing!

The king turned to Mika and gestured him forward, accepting the second infant, cradling them both in his arms, ignoring the princess's renewed growls. It was evident to Mika that whatever his quarrel with them, the old man would not take his anger out on the infants. Mika dared to hope that the infants might even temper whatever thoughts of revenge the king might entertain.

"And what be you wanting with us?" Lotus Blossom asked, ruining Mika's hope of introducing the subject in a gradual manner or even escaping without any mention of it at all. He turned and glared at Lotus Blossom but the look was wasted as she strode forward, hands resting on her broad hips like some great washerwoman, and planted one large foot on the bottom step of the throne.

A bolt of blue light crackled forth, so fast that Mika did not even sense that it was to happen. It filled the air with the stink of singed hair and the char of burning fabric and Lotus Blossom was thrown clear of the steps, somersaulting head over heels across the floor and coming to a halt literally pasted against the far wall of the antechamber.

"Ah yes, the purpose of your visit. Thank you, my dear, an old man's mind tends to wander," said the king, barely even blinking an eye at Lotus Blossom's astounding display of acrobatics.

He did not attempt to stop Hornsbuck as he hurried across the room and helped Lotus Blossom to her feet. Nor did he pay any attention to the fact that all three wolves were barking and howling and snapping their jaws, dashing back and forth between Lotus Blossom and the throne.

As they staggered back, Lotus leaning heavily on Hornsbuck, holding a hand to her singed and blackened brow, Mika, still thoroughly astounded, could see that while Lotus Blossom was severely stunned, she was obviously still alive.

Although Mika had been watching the king closely, he had seen no movement, no gesture, heard no utterance of magic words; there had been absolutely no warning at all.

"As you know, thanks to your interference with the demon Iuz," said the king as though nothing had happened, "I was unable to fulfill my part of the bargain with the demon Maelfesh. Demons are neither tolerant of failure nor interested in excuses. It did me little good to argue that the fault was not mine.

"As punishment for my failure, I was stripped of my powers, relieved of my kingdom and imprisoned in Exag where, as you will recall, we were all united and my daughter re-affirmed our filial feelings by tearing out my throat.

"As I lay dying, the prison collapsing around me, I vowed that should I live, I would become more powerful than ever I had been, and that none should ever gain control over me again."

"I will not bore you with the long details of my recovery; suffice it to say that recover I did and made my way back here to the island where none knew the story of what had transpired. I have told them only that I suffered a grave illness and such is their loyalty that they have no reason to question the tale.

"This poor body has grown old and frail without the demon's power to support it and it wishes only to be free of its pain. But I knew that you would come in time and so I used my pain and my hatred to keep me alive while I waited. You did not disappoint me."

Mika cleared his throat in the heavy silence that followed. "Why did you wait for us to come? What is it you want of us?" he asked nervously.

"Why, what else?" said the king. "I want what only you want. Descend into the depths of the island, pluck the magical red and blue stones from their hiding places and return them to me. You will find no quarrel with your reward."

I'll bet not, thought Mika. Dead men don't often quarrel at all!

"Why us?" Hornsbuck asked. "Why not just go and get them yourself."

The king looked at Hornsbuck as a teacher might look at a stupid child who has missed an obvious answer. "This body would not take me far," he said patiently. "It is a venture for the strong and the brave."

"Why us?" asked Mika. "Why have you waited for us? Why not just send some of your guards after the gems?"

"I cannot send just *anyone*," answered the king. "The stones carry great power and must not be allowed to fall into the wrong hands. You have handled the stone and come to no harm, as has Julia, so you are the logical choice."

No harm! thought Mika. Little does he know.

"Why do you need the gems?" persisted Hornsbuck. "You may be old but you seem to have all the power you need and you still have your kingdom even if you lost out to the demon."

The king shook his head as though unable to believe Hornsbuck's density. "How long do you think the demon will allow me to keep my kingdom once he learns that I still live? The stones will restore my strength and give me powers that will protect me against the demon in the fight that will surely come."

"This demon, does he sometimes go around all covered in flames?" asked Mika, as his demonic hand opened and closed of its own volition.

"One and the same," admitted the king with a nod, and Mika's head was filled with the thought of the magic gemstones and what they could do for him, restoring his hand to normal for starters', and restoring his manhood also, which had been slightly tarnished by using the blue, or female stone, instead of the red, male stone in his magic.

And, when they found the stones, why bring them back to this nasty old man? What was to prevent them from just taking the stones and leaving? Why, the world could be his for the taking with two such powerful stones!

"No, Mika, don't even think of it," said the king in his soft voice.

"Think of what?" croaked Mika, his throat suddenly dry.

"Don't even think of taking the stones for yourself. I have insurance to protect my interests, insurance that guarantees that you will bring the stones back to me."

"Insurance, what insurance?" Mika asked, wondering if he'd missed something.

"This insurance," replied the king, tickling a round, fat, down-covered belly and smiling at the answering gurgle.

"I know I'd just hate myself afterward, but as we all know, a man must look out for his own best interests." And as he looked down at them, his smile was cold and cruel.

Chapter 4

IN THE END, there was really very little they could do other than agree.

Leaving the infants was the hard part, although as Mika tried to point out to the princess who was nearly wild with rage and had to be restrained following the king's words, the cubs would certainly have been a liability on the dangerous venture. They would undoubtedly be safer in the hands of their own grandfather.

Mika could see the doubt in the princess's eyes and even as he was trying to persuade her that they would be safe, he was doing his best to convince himself. He trusted the king no further than he could throw Hornsbuck with the non-demon hand and that was not very far.

It was Lotus Blossom who finally said the words that they needed to hear. "Look, this king, he don't want to hurt those little ones," she said in her own blunt manner.

"He might not be the best father in the world, but

he knows that you'll never give him the magic stones unless he can give us back the kids in good shape. Let's quit talkin' and get on with it. The sooner we leave, the sooner we get back!''

Mika had persuaded the king to provision them with food, supplies, weapons and even the pouch that contained his book of spells and packet of healing agents. The king had been reluctant to give Mika the spell book, fearing some trick, but he agreed in the end, knowing that they might well have use for it in their quest for the magic gems.

The king was unable to give them any information on where they might find the magic gems. All he knew was that they had been found somewhere in the salt caverns that lay beneath the island.

They had been mined in the ancient past by dwarves who had entered the caverns long before his time, in the years of his father's father's father's father, and then they had vanished and had never been heard from again.

Legend had it that the mountain and indeed the entire island had been shaken by tremendous vibrations a short time after the dwarves entered the caverns. These vibrations were so strong that they had loosened masonry and tumbled rocks from the peaks, crushing many in the valleys below.

The rumblings and shakings increased in their intensity until that fateful morning when the entire top of the mountain disappeared in one gigantic explosion.

Hot ash blanketed the sulphurous air and molten rock poured down the slopes, swallowing everything in its path until it entered the ocean where it seethed and hissed like some great cauldron.

There was a great outcry from the people who had, of course, suffered the most losses. They demanded that the dwarven mining cease, stating their belief that mining the gems had disturbed some delicate balance that held the island intact.

Some even muttered that the gems belonged to the gods, and that the earthquake and subsequent eruption were but a sign of the gods' anger. Since the king could not prove them wrong, he was forced to give in to their demands. In truth, he was not at all certain that they were wrong.

But in the end, nothing was done, for none of the dwarves were ever seen again and none of the search parties, those few brave enough to enter the caverns, had found any trace of them.

It was this first king who had fashioned the blue stone into a magic amulet, and, as he reached great age and felt his power slipping from him, made the first bargain with the demons, trading his soul upon his death for longer life and demonic power, using the gem as barter and surrendering his family into demonic thralldom for generations to come.

As many of his offspring were to discover, unlimited power was difficult to turn down when you were young and powerless. An ephemeral thing like a soul seemed such a little matter to barter when old age and death were all but inconceivable.

But everyone must die in their time, even those with demonic power, and it was only when the blush of youth faded and the heavy hand of age pressed on one's faltering heart that the true cost of the bargain was felt. And by then it was far too late to change one's mind.

"Can you tell us nothing that will be of use in this quest?" asked Hornsbuck, not at all happy to be venturing into unknown territory without the slightest bit of knowledge.

"Nothing," admitted the king and even the princess could tell that he was telling the truth. "All I know is that the entrance lies beneath the throne where my forefathers have guarded it with their lives for generations past."

Just then, there was a resounding bang and the doors to the chamber burst open, and crashed against the walls on either side. "My baby, my baby! Where's my own precious child?" cried a tremulous voice and Mika and the others turned to see whom or what had created the unexpected intrusion.

A dumpy little woman could be seen at the far end of the room, hurrying toward them as fast as her chubby legs would carry her, her arms waving in the air above her head, still calling out for her baby. Mika and Hornsbuck looked at each other with raised eyebrows and exaggerated shrugs, wondering who or what the woman could possibly want.

The princess gave a sharp bark and rushed toward the woman, her tail curled high above her back. Mika uttered a curse and started forward, alarmed that the princess in wolfen form might attack the woman, harmless though she might be.

He soon discovered his mistake, for when he was still many paces away, he saw the princess leap up on the woman, all but knocking her over and begin licking her homely, wrinkled face.

Mika stopped dead in his tracks, staring in disbelief as the dumpy woman tried to fend the princess off, holding her hands in front of her face and crying, "Ooooh, get down you horrid creature, get down!"

Still the princess continued her ecstatic leaps and did not cease licking the woman until Mika reached her side and pulled her away. The old woman scarcely spared him a second glance, but hurried on to the throne where she pressed a hand to her chest and looked around in puzzlement.

She looked up at the king then, wondering if some cruel trick had been played upon her and asked once more in a quavering voice, "Sir, where is my baby?"

The king smiled down at them all, as though savoring some joke, and at last Mika understood. "There is your baby, your precious one," he replied, pointing to the princess and the woman stared at the wolf in horror, unable to speak.

The princess moved to her side and whimpered softly. Then, the woman began to cry. She sank to the floor beside the princess and hugged her with both arms, her sobs echoing the mournful cries of the wolf.

"A touching moment," the king said dryly. "Here, old woman, stop that driveling, you have work to do." And bending forward stiffly, he placed the infants in her arms.

The woman blinked the tears from her eyes and looking back and forth from the infants to the princess, laughed shakily and hugged them to her ample bosom.

"Go," said the king. "We will speak later."

The nurse was reluctant to leave and did so only after the princess accompanied her to the door.

When she was gone and the princess had once

more taken her place among them, the king pressed a combination of gems on the arm of the throne, and so quickly did his trembling fingers move that Mika could not have said with any assurance exactly what he had done, even though he had watched closely.

There was a deep rumbling and the marble slabs trembled beneath their feet as the throne slid backward, revealing a dark square in the floor. Humans and wolves drew near, clustering around the edges of the yawning hole, dread fear nibbling at them as they wondered what they would see.

The opening was draped with cobwebs as thick as woven fabric and a torch was required to free it from the clinging stuff. Still, nothing could be seen but crude steps hacked from the living rock and then even these were swallowed by the darkness.

They had taken their leave of the king then, burdened only with sacks of provisions provided by the king. They descended into the terrible gloom. They were aided in part by torches that glowed with magical fire (a simple spell that even Mika was able to accomplish), and they wore every good luck talisman that they owned draped from various portions of their anatomy. The light from the throne room had faded quickly and their only link with the world above soon vanished in the oppressive darkness.

At their first moment of rest, the princess, still in her wolfen form, had presented herself to Mika, standing before him and fixing him with a patient gaze. Mika refused to meet her eyes, trying desperately to ignore her. He knew all to well what she wanted and was more than a little uncertain that he wished it as well.

Mika remembered quite clearly how the princess had tried to kill him, first as a human and then as a wolf. He had gotten used to her as a wolf, as had Tam. Why couldn't she just stay a wolf? That was just like a woman, always trying to change things!

But the princess didn't budge and Mika, trying to avoid her eyes, looked around him and saw that Hornsbuck, Lotus Blossom and even Tam and Red-Tail were staring at him as well! Some loyalty! You'd think that at least Tam would want her to stay a wolf! But his bonded companion's eyes were unblinking and Mika sadly conceded that there was nothing to be done but return the princess to her human form.

"It's time, Mika," Hornsbuck said solemnly. "You gave her your word . . . said that you would try to change her back once it was safe. It can't get much safer than this," he added, waving at the darkness around them.

"But Hornsbuck . . . what if I can't do it?" Mika whispered hoarsely. "I, I don't have the stone anymore. I'm not sure of the spell. What if I get it wrong? What if I make a mistake?" All three wolves growled at him and the princess growled the loudest.

Changing the princess back into a human female from a wolf was easier said than done, for without the magic stone Mika's magical abilities were extremely limited. Mika knew from personal experience some of the unpleasant effects that could happen if you said the words to a spell wrong, but with all of his friends and all of the wolves aligned against him, there seemed little choice but to try. He sighed, opened his book and looked at the spell.

Finally, after staring at the spell for what seemed

like the length of time it took a tree to sprout, grow and die, he felt that he had memorized it to the best of his ability. He snapped the book shut and rose to his feet, giving a few flourishes with his hands just to make it seem special. His audience stared at him, totally unimpressed.

He cleared his throat, stuck his hands in his pockets and began to recite, uttering the words that would turn the princess from a wolf to a human. But halfway through the spell, the words seemed to vanish from his mind. He faltered and heard the princess growl. Unnerved, all but feeling her teeth at his throat, he stumbled over the last few sentences.

He heard a sharp intake of breath, an odd muffled bark and opened his eyes just in time to see the princess shrinking, shrinking, shrinking and turning into a pearl which promptly began to roll down the steps into the darkness.

Their shock and astonishment wore off quickly as they heard the pearl bouncing down the steps; and torches held high, fearful of losing her, the others rushed after the princess, cursing Mika as they went.

Fortunately, Mika's abilities were even less powerful than he had thought and the spell wore off quickly, returning the princess to her wolfen form with only a few bruises to show for her trouble.

"Look, I didn't do it on purpose!" Mika protested as humans and wolves alike glared at him. "Do you really think that I would do something like that on purpose?" No one answered and the angry looks convinced him that he had best not fail again.

He began again, concentrating even harder this time, changing the words to the spell slightly to eliminate the problem. But all he could think about was the possibility of failure and his throat was dry and his lips moved as though they were carved from stone.

As he uttered the final words, the princess disappeared in a cloud of acrid smoke that set them all to choking and when it cleared, nothing remained but a pile of ocher dust on the granite steps.

"Cumin!" proclaimed Lotus Blossom as she leaned over and sniffed the tiny pyramid. Mika looked closer, horrified at what he had done, and as the spicy scent filled his nostrils, he was seized with a terrible need to sneeze.

"Don't you dare!" yelled Lotus as she grabbed his nose in her powerful fingers and twisted so hard that tears came to his eyes. He suddenly lost all desire to sneeze.

"You stupid fool!" growled Hornsbuck. "You could have blown her away and we'd never have found all the bits and pieces! Now sit still and don't move until the spell wears off!"

Mika sat on the steps, touching his nose gingerly, and wondered why he'd never listened to his father, the very greatest of magic-users, who had tried to teach Mika about spells and magic, all those long years ago.

Even now, he thought about studying often, well, occasionally, but there were always so many more interesting things to do, like drink and sleep and chase women. And he'd gotten used to the amulet. Its magical abilities had boosted his own poor skills and made him forget how little he actually knew.

His father had taught him the basics, such as heal

spells and how to start a fire and flying, simple things like that. He could perform spells through third level complexity if he were very, very careful, but anything more difficult was all but impossible without the aid of the amulet.

He was still brooding over his ineptitude and his sore nose when the pile of spices reformulated and became a glowering wolf with dewlaps drawn back from teeth that glinted in the light of the magical torches. He was almost too depressed to be frightened. Still, it was all that Hornsbuck and Lotus Blossom could do to convince the princess that Mika was not being stupid on purpose, but came by it honestly.

"Look princess, we'd all like to have you back as a lady," growled Hornsbuck. "But I think that even you will have to admit that Mika cannot do it on his own. He needs another stone to help him. Gods only know what he might turn you into the next time."

The princess sank back on her haunches and grumbled to herself. Tam whined and hooked his neck over hers, commiserating.

"Hornsbuck's right, princess," added Lotus Blossom. "Yon laddie is a right fool. Damned if I'd let him play around with me." Mika was wise enough to keep a straight face and look down at his feet following this comment.

"Best you should stay a wolf than wind up in some strange form forever," Lotus continued. "Us'll find another stone soon and yon lad will do you up right or answer to me, right boy?" Mika nodded in reply, not trusting himself to speak.

In truth, despite his companion's harsh words, Mika was relieved. It would do no good at all if he continued to make mistakes. One of the permutations might not revert to her original shape and the princess would forever remain a cucumber or a snail or some such dreadful thing.

Growling and snarling at Mika in a great rage, the princess stalked off down the endless steps and the others were forced to follow. Mika brought up the rear, putting as much distance as possible between himself and the princess's fangs.

After a great length of time, the staircase finally came to a broad landing. The rough stone wall remained on their right and still there was nothing but the dark abyss at the left edge of the steps.

To their extreme displeasure, the landing was no more than that, simply a landing. It was almost as though the original builders, whomever or whatever they might have been, had grown tired of carving steps and had built a landing. The stairs commenced once more on the far side.

In the time that followed, they traveled great distances and time ceased to have meaning. They ate when they were hungry, slept when they were tired and continued on when they wakened, searching for the magical gems. They found many gems embedded in the walls and protruding from the steps. These they placed in their knapsacks, removing provisions to make room, but none of them were the precious gems they sought.

At last, they reached the bottom of the endless flight of steps and cautiously began to probe the depths that lay beneath the island of Dramidja. They traversed huge salt caverns that glistened and glittered like incredible diamonds, the vast arched domes curving far above their heads, the crystals reflecting and refracting the glow of their torches like millions of tiny glittering mirrors.

They inched their way across tenuous crystalline salt bridges that spanned dark chasms too deep to plumb. They swam across lakes of water, so laden with salt that they bobbed on the surface like corks, and their flesh and clothes grew stiff as they dried in the cold cavern air.

They encountered strange monsters that were unlike any they had seen before and would probably never see again. Some were overcome by strength, others by trickery, and still others preferred their own company and slunk away and hid in the shadows.

They found ample evidence of dwarven activity, great holes hacked in the glittering salt walls, huge excavations in the ground that had since been filled with pools of salty seepage, and columns pounded to dust.

They found the leavings of the dwarves in plenty, gormets, green as the grass above, sapphires blue as the all but forgotten skies, and querioz, the deep purple of the Suloisian mountains; but nowhere did they find the precious blue and red stones.

In the beginning, they had stuffed their pouches with the brilliant gems but they grew heavier with every step and their value dwindled as their weight grew. Soon the gems were discarded and then appeared as no more than sparkles in the darkness. But look as they might, they found no sign of the magic stones.

In time, their enthusiasm began to wane and the ties of friendship began to unravel as they penetrated deeper and deeper into the dark depths. In their hearts they began to fear that they would never find the stones and never again see the world above.

Thus, it was with almost incredible joy that they turned a bend in the dark corridor and saw sparkling with radiance before them, a pillar of solid gemstones, all of red and blue.

"Look! Look! It's there! The magic stones!" cried Mika, "Follow me!" and angry words and past grievances were all but forgotten as they dropped provisions, weapons, tools, the pouch that held the spell book, anything and everything that might slow their progress, and followed Mika, running toward the long-sought goal with hearts that sang with joy.

Chapter 5

THE DEMON MAELFESH was ecstatic. He hummed a few bars of a paeon written by a sole surviving monk to commemorate the death of an entire populace. They had drowned in their sleep as their island home dropped without warning and was swallowed whole by the seas around it. The funereal chords never failed to lift his spirits.

But he sang out of sheer happiness, having no need to cheer himself, for he had found the human he had sought, one Mika, the Wolf Nomad. It was as he had suspected all along, the clever fellow had not died, merely shed the amulet and thus escaped notice for a time.

It had taken some careful tracking to find him and his companions hidden deep under the island of Dramidja. He had also discovered that the king had survived as well. This gave him pause, for he did not want it thought that he, Maelfesh, the demon lord, was losing his touch!

It had taken little persuasion to extract the information that he sought, learning that Mika and the others were seeking the magic gems in the salt caverns that lay beneath the island.

Maelfesh was somewhat disturbed at this information. He certainly didn't want any more of the powerful gems to be found. It would never do. The right gem in the hands of the wrong person might conceivably equal his own power. It would have to be stopped once and for all.

There was no need to do anything to the king. The mere presence of the demon, coupled with his own fragile health, toppled him over the edge of sanity into madness and he wandered out of the castle, his eyes vague and empty, muttering some nonsense about heirs and future kingdoms.

Maelfesh shrugged and promptly forgot him, turning his thoughts to those who journeyed below. His first priority was in seeing that none ever gained entrance to or exit from the caverns. With a casual gesture, he brought the castle down, reducing it to a pile of rubble with a flick of his flaming fingers, burying guards and servants, the throne and the hidden entrance beneath piles of stone.

Next, he located the questing party, conjured up a magnificent illusion and placed it directly in their path, a seemingly solid pillar of the magic gems that they sought. In truth, it was merely a holding trap, one he had perfected over the centuries.

The trap was really very simple. It did not kill, that would have been too crude and far too merciful. Instead, it held its victim in place, as though suspended in liquid gel, unable to move in any way. And so they stayed forever, eyes open, seeing; heart beating, feeling; minds functioning, thinking, prolonging their agony, caught within the double prison of body and pillar.

The demon indulged himself and stayed for a time, admiring his handiwork, taking additional pleasure in the horrified expressions of his victims as they slowly realized what had happened to them and the hopelessness of their situation. It gave him that little added lift of pleasure.

Only one thing bothered him. Somehow, while entering the pillar of illusion, Mika's hand, the demon hand, had been left outside the trap. It protruded beyond the glittering red and blue transluscent pillar, a strange incongruous thing, rather like seeing a human nose growing out of a tree trunk.

Maelfesh lifted his own hand, ready to strike the thing off, but then the humor of it came to him and he decided to leave it as it was, as a signature of sorts. Not that anyone would ever see it, but still, he would know it was there and would be amused whenever he thought of it, a fitting end to Mika, the Wolf Nomad.

In the meantime, there was still much work ahead. Maelfesh sighed, a demon's work was never done. There were still storms of fire to be called down and oerthquakes to be summoned and probably a good old-fashioned, all-purpose curse to be levied on the island, just to keep the folks in their places. It would never do to let them get too complacent.

And so, busy with his plans for the devastation to be brought down on the hapless and helpless island (the best kind, to his way of thinking), the demon lord Maelfesh left his latest victims to the darkness of the ages to come.

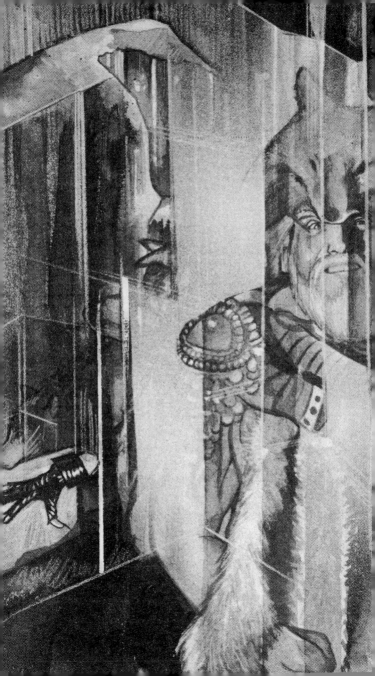

Chapter 6

IN THE FIRST YEAR, Mika developed a terrible itch in the middle of his back, but of course there was no way to scratch it. It plagued him for the entire year, vanishing for short periods of time only to return like the curse it had become.

In the second year, the itch disappeared, never to return, and was replaced by a cramp in his right leg. It was the leg that supported all his weight as the left leg was still raised behind him, frozen in midstep. He would have given anything to lower his leg and support his weight more evenly, but of course that was not possible.

During the third year, he became aware of the need to relieve himself. He knew in his head that such could not be the case, for all such functions were in stasis, but his body refused to listen to reason and he felt like a child on a too-long trip.

During the fourth year, he became aware of the growing resentment of his companions, all of whom had managed to slant their eyes so that they could glare at him. It seemed that they blamed him for their predicament. Mika became incensed and glared back. The injustice of it all carried him through the fifth, sixth and seventh years. Finally, he decided to ignore them and hummed loudly in his mind, shutting them out as best he could.

During the eighth year, he spent his time trying to remember the words to a spell that might have freed them from the pillar, but no matter what he did, he could not call the words to mind.

The ninth year was spent twisting his demon hand, trying to reach anything that might help them. He succeeded in catching an unwary bat once, but it bit him on the wrist and escaped, squeaking indignantly.

In the tenth year, it became all but impossible to ignore the hostility and resentment of his companions and he fell into a deep depression that carried him through the next eight years.

In the middle of the nineteenth year, he roused long enough to realize that unless he did something, anything, they would stay like this forever.

He began to think of those who remained on Oerth, those who might remember him still and care enough to help him.

He thought of those women he had loved, physically, at least, Celia and Starr, Wolf Nomad maidens, and Lefka, the rosy-cheeked baker's assistant in Eru-Tovar, and he knew in his heart that if they remembered him at all, it was not with undying love. He cast about trying to think of anyone, anyone at all who would care whether he lived or died; and he found, to his sorrow, that with the death of his family who had always loved him no matter what he had done, there was no one left to care.

He had lived his life in such a manner that all those who might have loved him, were used and then cast aside.

Those few to whom he had extended such loyalty and love as he was capable, were unfortunately trapped in the pillar with him, and from the mental vibrations he was receiving, he was lucky they were unable to move.

Somewhere deep inside Mika, in that callow selfish lump that passed for a heart, a great wave of despair and sorrow welled up, causing such pain as he had never before experienced. It was the pain that comes from recognition of self and the despair at what one sees.

This pain was too much for any one heart to hold. It burst up out of him in a great outwelling of anguish and then was gone, cleansing him in the passing, leaving him weak and vulnerable and somehow different than he had been before.

Knowing now that he could change nothing, but hoping that his companions would eventually find it possible to forgive him, Mika settled down to wait out eternity.

Chapter 7

THE LITTLE HARPY stroked the soft fur of the rabbit and mourned its death, wishing that just once she might be able to keep one alive. But such a thing was impossible, for even when the others brought live things back to the aerie, they either ate them at the first onset of hunger or the creatures huddled within themselves and died of fright.

The little harpy wondered what it would be like to have a live thing to talk to and stroke and share one's thoughts. It seemed that she had been searching for such a thing all of her short life and never finding it.

It was not possible to talk to the other harpies, of course, they were not much given to talk, and what little they did say involved squabbling over shares of food and who deserved the best perch in the aerie and who got which hunting grounds.

None of the others seemed to want to talk, or even understood such a need. Conversation about emotions and personal needs caused them to narrow their eyes and look at her askance. Over the years, she had learned to keep her thoughts to herself.

In one golden moment that would never be forgotten, her mother, prompted by feeding on fermented berries, spoke aloud, all but apologizing to the little harpy for her troubles, and blaming herself for mating with the man who had fathered her.

The little harpy had eagerly plied her mother with an abundance of the heady fruit until she learned all that her mother knew about the Wolf Nomad named Mika.

The little harpy listened to the story with wide eyes, her heart growing heavy at the tale of the baby harpy, stolen from the aerie by thieving humans and taken far away.

She relived the sorrow as her mother searched, unable to find the infant. Her pinfeathers prickled at the tale of the meeting with the Wolf Nomad whom her mother had chosen to be her slayer, unable to live with the heavy burden of grief.

The little harpy thrilled to the telling of the spell cast by the nomad, the spell that enabled man and harpy to communicate. Her heart filled with joy as her mother related how the nomad told her where to find the missing child.

She waited with baited breath as her mother confided how she had later found the nomad and rescued him from certain death, thus repaying her obligation.

As the tale progressed, chills of excitement ruffled the little harpy's feathers as her mother told of being overcome by an unusual passion and mating with the nomad high over the forests of Ekbir.

The harpy's mother left out that portion of the tale that told of dropping the nomad from the dizzying heights once her needs were fulfilled, mentioning only that the human had been alive the last time she saw him.

She then dropped into a snoring stupor and could never be persuaded to tell the story again. As the seasons progressed, she too sided with the rest of the aerie and ignored her daughter as her physical differences became more pronounced.

The young harpy's hair, instead of being properly tangled and snarled and nasty, was soft and silky, a glossy shade of red-brown that curled around her face like a gossamer halo.

Her features were delicate and fragile, all soft curves and velvety texture rather than stark and angular and rough to the touch.

Her body was graceful and sensuous rather than powerful and strong, and the feathers on wings and the lower half of her body were lustrous, all but glowing with a sheen that is found only in the very young.

She had no standing in the community and was forced to take the worst perch in the aerie, one that left her exposed to both wind and rain.

The other harpies ignored her completely, treating her with contempt when they noticed her at all; only her mother's high standing in the flock prevented them from driving her out or even slaying her.

Her hunting grounds were on the very farthest portion of their territory, that section that bordered Ekbir and was considered dangerous in the extreme, for its continuous proximity to humans, the harpies' worst enemy.

But the little harpy was strangely lacking in fear of humans and often spent her time watching them as they went about their peculiar activities.

She was puzzled by much that they did, pushing sharp, pointed sticks through the ground, burying little pellets in the resulting furrows and then fussing with the growth that sprouted thereafter.

She watched with interest as the people consumed parts of the objects, and sometimes crept down to taste that which they had left behind.

Initially, her efforts had been quite unrewarding. The townsfolk had eaten the things with relish, but she had found the rough white cylinders to be both hard and tasteless.

Only after much observation, perching quietly in a tree above them, was she able to discover that they actually ate a gold covering on the outside of the hard cylinders. The tasteless interiors were then discarded when the covering was gone, considered inedible by the people themselves.

Through subterfuge she managed to come by some of these objects with the soft portion still on them. Her world changed with the first bite. Afterward, she sought out other things that the people grew and learned how they were eaten.

Now there was a further difference that set her apart from the rest of the harpies. No longer could she pretended to enjoy gnawing on the poor broken animal bodies that her mother and older sister brought back to the aerie. No longer could she feign the desire to chew her way into the soft, rotting underbelly of a winter-killed deer or conceal her dislike at drinking congealed blood. Her revulsion was all too apparent.

She became aware of the mutterings in the aerie

when they thought she could not hear them. Her sensitive ears picked up the words "unnatural . . . tainted blood . . . keep the aerie pure," and other such alarming conversation.

But still she did not consider leaving, for the aerie was all the home she had ever known; and while her mother and her older sister were not overly kind, they were not overtly cruel and they were still her family.

As time went on, she became more bold and watched the humans more and more often, finding a fascination with them and the way they led their lives.

She peeked through dark windows at night and watched their peculiar oerthbound mating rites and wondered at the fact that the males still lived in the morning.

Their ways were strange, consisting of all sorts of peculiar rites and customs and habits. And each and every one of them had something quite special, precious even, a single individual word that summed up their very essence in a single word. It was called a name.

Harpies did not have names. But the longer the little harpy was around humans, the more she wanted a name, a name that would be hers alone, a name that would be uniquely her.

One day, in a burst of yearning, she gave herself a name. It warmed her. Thereafter, whenever she was unhappy, which was often, she said the word to herself and it comforted her.

But most confusing of all was the way humans showed affection and concern for one another, stroking and petting and touching openly.

The little harpy tried stroking and touching herself and once kissed the back of her hand just so that she might see what it felt like. It was not unpleasant but she thought that it must feel differently when someone else did it for you.

And then one terrible, terrible day in the middle of her twentieth year, the whole world changed.

She had been gathering some of the gold things that the humans called corn, when the stalks parted in front of her and there stood a group of angry men, their lips pressed tight in rage and their eyes glaring.

"There she be!" screeched an old man whom the little harpy had often watched fondly as he guarded the flocks of sheep and patted the large shaggy, flop-eared creature that was always at his side. It was called a Bark.

But the old man did not look so friendly now. He pointed a gnarled finger at her and shrilled, "four sheep her killed. I saw! An' she ripped poor ol' Rowdy up from one end to the 'tother. Never 'ad a chance. An' now she be 'ere stealin' our corn. Kill 'er!"

And they gave it their very best try as she foolishly tried to stammer out the unfamiliar words that would tell them that she had not killed anything at all for a very long time.

But her words were ill-formed and sounded more, to their uncaring ears, like the chittering of birds than the speech of humans. Nor would they have cared to listen had she been articulate.

They set upon her with staffs and stones and struck her delicate wings and beat her to the ground. They would have killed her had she not broken away from them and lifted into the air on aching pinions.

Tears blurred her vision as she circled above the humans, just out of spear range, and heard their angry voices cursing her and all her kind. Cradling a badly bruised arm, she slowly flew back to the aerie, sorrow piercing her heart, and she knew that she could never again visit the villagers of Ekbir.

For once, she longed for the safety of the aerie and the warmth of her mother's wing.

She flew as fast as her injuries allowed, making straight for the aerie, unaware of the villagers following below, determined to free themselves once and for all from the depredations of the hated harpies.

But she found no warmth and no safety at the aerie, for it had been her mother and sister who had killed the villagers' sheep.

Her sister had been killed outright by a well-aimed spear, and her mother had been grievously wounded by a broad-tipped hunting arrow that had driven between her ribs and lodged deep in her lung.

Her mother lay near death, sprawled in the nest which was only used for the laying of eggs and rearing of young, her wings twisted and crumpled beneath her.

The little harpy crawled into the nest and touched her mother's face, begging her to speak, ignoring the baleful looks that were flung her way by those who grudged her life while her mother died.

Her mother opened her eyes and an unusual spark of warmth lit the cold dark orbs. The harsh angles of her face softened as her lips contorted in the grimace of a smile.

Dark blood trickled from the corner of her mouth

and stained her rough lips as she said, "Leave the aerie, it will not be safe for you here once I am gone. Search out the one who was your father, he is a powerful magic-user. He will protect you."

"How do I find him?" asked the little harpy, her heart aching within her breast.

"The stone," whispered her mother, her voice all but gone as death drew near, forcing her daughter to bend close. "The stone will lead you to him."

She fumbled in the filthy straw that lined the nest and uncovered a thin gold chain. With her last bit of strength she pulled it free and placed it in her daughter's hands, closing her fingers over the bright blue gem.

As the last bit of lifelight faded from her eyes, there was a tremendous outcry, a great wailing and shrieking as of pain, and it took the little harpy a long, grief-stricken moment to realize that the sound was not of her making.

She held her silence as she lowered her mother's body to the nest and smoothed the variegated brown plumage for the last time.

The screaming and wailing grew louder and louder and now the dread scent of woodsmoke . . . fire . . . broke in on her grievous reverie. She looked up and saw that the shallow cave that compromised the aerie was in pandemonium. The harpies were fluttering back and forth crashing against the stone walls, maddened by fear and oblivious to the danger of damaging their fragile wings.

Angry shouts could be heard now, and as flaming arrows began pouring through the openings of the aerie, striking wood nests and harpies alike, the little harpy realized what she had done. She had led the villagers back to the aerie.

Unborn hatchlings boiled in their shells, nests blazed and harpies poured out of the aerie, their fear of fire greater than their fear of humans and their weapons. Half-blinded by the black smoke, they flew erratically and more than half of them were cut down by the waiting archers.

Still others stayed in the aerie and were struck by the continuing flights of flaming arrows. Feathers on fire and maddened by fear and agony, they fell over the edge of the cliff and plummeted to their deaths.

The little harpy, tears pouring down her face, scarcely caring whether she lived or died, knowing that she had brought death to her people, flew out of the mouth of the aerie.

At that moment, a freak gust of wind poured down the face of the cliff and blew the thick cloud of smoke back into the faces of the attackers.

The little harpy circled above them, the stone clenched, forgotten, in her hand, waiting for their arrows, waiting for death.

When death did not come, she spiraled higher and higher into the air, rising far above the conflagration into the highest of all altitudes, where the air blew thin and cold as it circled the Oerth. She gave herself up to its icy embrace, spreading her wings wide and allowing it to take her wherever it would.

Chapter 8

TAMSEN WAKENED with his arms wrapped around the base of a large pockmarked stone. His cheek was cradled on his arm which had gone to sleep long ago and failed to waken. His eyes felt itchy and gritty and the taste of sheep was in his mouth. He probed gently with his tongue and found bits of wool wedged between his teeth.

TamSen groaned and turned his face away from the bright sun that streamed down on his aching body, wishing he could somehow disappear. In spite of all his efforts, it had happened again; of that there was no doubt.

After a time, realizing that he was probably not going to disappear, he sat up and cradled his head in his hands, looking around fearfully, assessing the damage.

His flock, what remained of it, grazed on the flank of the mountain. Their stupid little sheep brains carefully ignored the fact that fully six of their number lay dead, throats ripped and bodies slashed by long, sharp fangs.

TamSen groaned again and buried his head in his hands, wishing he could remember the events of the previous evening, yet grateful that he could not. It was always this way after the first night of the full moon.

He wondered how long it would be before Quotar, the man to whom the sheep belonged, discovered his loss. It would not do to blame their deaths on wolves or other wild creatures, for they had been eliminated from the island many centuries before.

It seemed to TamSen that the dread secret that he and his sister had kept for so many years would soon be discovered. Assuming that they were able to escape with their lives, where would they go and what would become of them? The people of the island of Dramidja were understandably short-tempered when it came to magic.

Twenty years earlier, when he and his sister TamLis had been but babes in the arms of their nurse, the island had been all but destroyed by a major oerthquake, the second in the island's history.

The castle, on whose land he now sat, had been completely leveled, as had the city below. Every building, every home, had crumbled into dust. People had died in great numbers, as had their livestock.

Clouds of stinking, sulphurous ash had blanketed the lush landscape. It had poisoned the gardens, the fruit trees and vineyards, and coated the Oerth with fire and brimstone, causing all further growth to be both blighted and stunted.

Not even the sea had escaped unscathed. The oerthquake had wakened the volcano and masses of molten rock spewed down the flanks of the mountain and poured into the harbor, creating a black island where nothing that lived could exist.

Fish and other sea creatures had boiled to the surface, covering the ocean as far as the eye could see. After the water cooled and the stench of rotting fish vanished, it appeared that sea life had vanished as well. The water was sterile and void of life for many leagues in all directions.

Shipping, the island's main industry, now gave Dramidja a wide berth, bringing its custom to Ekbir, it being deemed a far safer port.

The islanders began to leave, judging the place to be cursed. And so did they curse the name of their former king, who had gone mad in the course of the devastation and wandered the island, his long, white hair blowing in the wind, blue eyes vacant and staring.

From time to time, the old man had appeared at the home of the nurse, one of those who chose to remain on the island. TamSen could remember the old man still, remember the feel of his fingers as they stroked the fine layer of down that covered his and his sister's bodies, setting them apart from all others.

"You are the heirs to the kingdom," the old man had whispered into their ears from the moment they were old enough to understand. "Never forget. The kingdom is yours, yours to claim, yours to return to glory."

He had filled their wide-eyed young heads with stories of the kingdom as it had been in days gone by. Told them tales of great heroes and valor, of bravery and legend, of courage and honor. He spoke the names of those who had gone before and told of their deeds.

Always there was the message: they were the heirs to the kingdom, and those who had gone before and those who were still to come were depending on their actions. Yet when they, in their childish naivete, asked what those actions were to be, and how they were to be performed, the old man had no words to answer.

They turned to their nurse when the old man had left and plied her with questions, begging her to explain his words.

To give the nurse her due, she did not lie to the children. Never did she tell them, as others did, that the old man was mad. Instead, she told them the story of their mother as she knew it and gave them the history of their ancestors as best she was able.

Of their father, she would tell them nothing, for she thought it best to spare them the knowledge that he was a wolf, as was the Princess Julia, their mother. Further, she begged them to keep their lineage a secret for it would earn them no friendship among the bitter islanders. The citizens of Dramidja cursed the king still, knowing intuitively that it was an action of his that had brought the devastation down upon them.

In spite of the nurse's silence, it was not hard for the lonely sister and brother to discern out that there were strong differences between themselves and other children.

Most obvious was the soft cream-colored down that covered them from head to toe. There was also the matter of their ears, which were longer and taller than human ears and ended in stiff peaks nearly half a hand's height above the crowns of their heads.

TamLis had learned to conceal her ears by wrapping her long heavy gold braids round her head. But her brother could not wear his hair in such a fashion and so, from his earliest days, TamSen was never seen without his cap, a soft formless thing that came down well over his ears and slouched comfortably to one side.

Their bodies were human in nature with no obvious differences except that they were extremely fleet of foot and very nimble.

But the greatest difference of all, and the one that set them apart, for there was no way to conceal it, was their faces. Their noses to be exact. Where other children had button noses, pug noses, short noses, long noses or even hooked noses, TamLis and TamSen's noses were darkened on the end and were always slightly moist.

It made no difference that TamSen was bright and cheerful and witty with a fun-loving, mischievous nature; none of the island boys came close enough to find that out.

It mattered not that TamLis was beautiful and sweet and gentle; none of the boys and certainly none of the girls ever ventured closer than it took to throw a rock or an insult.

Throughout their short childhood, they were teased and tormented by the island children at every turn until they learned to avoid others and became their own best friends.

Their nurse did the best that she could, loving them with all her heart and protecting them as best she was able. She tried to make them strong, to prepare them for the years to come when they would be alone.

TamLis and TamSen returned her love, doing her every bidding, and seeking always to please her. The three of them eked out a living, cultivating a small patch of land, setting snares for birds and rabbits and selling the nurse's cloth to the townspeople. Every woman on the island wove, but the nurse's weaving abilities far surpassed their own, producing cloth that was warm in winter, cool in summer, and could shed water and snow as well as a duck's own back.

There were those who whispered that such a talent was not natural, that it must be magical; but none said so aloud, for fear of being refused the wondrous material.

The death of the old man cast a dark shadow on their childhood, he whom they now knew to be their grandfather and, whether mad or not, was the former ruler of the island.

This event occurred during the month of Fireseek, the month of their borning, at the advent of their twelfth year.

The old man was found by a wandering shepherd, seated on what remained of his throne, a bare pock-marked stone thrusting up out of the broken marble that had once covered the floor of the throne room.

It was the place he was most often to be found, having excavated the site singlehandedly in the years that followed the destruction of the island. No amount of persuasion was able to keep him from the spot and he refused all of the nurse's offers to share her humble cottage.

His reply was always the same: "I must be there when they return. The stones . . . I must be there for the stones."

And so he was found by the shepherd, his body cold and covered with a rime of frost, the long sensitive fingers gripping the arms of the throne, blue eyes staring vacantly onto other worlds. His white hair stood out round his head, backlit by the sun till it shone like a platinum crown.

The villagers came then, for in death he was forgiven. They laid him out in simple dignity and covered his skeletal frame with a blanket of ermine; then they raised a massive cairn around him, built out of the stones that had once formed his castle.

The world seemed a lonelier place with the old man gone and TamSen had taken to visiting the cairn and talking to his grandfather as though he were still alive. Other than his sister and the nurse, the old man had been the closest thing he had to a friend.

His sister did not roam as often as did TamSen, for she was quick to notice the fact that the nurse's limbs grew more and more painful with every passing Fireseek. As the years progressed, Nurse's fingers curved in upon themselves and grew strangely gnarled and were never without pain.

TamLis's love bound her to the small cottage, tending to the daily chores and attempting to learn the craft of weaving. But despite Nurse's great patience and TamLis's continual efforts, she was never able to duplicate Nurse's skills and the villagers returned to their own crude homespun efforts.

With the loss of Nurse's income, the small household soon fell upon hard times, and it became obvious that one of them would have to seek employment. TamLis could not go, for it was she who cared for Nurse and maintained the cottage. That left only TamSen.

Through one of her old friends, Nurse was able to place TamSen with a cutter, one of the few men who still cut blocks of limestone out of the sea cliffs.

TamSen proved to be extraordinarily agile and could leap from one dangerous ledge to another without fear, but unfortunately, he was absolutely terrified of the water below. No matter how hard he tried, he was unable to overcome his fear and the cutter could do naught but let him go.

Next, he was given the post of guarding the village vegetable gardens at night. He was to guard them against the vermin who did great damage to the foodstuffs that were so vital to island existence through the cold winter months.

Shortly after the full moon in the month of Harvester, great holes were discovered dug deep in the soft loam of the garden.

TamSen was questioned but could not remember having seen anything strange. In fact, he could not seem to remember anything at all. It was assumed that he had fallen asleep.

There was a certain amount of grumbling, but as TamSen willingly helped replant the uprooted plants, he was merely chastised and told to stay awake.

The same thing happened again, following the first night of the full moon of Patchwall. This time, the grumbling was louder, but as TamSen seemed almost dazed and no one could think of a reason for him to have done such mischief, once again, he was held blameless.

But when it happened a third time, on the first night of the full moon in the month of Ready'Reat, TamSen was given his grushniks as well as his leave, the farmer staring pointedly at TamSen's broken fingernails which were still clogged with dirt.

This occurred in the middle of his fifteenth year and sometime soon thereafter, TamSen became aware of a terrible restlessness that seized him periodically, causing him untold discomfort. The cottage seemed to close in on him so that he could not breathe and it became necessary for him to be outdoors, no matter what the weather.

The things that happened during these times were not always clear to him. Sometimes he had vague memories of empty valleys and tall peaks with the moon hanging full and viscous behind them. Other times he remembered nothing; but his throat was sore and swollen and he found it hard to speak for several days.

The villagers began to speak of a frightful howling heard in the hills; and people began to wonder if ghosts were taking up residence in the empty villages. Nurse said nothing, but watched TamSen with worried eyes, afraid that he would come to harm.

By the time of their twentieth year, Nurse was very much worse. The crippling illness had spread to most of her joints, twisting her limbs in painful contortions and confining her to bed where she required much care.

TamSen had held and lost every job that had been offered to him by Nurse's well-meaning friends. They were more than willing to take her into their own homes, but she refused to leave her charges. All they could do to help was to try to employ TamSen.

On that fateful morning in the month preceeding the full moon, TamSen had taken the very last job available to him, guarding the sheep of that same shepherd who had found the dead king, one Quotar.

TamSen had a terrible feeling about the job. Somehow, he just knew that it would never work out, but it was the only available job. Without the meager income that it would provide, they would surely starve. TamSen had shaken hands with Quotar, taken the staff and gone up the mountain to guard his fleecy charges.

All had gone well until the full moon. TamSen was still unable to recall anything that had occurred that previous night, but given the fleece between his teeth and the dead sheep, even he was able to figure out the connection. He had no doubt that Quotar would make a similar assessment. And then it would all be over.

The villagers would not be so forgiving this time, the evidence was too clear. He would be killed or driven up into the empty hills to live as an outcast for the rest of his life.

TamSen sat on the cold stone throne, looked deep in his own misery and wondered for the millionth time how life could be so hard. Was there no justice?

If his family had truly ruled the island for so many generations, why were they forced to live like this now? Where was the rich heritage that his grandfather had spoken of so often? Where were the wealth and glory that were to be his to command? TamSen drummed his fingers on the pockmarked arm of the stone throne, beating out a strange irregular tattoo, the measure of his frustration as he wondered what to do about his life.

If only there were something he could do to save them from the misery that hounded them. If only . . .

Suddenly, there was a terrible rumbling sound, deep as thunder, but it erupted from the stones around him, not the sky.

As he sat upright, gripping the stone arms and wondering what was happening, the throne slid backward on the marble slabs revealing a dark gaping hole in the oerth.

Chapter 9

TAMSEN SAT IN THE STONE CHAIR and stared at the hole. He rubbed his eyes with the back of his hand and blinked several times, wondering if he were seeing things. But the hole remained.

He stood on trembling legs and cautiously stepped to the far edge of the hole, wondering what he had done to make it appear. He had sat in the stone chair countless times before and never had such a thing happened. He wondered where the hole led.

Dropping to his knees, yet staying well back of the dark opening, TamSen craned his head forward and looked down. He saw a rough cut stone step and then others that were soon swallowed by a darkness too thick to be illuminated by mere sunlight. A dank smell, reminiscent of oerth closed off too long from the sun, wafted up and filled his nostrils.

Conflicting emotions struggled within him. An inner voice urged him forward, telling him, no, demanding, that he descend instantly and find out where the mysterious staircase led.

Another voice demanded equally strongly that he do no such thing, that it would be both dangerous and foolhardy, and should something happen to him there would be no one left to take care of his sister and Nurse.

Still another voice spoke out, bringing up the fact that he was not exactly doing very well supporting TamLis and Nurse. They would soon be without him in any event, after the villagers found out about the sheep.

TamSen grew more and more confused with every passing moment; he simply didn't know what to do. He sank back onto the throne and contemplated the open hole that stared back accusingly, like an empty eye, waiting for him to do something.

TamSen groaned and propped his head in his hands, closing his eyes against the distressing sight while he tried to figure out what to do. Why did life have to be so hard? If only he had a clue, some sort of idea what was expected of him.

"Oh, grandfather," he muttered, more to himself than in any expectation of being heard by that departed figure, "Give me a sign, tell me what to do."

And at that very moment, a great weight struck him full on the back of the neck, toppling him off the throne and tumbling him headlong into the dark cavity.

Though stunned and astounded, TamSen was still in possession of his quick reactions and he reached out and grabbed the edge of a step, clinging to it with all his strength to prevent himself from falling into what well might be a bottomless abyss.

At the same time, he wrapped his other arm

around the object that had struck him and pressed his body against it, to prevent it from attacking him again. But the thing did not move, and lay still and unresisting beneath him.

For a moment, TamSen wondered if it were the shepherd Quotar, but the thing smelled too good to be Quotar. It smelled of wind and rain and sea air and feathers. Feathers?

After several heartbeats, when nothing further happened, TamSen dared to move, curious to see what it was he held, but unwilling to do so at the risk of plunging to his death down the dark staircase.

Using his feet and his one available hand, TamSen inched himself and his acquiescent attacker along until they were securely lodged on a broad step. Only then did he sit up and look at what he had captured.

He drew a sharp breath and for a moment, forgot to breathe. It was a girl, well, some sort of a girl, and the most beautiful he had ever seen.

Of course, he realized that he had not seen all that many girls in his lifetime, mostly Nurse and TamLis and a few village girls who always ran and hid at the sight of him. But there was something about this girl, something other than the fact that the lower half of her body was covered with feathers, that took his breath away.

Her hair, which hung well past her waist was a mass of tangled curls the color of gapa leaves when they turned reddish brown in the month of Patchwall; and tiny tendrils curled damply on her brow and cheeks.

Her eyebrows were delicately arched like small replicas of the enormous wings that sprouted between

91

her shoulder blades. Her eyes were closed as though she slept and fringed with thick lashes that cast dark shadows on her soft rosy cheeks.

Her nose was short and rounded and was not dark on the end; nor was it moist. Her lips were pale pink and beautifully shaped. They were parted slightly as though she were about to speak, or perhaps waiting to be kissed.

TamSen felt his cheeks burning beneath the downy covering that of late had become thicker and longer. He looked away from her mouth in confusion and found himself looking directly at the girl's chest which was quite bare of any sort of covering.

TamSen's confusion grew and his eyes darted from side to side, not knowing where to look. His whole body seemed to grow hot and his clothes felt tight and uncomfortable as though they were suddenly too small. He was all but overwhelmed by a panicky desire to run away, but at the same time, he did not want to go.

Suddenly, it occurred to him that the girl or whatever she was, had not moved. Maybe she was dead! Maybe she had been killed by the fall! Maybe something else had killed her and that was why she fell from the air and struck him in the first place!

Almost too fearful to find out if she were alive or dead, TamSen placed a trembling finger on the side of the girl's neck. But he felt only his own pounding pulse. Steeling himself, he placed a shaking hand against the girl's left breast and leaned close so that he might feel any air that passed between her parted lips.

The touch of her soft skin beneath his palm was almost more than he could bear. He felt as though he might die on the spot. It took more than a heartbeat for his mind to clear before he was able to concentrate on the task at hand. Elation rushed through his body as he felt the faint heartbeat against his palm. He clutched the girl to him, overcome with joy that she still lived. At that moment, he felt her stir in his arms.

Still holding her in a light embrace he lowered her slightly, unwilling to let her go for even an instant. He saw with rising excitement that her eyelids were fluttering and her breath could be heard in little soblike gasps. Her hands rose before her as though to ward off some great danger.

"Be still," TamSen said softly. "You are safe with me," yet he realized what a ridiculous thing it was to say; even he was not safe with himself.

The girl's eyelids flickered and then opened, revealing eyes that were startlingly different from his own. The pupils were quite large, black in color and were surrounded by thin circlets of amber irises. As she blinked, he saw that she had a third, transparent, inner eyelid as well. It did not matter; he stared into her eyes, transfixed.

She seemed to see him for the first time, and became aware of his arms around her. She placed her small hands against his chest as though to hold him away from her and her eyes were filled with terror. She opened her mouth as though to speak, but all that emerged were alarmed twitters and chirps.

"No, no! It's all right. I won't hurt you!" cried TamSen, horrified to think that she might be afraid of him.

But in spite of his words, the girl struggled even

more strongly, looking about in panic and fighting to free her wings which were pinned beneath her by the weight of her own body.

TamSen was terrified that in her efforts to escape, they might fall off the steps and plunge into the darkness to their deaths. Much as he wanted to hold her, he could not bear the sight of her fear or the thought of hurting her. He opened his arms and released her.

She leaped to her feet in a single fluid motion and opened her wings as though to fly; but only one wing extended itself, the other hung limp and dangled at a peculiar angle.

The girl looked over her shoulder, gave a shrill cry of despair as she glimpsed her damaged appendage and grasped it with both hands. She pulled, attempting to straighten it, then gasped sharply with the unexpected pain and stumbled dizzily. She would undoubtedly have collapsed and fallen from the narrow step had TamSen not caught her in his arms.

She brushed a limp hand against her brow, chirped softly in distress and then sagged against his chest, senseless.

TamSen stared down at her in alarm, seeing in her the same response that he had often observed in other injured wild creatures.

In his ramblings through the wild valleys, TamSen had frequently encountered rabbits, squirrels, birds, chipmunks and other small animals that had been hurt in some manner.

It was all but impossible to save them. So great was their fear of captivity and humans that they generally lapsed into shock and died in spite of TamSen's gentle caring.

He was frightened that such a thing might happen to this beautiful birdgirl and he was determined to do nothing that would alarm her. Wrapping his arms around her gently, he sat back down on the step and waited for her to waken.

Chapter 10

TAMSEN SAT QUIETLY, admiring the strange beauty of the birdgirl, almost unable to believe that anything so lovely could have come to him, even if by accident. He was still half-lost in his musings when at last she stirred. So strong were his feelings for her that he almost forgot that she did not share his sentiments.

This fact was brought home rather abruptly as her amber-flecked eyes snapped open at the same instant that her talons ripped into the sturdy cloth of his trousers. His eyes told him that she was a girl, but the feel of her claws and the sound of her angry chittering were anything but human.

The birdgirl drew her powerful feathered legs up and attempted to drive her curved talons into his stomach. Instincts of survival caused TamSen to pull the birdgirl close against his chest so that she was unable to bring her talons into use and he continued to hold her tight.

As her breasts pressed into his chest, thoughts, not quite as lofty as self-preservation, flashed through his mind. But this interesting revelation was interrupted by a sound from above.

"It oughta be around here, someplace, Pa; I saw it fall!" whined an unpleasant voice.

TamSen immediately recognized the voice as belonging to Shmerk, Quotar's eldest son, a great slouching lout who had often tormented TamSen with cruel words, insidious pranks and well-aimed rocks.

TamSen realized instantly how much this oaf would enjoy inflicting pain on the beautiful creature he held in his arms. He was equally determined that it would not happen.

"Well, why in the name of all the gods that be holy, didn't you kill it?" shouted Quotar. TamSen groaned inwardly, for dull, stupid Quotar with his malevolent eyes and mean nature was the only person whom TamSen would less like to see than his nasty son.

"I put my stuff down to look at the sheep, Pa," Shmerk sniveled. "I din't have time for nuthin' more'n pickin' up a rock an' chunkin' it. Damned thing's gotta be 'round here, somewhere's. I'll kill the blood-suckin' sheep-eater if'n I kin find it!"

"Not if I find it first," growled Quotar. "Look down there in them bushes!" And the voices slowly faded away as the two men moved off into the dense underbrush, looking for the fallen harpy.

Their prospective prey had ceased her chittering and become very still at the first sound of their angry voices. She and TamSen sat on the steps, momentarily wrapped in a conspiratorial silence.

It had never occurred to TamSen that the harpy might have been seen by anyone else, much less blamed for the death of the sheep. He himself had never before seen a harpy, although their ferocity and love of live game was much vaunted. Fear for his own safety was now all but overwhelmed by fear for the beautiful creature he held in his arms.

TamSen knew that Quotar and Shmerk would gladly display the harpy's dead carcass in the town square should they find her. This terrible thought caused him to hold her tighter yet and placing his hand behind her head, drew her face tenderly against his shoulder. For some reason, the harpy did not resist.

TamSen and the harpy lay on the steps in a close, fearful embrace until Shmerk's and Quotar's voices could no longer be heard. When it appeared that the immediate danger had passed, they sat up slowly and looked at each other. This time the harpy made no attempt to claw him but only looked at him with a quizzical, uncertain gaze that held a degree of gratitude.

But the moment, one that every red-blooded boy dreams of, no matter what amount of wolf flows in his veins, was short-lived. Directly above them there came a sound, that of stone rumbling against stone.

Their first reaction was to cower back, thinking that some rock above had given way and was about to fall upon them. It was this mistaken impression that sealed their fate, quite literally, for the rumbling sound was that of the throne as it slid back into place, sealing them in darkness as it shut out the light from above.

They dove for the opening as soon as they realized what was happening, but it closed completely before their grasping fingers could reach it.

For long heartbeats they clawed and pushed and even beat on the stone in desperation, but these futile efforts proved more tiring than useful and eventually they were forced to give up.

Remembering how he had opened the secret passage, TamSen began to feel around on the wall beside him for some secret lever or button in the hopes of opening the hidden door. He knew that there was great danger outside, but the darkness was more immediate and much more frightening.

The harpy, unaware of the concept of levers and other such human devices, did not understand what TamSen was doing. But she realized that his efforts, which she was able to picture accurately due to her acute hearing, were somehow meant to free them, so she too began to pat the walls imitating his actions. However, despite her efforts, she too achieved the same results; the stone and the darkness remained unbroken.

Finally, TamSen gave up and sat down on the steps with a sigh that reverberated throughout the stairwell. Still imitating him, the harpy sat down beside him and uttered a strangely melodic sound that clearly echoed the same sad note.

"Well, I guess you know we're in big trouble," TamSen said in a quiet voice. "They'll kill you if they can. Me too. I killed their sheep. I didn't mean to . . . I don't know what to do. . . . Do you understand anything I'm saying?"

The harpy however, chose that moment to cease imitating him and returned his question with silence.

"I guess it doesn't matter much, we're both in a mess. I don't want to face them, but I don't want to

stay here, either. If we get out, I could probably say
that you killed the sheep and that I caught you.

"Nah, I can't do that, even if you aren't human.
'Sides, there's bound to be tracks around the sheep
and they sure won't look like yours. But none of that
really matters since we'll probably never get out of
here."

He soon ran out of things to say and the two of
them sat together in silence in the darkness; aware-
ness of the harpy's presence growing on TamSen with
every passing heartbeat.

TamSen tried to picture her. She was easy to remember from the waist up; a girl doesn't walk
around half-naked without making a definite and
lasting impression on a red-blooded lad like TamSen.
But from the waist down, ah, now that was a different
matter; it would take him a while to get used to that
half.

They sat in companionable silence for what
seemed like days; thoughts chasing themselves round
and round in TamSen's mind as he tried to think of a
solution to their problem. But no matter how hard he
thought, it appeared that their only option was to descend the staircase and everything in him cried out
against the awful idea.

Suddenly, everything seemed too much to bear
and the full weight of his troubled life crashed down
on TamSen full force, filling him with despair.

Everything seemed hopeless. He couldn't go back.
He couldn't stay where he was, and there was nothing but darkness ahead. It was the story of his life. At
long last, filled to bursting with despair, he began to
talk, though whether to himself or to the harpy, he

could not have said.

"I've never had my arms around a girl, before, you know. Not even one with her clothes on. Oh, I've hugged Nurse and my sister, but they don't really count. I mean, I've never hugged a *real* girl, but then, I guess you're not a real girl either."

The harpy sat beside him without answering, but then he hadn't expected her to. Now, there's a funny thing about talking aloud in a dark place; it's hard to do, but once the first word is spoken, the silence broken, it sounds as though someone else is talking and the words continue, almost on their own, as though separate from the speaker.

In the following span of time, TamSen poured his heart out to the birdgirl who sat beside him on the rough stone steps, much as any nomad would speak to his wolf or a townsman to his dog.

TamSen spoke of many things, of Nurse, and TamLis, of the old king and his stories, of being heir to a kingdom in which he could barely eke out a living.

As he spoke in the still darkness, the feelings spilled from him in torrents, freed at last from the hurtful bonds that had held him all his life.

He told her things that he had never voiced aloud, nor consciously formulated in his own mind. He spoke of the intense loneliness and of watching other boys with their girls. He told of his great longing for a girl of his own or one who would be his friend. He told of his secret desire to touch a girl, stroke her cheek or hair and hold her close.

Then, growing more bold in the covering darkness, he told of the feelings that had stirred him when first he saw her, how her beauty had taken his breath away and the fascination of her eyes. He whispered of his longing to touch her and hold her again.

He was stunned at his own boldness, for he had learned at an early age to hide his emotions lest they be laughed at by the uncaring villagers. But his unhappiness had come unstuck and floated to the surface where it demanded to be heard after all the years of confinement.

Now, more to himself than to the harpy, TamSen spoke of the worst pain of all, the knowing that no matter how long he might live, the unhappiness and despair would never end.

"I wonder if you have a name," he said, more to himself than to the silent birdgirl.

"Chewppa," she twittered in a high, melodic, birdlike trill.

"Easy for you to say," he replied, half jokingly. "Anyway, my name is TamSen, and whatever this is we've gotten ourselves into, we're in it together. Let's see, what should I call you."

"Chewppa," the birdgirl twittered again in the same birdlike song.

"I guess I could call you 'Birdy,' " TamSen said with a chuckle, "Or, 'Body,' gosh, what a body. Or maybe I should just call you, 'Girl.' "

"Chewppa," she repeated aggravatedly, "my name Chewppa!"

After the initial shock of hearing her speak had worn off, TamSen realized that he had just poured out the innermost guarded secrets of his soul to the harpy who had most probably understood every word. It took far longer for him to realize that in spite of hearing and understanding, the harpy had shown no sign of ridicule.

TamSen cringed in the darkness, waiting for the inevitable laughter or some cutting remark, but instead, he felt her hand upon his arm and she placed her head upon his shoulder much as he had done earlier. A strange unfamiliar thrumming sound began to emerge from her throat. Had it not been for the high pitch, TamSen would have thought she was purring. But whatever the sound was, it didn't sound the least like laughter and for that he was most grateful.

After another long period of silence in which he subdued some of his reeling emotions, he was able to summon up enough courage to speak. "Who are you and how did you get here?"

"You told my story, too," she said. Use of the human language was clearly not her strong point and she spoke it with an accent that was so foreign to his ear that at first he had trouble comprehending what she was saying.

Slowly, struggling along with very broken speech, formulating each thought in her mind before speaking, the harpy told him of growing up a virtual outcast among her own kind, of the taunts and pranks, the hatred and the laughter.

She related how those of the aerie would have killed her as soon as her differentness became obvious had it not been for her mother's grudging protection.

She spoke of her fascination with the humans in the valley and how she had spied on them, of learning their ways and their speech by listening to them talk among themselves. She told of giving herself a name, a secret name never before spoken.

She told how the humans had tried to kill her, shattering her dreams of finding friendship and acceptance among them.

Chewppa described how the villagers had followed her to the aerie, killing her mother and sister and all the rest of her kind.

She enumerated the many encounters she had had with humans during her flight from the aerie to the island, ending with Shmerk's rock which had struck her upon the wing and tumbled her from the sky.

"Human hurted my wing," she said. "Wing breaked, I think."

TamSen flexed her wing gently and finally concluded that it was, in fact, most probably broken. She was obviously in great pain so he took off his leather belt, circled her narrow waist and strapped it across her folded wing, holding it immobile.

"All human try kill me," she said, "but not you. You, me, same. You not try kill me."

"But why did you come here?" TamSen asked. "Why didn't you stay in the mountains, away from humans?"

"I try find human father. I try find Mika-oba. He make good. He good. He magic," she added proudly.

Suddenly it dawned on TamSen that in all his soul-baring, the one thing he had neglected to tell his listener was the relationship of his father to the man whom Nurse had called only Mika, the wolf-magician.

Quickly, TamSen told Chewppa of the man Mika and asked if they could be one and the same, but the harpy gave no answer and the sound of soft breathing told him that she was asleep.

TamSen lifted his hand to her face, and the soft moist warmth of her breath filled him with a sense of satisfaction and peace that he had never felt before.

He shifted her head from his shoulder to his chest and slipped his arm around her, careful not to jostle the huge wing that fanned out behind him as he leaned against the wall. That barrier, hard, cold stone that it was, was more comfortable than any feather mattress. Sighing contentedly, he smiled into the darkness, and gave himself up to sleep.

Chapter 11

TAMSEN WAKENED to feel something moving behind him. For a moment, the darkness and his dream mingled. He had slept more soundly than ever he could remember. He was startled, but the feel of Chewppa's warm flesh brought him quickly alert.

It took another heartbeat for him to sift all information about his circumstances and then realize that the thing behind his back was Chewppa's wing.

The harpy was shifting restlessly and whimpering in her sleep and TamSen discovered that he had slumped backward in his sleep and pinned her wing beneath his body.

Attempting to remove himself from Chewppa's wing, TamSen received his first lesson dealing with strange body parts

No matter how he moved, TamSen could not get a firm grip on the wall, and in placing his hand behind him he only brought more pressure to bear on the injured wing.

Soon, TamSen became aware of his own body's

complaints and he stifled a groan of his own. Despite the happiness of his slumber, sleeping on a cold stone staircase was not conducive to comfort. It was all he could do to move.

TamSen's movements startled Chewppa into wakefulness and she sat straight up and uttered a loud screech of alarm. In the absolute quiet of the dark staircase, the horrible sound rang out magnifying itself many times over until it sounded like the annual Island Pig Slaughter Event. The noise so startled TamSen that he lurched forward, forgetting that there was no floor, only steps leading down. His head thumped against the ceiling of the sealed entrance, then his feet landed on, on nothing!

TamSen tumbled forward and down, wrapped in the total darkness of the staircase, falling for what seemed forever still on the edge of the unseen abyss.

When he finally managed to stop, fetching up against the stone wall with a tremendous crash, he had fallen down at least two hundred steps, judging by the large assortment of red-hot bruises on his body, each one screaming for attention. He lay still for the moment, quite unwilling to move.

"I know we had to go down the steps," he muttered to himself, "but not like THIS!"

He heard some fluttering and nervous chittering far above him. "Are you all right?" he called out.

A heartbeat later the harpy formulated the human words in her mind and replied, "Yes, I all right. I not falled. You falled."

"Yeah. I'm all right, too. Thanks for asking. Look, why don't you come on down, instead of me coming back up. I think I'd better stay here and see if everything still works," TamSen said as he righted himself painfully.

"I not see," said Chewppa.

"I thought owls and hawks could see in the dark," said TamSen, relieved to find that all parts of him were still properly connected and that none of those parts seemed to be broken.

"I not owl! I not hawk!" Chewppa proclaimed indignantly. "Even so, must have some light to see at night. No light is here!"

"Yes, well, that's something we're going to have to live with until we can find a way out of here," replied TamSen.

"I hungry."

Among the multitude of unhappy signals sent by his body, he added a new one. TamSen suddenly realized that he was hungry too. In fact he was ravenous!

"Maybe we can find something down below," he said, knowing that he was deluding himself.

After several long heartbeats of scraping sounds, Chewppa stood at his side. Giving comfort to a living thing was a new concept to Chewppa, but her heart went out to this human who was trying to help her and whom she had caused to injure himself through her careless cry of fright. Not knowing what else to do, she wrapped her wing around his body and drew him near.

The unexpected gesture and the warmth of her sympathy as well as the nearness of her beautiful body were more welcome to TamSen than all the bandages and balm in the world.

But soon, hunger returned, and TamSen knew that they would have to continue their journey down the seemingly endless staircase. He stood carefully, painfully and regretfully, pulling her up beside him.

"We have to go on," he said gently. "Follow me." He turned and began walking down the steps, with Chewppa pulling and tugging on his arm with every step.

"What are you afraid of?" he asked. "We can do this, just follow me."

"Cliffs," she said. "Can be cliffs. Us can fall off cliffs."

TamSen stopped dead still, and it dawned on him for the first time that just because he was on a staircase, didn't necessarily mean that his next step would land on a stair.

What if the stairs ended? What if he were to fall into some bottomless pit, pulling Chewppa with him! A sudden wave of fear immobilized him, and he broke out in a sweat as he realized the extreme danger of the situation. His knees gave way beneath him and he sat down on the steps and shivered.

From that point on, they crept downward at a snail's pace, one step at a time, feeling carefully before them to find the next step.

They inched forward at this slow pace for what must have been an entire day, until the moment came when TamSen felt forward only to discover an expanse of stone that continued on without a drop-off.

Exploring the space with caution, he realized at last that they had reached the end of the staircase. They were on solid ground.

The two, weary, begrimed, and hungry, crawled out onto the floor and rested. After a time, roused by the continuous growling of their stomachs, TamSen began to explore their surroundings.

Disappointment lanced into him with the sharpness of a knife as he discovered that the staircase had not ended after all. They were on a landing which dropped off to further steps on the far side. Then, just as his despair was at its highest peak, his hands encountered something.

Even though there was no light, identifying the objects was not difficult. There were several stones with very sharp and regular corners; crystals of some sort as well as a pile of hand-round objects, very light in weight that felt suspiciously like . . . loaves of bread!

Unknown to TamSen, the pure and simple greed of the previous travelers of these same stairs, twenty long years before, had saved him and Chewppa from starvation. As Mika's party traveled down the staircase, they discovered gems protruding from the stone walls and gathered them in great quantities.

On this same landing, they had emptied their pouches of several loaves of bread, filling the space with the most precious of the gems, reasoning that they would not need all of their provisions and could retrieve them on the way back.

As their journey continued, the gems grew more numerous and more splendid and more and more of their provisions were left at every landing. The bread, though two decades old, dry and extremely stale, had been preserved in the dark cold underground air, and was edible if not a gourmet delight.

After eating and resting for a time, TamSen and Chewppa searched the floor of the landing more thoroughly, took what supplies they could use and then resignedly resumed their downward trek. After a moment's thought, Chewppa picked up one of the crystals and tossed it before them. The sound of the gemstone bouncing down the steps continued for several heartbeats.

"No cliffs," Chewppa said. "We no crawl."

But even at the faster pace, the stairs seemed endless. Time ceased to have meaning. How many times had they slept? How many stairs had they descended? How many days had passed on the surface? The surface. Now almost a foreign concept. How far was it above them? TamSen gauged that they must be leagues into the oerth.

The steps curved and turned at odd angles and often doubled back beneath themselves. Were they still under the island, or were they somewhere beneath the sea? There was no way of knowing.

After what seemed like a lifetime of the unending darkness, they came to another landing which had a strange hollow sound. This time their voices did not echo. TamSen felt outward from the stairs and could find neither walls nor further steps. He was unable to touch or even sense the ceiling.

"We're at the bottom," he said with a sense of wonder. "We made it, Chewppa, we made it!" Joining hands, they twirled round and round joyfully till they became dizzy and collapsed on the ground, breathless.

"I can't believe you trusted me this long and followed me without question. No one's ever trusted me like this before. Now maybe we can start to look for a way out."

"No!" said Chewppa in a harsh firm tone that took TamSen aback. "My stone say we find Mika-oba here. We go find Mika-oba now."

"HERE?" said TamSen, very much surprised at her words.

"Here," Chewppa said firmly. "We go this way." And TamSen was left listening to the sound of her talons clicking against the stone floor as she vanished into the darkness. Unwilling to be left by himself. TamSen had no choice but to follow.

Chapter 12

AS TIME PASSED, a thought began to gnaw at Tam-Sen, causing him great worry and discomfort, yet he was afraid of mentioning it to Chewppa for fear of frightening her. Finally, worry overcame fear and he spoke.

"Uh, Chewppa, there's something you probably need to know about me," he began falteringly. "You know I'm part wolf, right, and that I'm the one who killed those sheep. Well, I didn't really mean to do it, but every now and then, something happens to me. It just comes over me no matter how hard I try to prevent it. Then, I wake up the next day not knowing what I've done the night before.

"I guess I actually become a wolf and I usually do something bad. I'm really worried Chewppa. The last thing in the world I want to do is to hurt you, but, I don't know what I'm doing when I'm a wolf.

"I'd hate me for the rest of my life if anything were to happen to you, when I'm a wolf. Do you understand what I'm saying?"

Chewppa did not reply.

Disturbed by her silence, TamSen babbled on. "Do you know what wolves are?" he asked.

"Yes," replied Chewppa. "I meeted wolf many oftens."

"Then you know how bad they can be," said TamSen.

"Wolf all right," said Chewppa. "But not good like rabbit."

"I know," said TamSen, relieved that she understood. "Wolves are a lot meaner. Now listen, if you suddenly meet a wolf down here, and it tries to hurt you, you must try to get away from it."

"Why?" said Chewppa. "Mother say, wolf not good like rabbit, but make bigger meal. Sister say wolf taste better than rat."

TamSen was shocked into silence. He walked beside her in the darkness, suddenly wary, wanting to believe that there had been a teasing tone in her voice, that she had been joking, but he couldn't really be certain.

In the silence that followed, they became aware of a sound in the cavern that was not being made by them. It was far distant and barely audible at first, then slowly the sound increased in volume until they knew without a doubt that they were no longer alone.

Conflicting emotions filled TamSen's breast as he stood still and tried to figure out what was making the noise and whether it was friend or foe. But no matter how hard he listened, he could not tell. Only three things were clear: whatever it was was moving fast, heading straight for them and was very, very big.

Now, for the second time, their blind helplessness

brought them true panic. They froze in place and clutched each other fearfully, waiting to see what would happen. Surely the thing was as hampered by the dark as they. But maybe not.

The unknown thing drew closer and closer until it was possible to separate the single loudness into several distinct sounds. High above them was the sound of heavy, raspy breathing, interspersed with hoarse whistling exhalations.

At head level there was the sound of claws or heavy scales brushing against the walls on either side as though the creature filled the tunnel from side to side.

Then, slightly distant and less distinct, was the sound of something heavy dragging, like an immense tail scraping along the ground.

They cringed behind a fortuitously placed boulder, in the faint hope that the thing would pass them by, but their hopes were in vain for the thing came to a stop directly in front of them.

They could hear its raspy breath high above them and could sense the immensity of its bulk. A rank stench filled their nostrils as something swished through the air in front of them, slammed against the boulder and sent it flying, leaving them exposed and defenseless.

TamSen grabbed Chewppa's wrist and pulled her after him as he tiptoed toward the unknown menace, the direction it would least expect them to go. They pressed against the stone wall and crept past. Then, carefully avoiding its tail, he pulled a handful of gems out of his pocket and threw them beyond the monster, in the direction from which they had come.

The gems struck the floor of the cavern some fifty

paces beyond the creature and it immediately lunged toward the sound showering them with stones kicked up by its powerful feet.

TamSen and Chewppa hurried away, crashing into walls in their panic, tripping over stones and making nearly as much noise as the creature they were fleeing. Unfortunately, the sound of their flight soon reached the monster's ears; angered by the subterfuge, it turned and uttered a low, hissing growl.

TamSen was doing his best to hold onto Chewppa as well as move along at a rapid pace. But when the monster growled, Chewppa stopped with a jerk and turned to face it, uttering the worst, most bloodcurdling screech TamSen had ever heard in his entire life, a scream that made all others before it pale into obscurity.

Magnified a thousandfold by the narrow strictures of the cave, the scream echoed and reverberated, growing louder and louder by the heartbeat till it seemed impossible, even to TamSen, that the sound had been made by only one being. It sounded like an entire army going into battle.

TamSen's head felt as though it were going to explode with the awful sound and he stumbled backward and came to rest against a stalagmite, knocking his head quite hard, which he barely noticed. Even Chewppa herself was more than a little startled by the unexpected volume.

The monster was evidently no less surprised than they were, never having heard anything like the terrible sound in its entire life. It must have leaped straight up in the air for there was an awful squishy, bone-crunching "thunk" from the vicinity of the cave's roof, followed by a heavy thump and a low groan as the monster fell to the ground.

This was followed by a number of loud crashes, interspersed with shrieks of pain as scores of stalactites, both large and small, rained down upon the hapless monster.

TamSen scrambled to his feet and groped through the darkness, anxious to find Chewppa, for if the monster were still alive, it would no doubt be very angry. They would do well to get as far away as possible before it recovered.

TamSen found Chewppa exactly where he had left her and grabbing her arm, pulled hard, trying to drag her after him. But it was no use, Chewppa would not leave.

Chewppa's stubborn courage sobered him and he suddenly realized that there would be no easy escape from this thing, no matter what it was. Chewppa would not go, and if she would not go, he too would have to stay. He might be deaf before he was dead, but that really didn't seem to matter.

Suddenly, he realized that they might never get out of the dark caverns, might not survive the monster's attack. Without thinking, forgetting the need for silence, he turned to Chewppa and blurted out impulsively, "Whatever happens, I think I love you!"

But the words, even if Chewppa had heard them and known what they meant, were lost in the sudden renewed hissing and shuffling as the monster drew near yet again. This time TamSen was almost prepared as Chewppa let out another screech, this one even more horrible than the one before.

The sound deterred the monster for a heartbeat

and it fell back several steps, but the sound also enabled it to locate them and it charged toward them with renewed vigor.

Its presence towered above them. The very immensity of the thing filled them with the knowledge that they would soon be crushed beneath its feet, yet still, Chewppa refused to move.

Determined to protect her to the best of his limited abilities, TamSen flung himself on her, placing himself between her and the monster, forcing her to the floor with the sheer weight of his body. TamSen was surprised to discover that his fear had left him.

As they fell, the air was filled with a strange humming sound. Even as TamSen wondered what had caused such a strange sound, there were numerous meaty thunks as though the monster were being struck repeatedly. This was followed by a deep, heartfelt moan and then a loud rumbling crash as the monster fell to the ground. There was a single gust of breath and then there was only silence.

"What was that?" TamSen said in a loud whisper as he pushed himself upright, wondering if the monster could truly be dead. "It almost sounded like bowstrings. What do you suppose happened?"

"Humans happened," Chewppa replied tensely, even more alert than she had been when facing the monster. "I heared that sound before. Humans shoot. Humans kill."

"Humans?" said TamSen. "There aren't any humans down here besides us, uh . . . me."

And then, as though it were an echo, a deep rolling voice came out of the darkness, saying, "human," in a twisted, ironic, tone as though the speaker were sneering.

A strange laughter broke out, cascading from hundreds of throats, snurkling, snorting laughter, like that of pigs rooting in mud or bulls in rut. And from the sound of it, they didn't like humans very much either . . . unless, of course, and TamSen's blood grew cold at the thought, unless humans tasted better than wolves or rabbits.

Chapter 13

THE FACT THAT TAMSEN and Chewppa had just been saved from one certain death didn't make the possibility of another death any less certain. Nor was their situation very good. At that moment, they were in total darkness and couldn't even see their own hands in front of their faces. They had no weapons at all, with the exception of rocks, and would have to scrabble around on the floor to find even those. They were confronted by hundreds of unknown Something-things who were armed, capable of seeing in the dark, and probably hostile.

They couldn't see to fight or run; and even if they could see, there was absolutely nowhere to run to. Their situation seemed hopeless.

TamSen could hear the sound of weapons being laid down on the ground. Obviously, these What-evers were not the least bit worried about the danger of confronting TamSen and Chewppa.

Next came the sound of rock striking rock. To TamSen's eyes, the resulting sparks glowed as bright as flares. A torch was lit, nearly blinding him and the one thing TamSen was able to discern before shielding his eyes was a very large, dark rock standing directly in front of him. It was large and lumpy and seemed to be pointing a spear at him!

Even as he stumbled backward, trying to avoid the spear, TamSen realized that what he had seen was neither rock, nor human, but one of the Whatevers, although he had heard no sound of its approach.

He cursed himself for falling about like a clumsy ninny, caught his balance, lunged for the figure and missed. As he stumbled past, a large hand as heavy and rough as stone grabbed him by the neck and held him firmly in place, as though he were but a small child. He struggled against the hand, but could not dislodge it. The more he struggled, the more exhausted he became, and still the thing did not weaken.

His breath came in gasps and he hung from the outstretched hand. Slowly, he became aware of the fact that the Whatever was chuckling softly. Mika twisted in the thing's grasp, hoping to catch a glimpse of his opponent. In this, he was not successful, but in the light of the glowing torch, he saw Chewppa, confronted by yet another of the strange figures.

The thought of Chewppa's danger drove him wild. Without a thought for his own safety, TamSen struck out with all his might, arms flailing wildly, trying to free himself so that he might protect Chewppa, but once again he met with failure.

The second figure was standing directly between Chewppa and the torch, so that its thick shadow was cast across her slender body like an evil stain. But

Chewppa seemed totally unaware of the horrible thing, so intent was she upon freeing her wing from the restraining belt.

When the wing was freed, Chewppa looked up, saw the thing standing before her, and swung at it with the rope. But the thing caught the rope in midair and giving it a mighty jerk, pulled Chewppa to its side.

The torch shone full upon her; there was a brilliant flash of blue between her breasts, and the sound of a hundred gasps.

The creature who held TamSen released him, shoving him aside roughly. Hurrying forward, it knelt before Chewppa and touched its forehead to the ground. There was an immediate hush among the creatures, and total silence reigned in the cavern.

TamSen and Chewppa stared at each other in open-mouthed astonishment, neither understanding what had happened. They looked around and saw at least a hundred lumpy creatures, bowed down before them, heads pressed against the ground and fat rumps upended in the air.

Neither TamSen nor Chewppa knew what to say or do and an awkward silence filled the cavern as though all of them had been stricken with a spell of paralyzation.

Slowly, uncertainly, a few of the creatures began to move, with eyes cast down. More torches were lit and one of the things approached them with a torch held high.

The mysterious creature was nothing more ominous than a squat little man with vastly exaggerated features. His eyebrows were bushy beyond belief, extending far out over his eyes. His nose resembled a huge potato stuck in the center of a pumpkin and his mouth was wide and mobile above a jaw that jutted out like the ledge of a cliff.

His body was equally remarkable, short, thick neck, massive chest and shoulders, arms thick with muscle and sinew and hands like hams and his thighs and legs were powerful, like those of a wrestler. He was quite short, the top of his head barely rising to the middle of TamSen's chest.

The color of his skin was like that of a mushroom, pale white and clearly grown without benefit of sunlight. He was not human, that much was clear, but there was a close resemblance.

The thing wore a multitude of weapons. Knives and sharp-pointed hammers protruded from his belt. A number of unidentifiable metal weapons hung from loops attached to a wide bandolier worn across the creature's shoulders. They would later learn that these were not weapons, but tools.

All this was learned in quick glimpses, as it was painful looking at the light after being in the dark for so long.

The sight of the approaching torch terrified Chewppa. She did not like fire or humans and certainly not in close proximity to each other. The last humans she had seen holding fire had used it to kill all the harpies in the aerie and she was certain that the moment of her own death had arrived.

Her third eyelid closed involuntarily against the sudden brightness, blinding her as effectively as though all the torches had once again been extinguished.

Vivid pictures of her sister and mother flashed through her mind. Her wings fluttered nervously and she uttered a low moan of despair.

A sudden image came to her, that of a farmer stroking a chicken's belly until its head fell back limp, its eyes glazed; then the farmer had chopped off its head. Unable to move, shivering with fear, Chewppa felt herself as helpless as the chicken.

Sensing her distress, TamSen moved quickly to her side and placed his hand on her arm. His touch was like that of a pin pricking a festival balloon. The resulting explosion of feathers and fury scattered the ugly creatures in all directions.

Chewppa flew straight up in the air and hovered above them, screeching and cawing. The things cringed and clapped their hands to their ears. Several attempted to reach their weapons, but it was impossible for even the strongest to ignore the terrible noise; and soon they too had dropped their weapons and were trying to shut out the horrendous sound.

Mouths grimaced in agony, but their screams of fear and pain went unheard above Chewppa's loud screeches. Not even TamSen was spared; their friendship offered no protection against the horrible high-pitched threnody. He quivered and shook on the ground among the rest of Chewppa's victims.

Not content with screaming, Chewppa swooped down, plucking the things off the ground in her powerful curved talons then flew to the peak of the cavern and dropped them onto the rocks below.

The terrified creatures, who had been the oppressors such a short time earlier and were now the victims, looked up in abject fear and saw only wings, claws, and the brilliant blue flash of the magic gem.

This one moment in time would live in tales and legends for centuries to come, and more specifically, in the worst nightmares of those present, throughout the rest of their lives.

At long last, after many of the creatures had met their doom, Chewppa grew tired and broke off her attack on the cringing lumps below. Her claws had opened many a gaping and bleeding hole in their tough hides. The boulders dripped with blood. Many of the creatures remained on the rocks, unmoving.

Chewppa landed on a ledge high on a wall of the chamber. She crouched there, chattering in a threatening manner at the cringing figures below, watching them with hawklike attentiveness.

The creatures who had suffered the greatest fatalities were those who had been nearest TamSen. At long last, the one who had first approached Chewppa and had by some miracle escaped injury, dared to speak, although he did not move.

"Help us, sir. Please make her stop. We are not your enemies and wish you no harm!"

TamSen hesitated for a heartbeat, then, because it seemed unlikely that the creatures could do them any harm under the present circumstances, called out to Chewppa. But Chewppa refused to listen, speaking not at all, uttering only the angry chittering.

The creature rose to his feet with many careful pauses and took a tentative step toward TamSen, then froze in his tracks at the resulting change in the tone of Chewppa's voice.

Realizing that only he could end the stalemate, TamSen got to his feet and approached the creature with no more than a cautionary chirp from Chewppa.

The creature's arm had been laid open along its entire length and there were three deep gouges across his chest. His thick leather shoulder belt had been completely severed and hung down around his knees.

Seeing that the fellow was not acting in a threatening manner, TamSen pulled a cloth from the man's tool belt and wrapped it around the injured arm.

As for the rest of the creatures, even those who were still able to move lay perfectly still and silent, hoping to avoid the fate of their less fortunate comrades who lay scattered about the cavern in pools of their own blood.

Chewppa's angry chitters finally dwindled away and ceased entirely. But she did not cease her relentless scanning of the area and she remained on the narrow ledge with wings spread wide and her magnificent body highlighted by the flickering torches. TamSen's gaze was drawn to the magic blue gemstone as it glittered in the torchlight and swung between her equally magnificent naked breasts.

Had the poor battered creatures below the courage to look up, their eyes would also have noticed the powerful feathered legs with their sharp and dangerous talons, but that part of Chewppa's anatomy somehow escaped TamSen's attention.

"I am sorry we have given you such fright," the creature said, fixing TamSen with large, doleful eyes. "None of us, including my poor friends whom the wizard has slain, meant you any harm.

"We were hunting the giant black cavernquatch. The monster has been raiding our caverns and killing our people. We were determined to put an end to it, as well we have, although at an unexpected cost. Had we not startled this magic lady and brought her wrath down upon us, this day would have been cause for a mighty celebration. Now, it will be remembered with sorrow and grief."

"I'm sorry, but I don't understand," said TamSen. "Who and what are you and what are you doing in this place?"

The creature drew himself up as tall as was possible and said: "We are dwarves of the lineage of Suloise. We are brave and fear nothing, but we will not and cannot fight against the magic of the stone. One who wears the stone commands our honor."

Looking down at the earnest little fellow, so grievously injured and seemingly innocent of any wrongdoing, TamSen called out to Chewppa. "Come down, Chewppa. They are friends. They will not hurt us."

Chewppa listened intently, peering this way and that. Finally, she seemed to be convinced and even the nervous fluttering of her wings ceased. But she refused to come down from her perch and remained where she was, on guard above them.

The dwarven leader approached her hesitantly, drawing as close as possible on the ground below. Cap in hand, he began to speak. His voice was very quiet, as are the voices of all cavern dwellers, yet it was the full, deep bass of a man accustomed to the role of leadership. As he spoke, his voice took on the rolling cadence of one reciting a confessional litany before a deity.

"Magician Chewppa," he began, "we are heartily

sorry if we have given you offense. We meant you no harm, and ask only that you accept our apologies and spare us further harm.

"We have been aware of you for some time now and followed you, hoping that the noise of your progress would bring the giant black cavernquatch, luring it to our arrows. We remained in darkness and silence so that it would not note our presence.

"We did not know who you were, nor why you were here. Never did we expect to find a wearer of the magic stone in our caverns. Had we but known, our actions would have been different. We did not mean to interfere in your plans, whatever they may be.

"I must admit to being confused even now," continued the dwarven leader. "Although I am but a lowly dwarf and cannot hope to understand the mind of a wizard.

"Since you did not choose to use the torches and flints which are placed at regular intervals on the walls, we naturally assumed that you were but ordinary, stupid humans and thus used you to our own benefit against the cavernquatch. For this, too, we are sorry.

"We did not realize that you were a magician who could turn yourself into a harpy, and that your assistant was a . . . uh . . ." He looked briefly at TamSen as though trying to figure out exactly what he was, then returned his gaze to Chewppa, as though fearing he had committed a sin by turning away.

TamSen thought about trying to explain his lineage to the dwarf, but he was too interested by the dwarf's revelations to interrupt.

"We did not mean to insult your great power by

thinking to save you from the cavernquatch," continued the dwarf. "We know now that, with your magic, you did not need us to save you from the beast. Nor were our poor brave dead lads ever a threat to either of you. Please accept our apologies for all that we have done so wrongly." And concluding his long speech, the dwarf backed away slowly.

Chewppa had studied him closely as he spoke. She did not understand all the words, but enough of them to realize that she would have no further trouble from the dwarves, at least for the time being. They seemed well-meaning enough, but would they turn on her as the humans had?

Chewppa spread her wings and glided silently through the cavern, landing beside TamSen. She put her hand on his arm as she turned to glare at the dwarves, who were careful to remain glued in place.

So frightening was her appearance that the dwarf leader averted his eyes and quickly decided that all future verbal transactions would best be carried on with the male, whatever he was.

Anxious to ease the situation, TamSen spoke up. "Forgive me for being dense, but I still do not understand exactly who you people are and how you come to be here in such an awful place."

The dwarf leader looked up, seemingly grateful for the opportunity to explain himself further.

"My name is Giebort, good sir. My men and I and all of our families are mountain dwarves, descendents of the ancient line of Suloise."

TamSen looked around him, wondering if he had somehow missed women and children dwarves.

"Many years ages ago, our forefathers traveled through the great high mountains of the Crystal Mist into the lands of the east, called Yeomanry," said the dwarf, wondering to himself what TamSen's furtive glances signified, wondering if there were perhaps other wizards lurking nearby who would slay even more of his men. He gulped and blinked rapidly at the terrible thought, causing Chewppa to chitter nervously, wondering why the fellow was acting so strangely.

Giebort, alarmed by the sounds and smart enough to realize that it was his own behavior that was disturbing the harpy wizard, brought his voice under control with great effort and continued the story.

"We lived and worked in Yeomanry for many years, mining the precious stones. But the work was hard and the profits were few and eventually, all attainable riches had been taken from the mountains.

"The high council was seeking a new direction, a new homeland, when they were approached by emissaries from the island of Dramidja. Great riches lay in the ground, unmined, said these emissaries, there for the taking. The king of this island was seeking workers who were brave enough to extract the riches from the oerth.

"Other than reports of the more ordinary sort of gems, the emissaries told of magical stones that could turn even the most ordinary of dwarves into powerful wizards. And this was of great interest to our Wizard Korlim."

"I take it that you decided to accept the emissaries offer," said TamSen, growing more and more interested in the dwarf's tale.

"Much to our sorrow," Giebort said with a sigh. "Our wise men, the elders, decided against the project for reasons that we now understand all too well, and returned to our ancient homeland.

"But we," he said, gesturing at himself and then at the others around him, "Ah, we were all very young then, mere children, but we were full of ourselves and felt ourselves old enough to make our own decisions.

"We wanted to make our own way, to be independent of the mines and the claims of our parents. We wanted to mine where stones were easy and plentiful. We wanted to be rich without work. And as you can see, we came to the right place."

As Giebort waved his hand, TamSen noticed for the first time that the walls around them glistened in the light of the torches, and that the ground was littered with crystals as well as rock. Crystals lay heaped in mounds like grains of sand and some had even been crushed beneath their feet.

TamSen reached down and picked up a beautiful green crystal, as long as his hand and extremely heavy. He held it up to the torchlight, and watched in awe as it took on the life of the fire. Its deep rich color was that of dark forests on a cloudy day.

As he looked into its cool depths, TamSen was overwhelmed with an intense longing for the forests far above. On the surface, this one stone would be worth the wages of a lifetime.

"Why do you not go back into the world and live like kings?" he asked. "There's enough wealth here for all of you."

"Ah, well, that's another story," Giebort said sadly, "and one that had best be told by the Wizard

Korlim himself, for it is not my place to speak further. If you would deign to honor us so, we will return to the safety of DwarvenHome and there, all will be explained."

Chewppa was not all certain that she wanted to go anywhere that would bring her into contact with even more of these strange, ugly creatures; and she made her feeling known to TamSen as the dwarf withdrew with many a polite word.

While the dwarves moved about the cavern treating the living and collecting their dead, Chewppa and TamSen were locked in a heated discussion.

Chewppa told TamSen in no uncertain words, or chitters as the case may be, that she could care less about the reasons for some stupid dwarves living in secret under the island. "Find father, find Mika-oba!" she repeated over and over, stubbornly refusing to listen or even consider any other suggestion and finally covering her ears with her hands and closing her eyes, as well.

But TamSen, disturbed by her obstinate behavior, grasped her wrists with his hands and forced her to listen.

"Chewppa, listen to me, we've done a terrible thing here. We've killed a lot of these little guys for no reason," he said gently, gallantly including himself in the dwarves' demise, even though he had had little or nothing to do with the slaughter. "I think that if they want us to go with them to this DwarvenHome place, then we ought to do it. We might even learn something.

"Think about it, these dwarves have been living down here for hundreds of years. If Mika-oba is down here, who would know about it better than they? They're our best hope of finding him."

Chewppa opened her eyes and looked at TamSen intently, considering his words. Her eyes grew bright and she became agitated. Leaping to her feet, she demanded in strident tones that they leave immediately.

Relieved that he had convinced her and hoping that he was right about the dwarves' knowledge, TamSen rose and approached Giebort.

"We will go with you, Giebort, but only for a time. We are here on a quest of our own, searching for someone, and that must take precedence."

"Searching for someone? Here in the caverns?" Giebort said, thinking with horror that he had been right after all. There were more wizards!

"Yes. A human, one Mika-oba by name. Do you know of him?"

"I know of no such name, but perhaps the Wizard Korlim will know," replied Giebort.

"We know that he is here," said TamSen. "My own grandfather told me that a man named Mika entered the caverns with a party of people and wolves, and has never been heard from again. It is they whom we must find."

"Oh!" exclaimed Giebort, his face brightening with comprehension. "You must mean the people in the Pillar of the Demon Hand. That is very far from here, and must not be approached, for it is a magical and dangerous place. Even the Wizard Korlim takes care to avoid it."

TamSen, overjoyed that his guess had proved correct and that their quest was to be so easily resolved, did his best to conceal his expression. He agreed to accompany the dwarves to DwarvenHome and seek the Wizard Korlim's advice on the magical pillar, then he hurried back to share the good news with Chewppa.

Chewppa was unable to conceal her happiness. Her fear and distrust of the dwarves vanished in her great joy and she rushed over to Giebort as he knelt beside one of his wounded comrades.

Giebort looked up to see her standing above him and knelt before her, an expression of abject terror frozen on his face.

"Where Mika-oba?" she demanded.

"In the Pillar of the Demon Hand," Giebort replied shakily.

"More! You tell more!" demanded Chewppa.

"I, I really don't know any more," stammered Giebort. "The pillar only appeared in the last great quake, some twenty years ago. They say that there are people and wolves trapped inside. But none of this can I tell you in fact, for I have never seen it."

"We go now!" commanded Chewppa.

"I cannot, my lady," whispered Giebort. "I do not know the way. And even if I did, there is great danger. Anything that touches the pillar which is not solid but made of some magical substance, is sucked inside and lost forever."

"We go get wizard!" shouted Chewppa. "Wizard get Mika-oba out!"

"I wish that it were so," Giebort said miserably. "But even the Wizard Korlim cannot break the magic of the pillar. Ten years ago, bearing Korlim's spell of protection, one of our own brave people, Bij, the Wizard Korlim's own son, tried to enter the pillar and rescue those trapped within, but he too, was sucked into the pillar and never returned. Since that time, we have been forbidden to go near the pillar without the Wizard Korlim's permission."

"We go Wizard Korlim!" said Chewppa, glaring at Giebort, arms folded across her chest and talons clicking impatiently on the hard stone floor.

Travel preparations were quickly made and what little edible meat exists on a cavernquatch was collected and packed away.

As the group got underway, heavily burdened with dead and wounded, Giebort turned to TamSen and said, "We have far to go, and there are many dangers along the way. It is fortunate that we are in the company of a wizard, for some of the monsters with whom we battle have magic abilities of their own and losses are frequently great. The wizard Chewppa's powers may well be needed."

TamSen said nothing, having no knowledge of Chewppa's wizardry, other than the magic he himself felt whenever she was near. But if the dwarves chose to believe that she was a wizard, who was he to deny it, especially if it helped them achieve their goal. And if they were lucky, they wouldn't meet up with anything that couldn't be stopped by good, old-fashioned violence.

Chapter 14

QUOTAR'S SON, SHMERK, had become a local hero. He, of course, had repeated his story of how he drove away the monstrous giant harpy singlehandedly and without weapons.

The harpy had, by now, grown to more than fifteen feet in height with a wingspan that nearly blotted out the sun. Shmerk insisted that she had surely been the forerunner of whole flocks of harpies, intent on taking over their island. Only his brave efforts with no thought of his own personal danger, his overwhelming defeat of the harpy, had kept the rest of the flock from descending on the island and picking it clean.

But much to Shmerk's dismay, TamSen had become a hero as well. When he had first disappeared, it was rumored that he had run away out of shame for having lost the sheep to the harpy. This rumor, which Shmerk had actually begun himself, lost credence as the weeks went by. For the island had been thoroughly searched and still, there was no sign of him.

Slowly, the story began to change.

Eventually, it became obvious, even to Shmerk and Quotar, that TamSen was no longer on the island. The Dock Captain's records had been checked and it was found that no ships had approached or left the island in months. TamSen had to be on the island . . . if he were still alive.

Quotar's woods and fields were combed by scores of searchers, then in turn the surrounding lands, but still there was no sign of TamSen.

At last it was determined that the harpy had killed TamSen sometime during the early morning hours, and was in the process of attacking the sheep when Shmerk drove it off.

Only the fact that the harpy's appetite had already been slaked had kept Shmerk from being killed and devoured as the unfortunate TamSen had been.

It was equally obvious to everyone that despite Shmerk's bold words, the harpy had not been killed and had escaped with TamSen's body, or what little remained of it.

While searching for TamSen, the townsfolk had trampled most of the underbrush, crushing it beneath their heavy hobnailed boots. This same crushed underbrush led those same searchers to conclude that a tremendous struggle had occurred between TamSen and the harpy.

And suddenly, in death, TamSen's unsung heroism overshadowed Shmerk's loud tale, tenfold. There was even some talk of erecting a statue in TamSen's honor, but that soon faded away when the town accountant dared ask how it was to be paid for.

Then, just as suddenly, everyone on the island became concerned over the sick Nurse and TamLis, the all but unknown sister of the great hero TamSen.

Why, mothers asked themselves, had TamLis been so distant and not become friends with their daughters? Why, fathers asked, had their sons not noticed how beautiful she was?

To TamLis, however, the whole affair was grievously painful and she shrunk from the townsfolk's attentions.

She stood looking out the window of the cottage one morning, pondering the whole unhappy situation. Her thoughts had become so muddled during the past weeks that she scarcely knew what to think anymore.

Nurse's health had taken a turn for the worse. But now that such concern had developed within the community, the healer made regular visits and supplies, and firewood appeared at their door.

Their hunger was gone, but the enjoyment of a full stomach was tainted with guilt, knowing that this new beneficence had been gained at the cost of TamSen's life.

And then there was the whole matter of TamSen's death to be dealt with. TamLis was still struggling with what now appeared to be incontrovertible fact, that TamSen had indeed lost his life to the harpy.

All her life she had dreamed of a family who would love her, yearned for the acceptance of the townsfolk, and now that she had it, she found that it could not begin to make up for the loss of the one person who always had loved her.

Tears welled up and she fought them back, as

though in denying their flow she could deny Tam-Sen's loss.

Never in her life had she known such kindness. People had been nicer to her than ever before, especially when the subject turned to TamSen. The same people who for years had hurled barbed and cutting words at her and TamSen were now covering their words with velvet.

Even Dame Quotar had visited, bringing with her a platter of mutton steaks, saying only that they had come by the meat unexpectedly and didn't want it to be wasted. TamLis accepted the meat, though she knew that she would not be able to eat it. In a way, she thought, the bare truth is easier to take than half truths or lies.

"Well," she said in a low tone as she turned from the window, "I should really stop fretting about what people think and wondering about their motives. Nurse is comfortable for the first time in years, and that is all that really matters."

Shaking her gloom from her with a deep sigh, TamLis crossed the room, intending to begin supper for Nurse. She opened the pantry door, full of strong resolve, entered the pantry and as she stared at the strange sight of fully-stocked shelves, was immediately lost in thoughts of TamSen.

Ignorant of the fact that he was a dead hero, and that Nurse and TamLis were grieving over him, TamSen rose from the rock where he and Chewppa had been resting as the dwarves gave the command to move out.

The relationship between he and Chewppa had, to

his amazement, continued to improve. He had agreed to help her learn the human language and she had responded with enthusiasm. She pressed on, determined to learn, even when she was tired and found it difficult to formulate sentences in the foreign tongue. More and more they spoke to each other as the language barrier shrunk, sharing with each other all the bits of their lives.

TamSen loved listening to her no matter whether she was speaking human or harpy. He loved all of her sounds, with the single exception of the horrible screams. He found her voice more melodic than any island song he had ever heard, at least when she spoke to him. It was not always so when she spoke to the dwarves.

In spite of her lack of open hostilities, the dwarves continued to regard her with great trepidation. They had a fear of her supposed magical powers, and Chewppa did nothing to lessen those fears.

With TamSen, however, she was as tender and loving as could be. All of the love that had been stored inside her all of her life was now directed toward TamSen. All the love that TamSen had been deprived of, was now his to enjoy.

Only by being loved did TamSen realize how fully he loved in return. The joint emotion was so overwhelming, he was unable to determine which was more fun, loving or being loved. It was a delightful dilemma.

On one of their rest stops, Chewppa asked TamSen how human women wore their hair. He had made a crude comb using the dwarven tools and had tried to show her, only to have the comb snag instantly in the years' accumulation of snarls and knots. Now, much of their free time involved trying to separate the tangles from the curls. It took many, many days to undo the years of neglect, but when it was done, TamSen wished that it could have lasted a lifetime.

Once again the dwarves gathered their gear and removed the torches from standards mounted on the walls. Traveling with light certainly had its benefits. TamSen could not only see where he was going, and get there without falling on his face, but he could also see Chewppa. She was beautiful.

Although they were no longer descending, the caverns were still very cold, even to TamSen who was fully clothed. He had repeatedly offered his jacket to Chewppa. She had steadfastly refused, being accustomed to the thin, cold air of the mountains, and had not felt the slightest discomfort.

But TamSen did not understand, nor did he like the thought of the dwarves looking at Chewppa's bare body. He, of course, did not know that dwarves considered human anatomy ugly and unattractive, and that they were only looking at the magic gem.

TamSen continued to insist that Chewppa take his jacket. Finally understanding that the jacket was a symbol of his caring, she agreed at last.

She could not wear the jacket as it was intended to be worn because her wings got in the way, and was forced to wear it backward. Her arms were thrust through the sleeves which were far too long and had to be rolled up.

The jacket was buttoned behind her. One side of the frontpiece covered her wounded wing and compressed it tightly into the too-small space. The buttons and opposite side of the jacket passed beneath the base of her other wing.

But worst of all was the rough, homespun wool from which the jacket was made, which chafed and irritated her tender skin as though she had chicken mites.

It was probably the most uncomfortable thing that had ever happened to her in her life. Of all the things she envied about being human, she soon decided that wearing clothes was not one of them. She vowed that should she succeed in freeing herself of the awful garment, she would never wear clothes again.

But TamSen had come to believe that it was more than necessary for Chewppa to wear clothes, for time and again he would look up only to find the dwarves looking at her and it ate at him like acid.

In reality, the dwarves were looking at him, not Chewppa who held no attraction in their eyes, and they averted their eyes when they caught his gaze. More and more they had begun to wonder whether their initial assessment of his role had been wrong.

It was now obvious to them that TamSen was not the wizard's assistant and was most probably her consort. Now, to be the consort of any woman was, to the dwarves way of thinking, a condition worse than death.

How any male could allow such a thing to happen was beyond their comprehension. It was totally humiliating. No red-blooded dwarf would allow his woman to be dominant, love notwithstanding. The fear they felt for Chewppa's magic was now matched by the pity and loathing they felt for TamSen.

As they settled into place around a small fire before

a sleep break, the dwarves began discussing the subject yet again. They recalled that during the attack in which the harpy wizard had almost destroyed them, TamSen had just stood by, watching. While they were glad that there was only one adversary to worry about, it was generally agreed that anyone worth his salt would have taken part in the battle.

True, it was he who had calmed the harpy at last and he to whom they appealed when they needed to speak to the wizard, but none of those facts alleviated their scorn.

From the facts available to them, they had concluded that TamSen was no fighter. Nor could they depend on him to do battle with the monsters that they were likely to meet on the journey home. Their scorn turned to cold dislike.

The discussion raged back and forth. A goodly number of the dwarves felt that if they encountered a monster, they would just ignore the consort and let him take care of himself. With any luck at all, the monster would do away with him before the battle ended.

This thought was met with a certain amount of cautious disagreement. Might the wizard not resent the fact that they had allowed her consort to be killed and punish them for his death? It was suggested that they might actually consider protecting the consort so that he did not come to harm.

This point of view was met with jeers and sounds of derision.

"We don't need the consort's help," said Giebort, growing tired of the entire discussion. "If the consort needs to be protected, the wizard will do it, not us.

"And for that matter, we can get along without her help too. We've never needed a wizard's help getting home before this and we don't need it now.

"I don't want to see anyone dropping back from the fight, if and when it comes. Anyone who does will face me later, and let me tell you, it's better to die at a monster's hands than mine.

"Any questions?" And without waiting for a show of hands, the question period ended. Giebort snapped his cap down over his eyes, and settled in to sleep.

Chapter 15

TAMLIS SAT NEAR NURSE in the growing darkness. Nurse's breathing had been very uneven all day, and TamLis had grown increasingly worried. She had run to a neighbor's earlier and the healer had been sent for, but he had yet to arrive. Nurse stirred and slowly opened her eyes.

"He's alive, darling. You musn't fret so. I know he's alive, I can feel it."

"Yes, I know," said TamLis, reaching up to hold Nurse's hand. "I feel it, too," she lied. "I'm sure he'll be back soon."

Nurse closed her eyes and said, "I've loved you and that boy from the minute you were placed in my arms. You were so beautiful, so tiny . . ."

TamLis knew that her beloved Nurse would continue like this, talking to herself, living in her memories until she dropped off to sleep again.

Still holding Nurse's hand, she lay her head on the bedside. She was so tired, staying up day and night with Nurse, never knowing when she would waken and call her name, perhaps wanting nothing more than to talk had taken its toll on her.

It had been weeks since TamLis had slept in her own bed or eaten a meal at the table. Where was TamSen? Was he really dead? Was she to lose the only two people whom she had ever loved in such a short period of time? How long would it be before there was no more Nurse? Tears came to TamLis's eyes and she realized that all the heartaches caused by Nurse's age and illness were preferable to being without her.

All of a sudden, in the middle of Nurse's rambling speech, her eyes opened and she looked at TamLis and squeezed her hand gently.

TamLis sat up quickly and looked at Nurse in alarm. Nurse smiled. "You must have faith, my dearest. Have faith. Do not give up on one you love so easily. He's alive, TamLis, and he's all right. I would know if he were dead."

Nurse's eyes closed again and once more she began her rambles, but TamLis felt a surge of hope, and a smile came to her lips. Nurse was right, TamSen had to be alive for surely she would know it if he were dead. She lay her head on Nurse's bed, and fell into a deep and dreamless sleep.

The next day dawned sunny and crisp and Nurse had awakened in her right senses, feeling no pain. The night's sleep had refreshed TamLis as well; she sang as she cleaned the cottage, and roasted a hare and some potatoes over the fire for their dinner.

Toward midday, a young man named Tallo appeared, hat in hand, on their doorstep to see if they needed any help.

TamLis recruited him instantly and they moved

Nurse's bed outside, so she could enjoy the sunshine while they picked the last of the beans in the small garden.

They worked in companionable silence, looking at one another when each thought the other was not looking; and they liked what they saw. There had been a time several years earlier when TamLis had accompanied Nurse on a trip to town and had looked up from her packages and caught Tallo looking at her around the side of a tree trunk. She had smiled, and he smiled back, but quickly dropped his head and didn't look up again.

This had occurred several times, on her each and every visit to town. It almost seemed as though Tallo watched for her, for he was always there when she passed. She had always smiled in an encouraging manner, but never had he spoken.

That Tallo was very shy was obvious. TamLis had determined that on her next trip she would try to speak to him, but as she approached he was thrust out at her from behind the tree, thrown by a group of larger boys, led by Shmerk, who had laughed uproariously and called out, in loud, jeering voices, "Kiss the fuzzy face, Tallo."

Tallo had gotten to his feet, his face scarlet, and had run away as fast as his feet could carry him. Never again had he waited for her behind the tree.

She realized that day that there would probably never be anyone who would be strong enough to fight the taunts and jibes of the others and be her friend. She had never again accompanied Nurse to town, but she had never forgotten Tallo.

Nor had Tallo forgotten her or forgiven himself for

having run from Shmerk and his gang of bullies. TamSen's absence and the town's renewed conscience over the plight of Nurse and TamLis had allowed him the opportunity of seeing her again.

His shyness kept him from speaking overly, but somehow it did not seem to present a problem, TamLis was always glad to see him. He began to visit more and more often until his presence, working beside her in the garden or sitting quietly by Nurse's bed, had become a silent commitment.

TamLis bloomed in his steady, quiet company, knowing that at last there was someone for her. Nurse smiled at them from the bed, watching with pleasure as the two young people forged the bond that would never be broken.

It was late in the month of Harvester on a bright and sunny day. TamLis was hard at work in the garden, pulling the last of the onions from the oerth and Tallo was high on a shaky ladder repairing the thatching on the roof, when Nurse suddenly called them to her.

"It is a good day, children, always remember that there are days like this," she said as she lifted her small withered face to the sun. Then, taking each of their hands in hers, she said, "You must listen now, for it is most important."

TamLis smiled at Nurse, prepared to humor her; when she realized that the woman was both lucid and extremely serious.

"TamLis, as you know, you are the heir to the throne of Dramidja, and it will soon fall upon you to see to the needs of your people.

"They are not always good people, TamLis, but they are yours to care for and you must show them more compassion than they showed you or your poor brother. Always remember that compassion is the mark of true royalty.

"There have been few ships and no trade since my king fell from power. But the ships will return one day soon, not to trade, but to conquer.

"You must be strong, TamLis. The people of Dramidja do not yet look to you as their queen. They have not treated you with honor.

"But the time will come when there is both danger and need, and they will know the fear of death. Then they will turn to you and you will lead them, for the blood of kings flows in your veins.

"Tallo, you will be the one upon whom TamLis will depend when the time of fighting comes. You love her. You must stand by her and be strong.

"I have seen a great invasion of this land," said Nurse, her voice growing weaker and her eyes taking on a strange faraway look. "I have seen battalions of soldiers, with you and TamLis at their head. I have seen fierce battles, and many deaths. I have seen terrible things that I don't understand, and I fear them."

Nurse turned her head to look at them and TamLis saw that tears were pouring down her cheeks. "I have seen you, TamLis, fighting against TamSen, and that I understand least of all. You must never fight against your brother, TamLis, he loves you most on all this Oerth and would never cause you pain."

Nurse lifted Tallo's hand to her lips. "I cannot help but leave her. Promise me that you will never do so."

Tallo looked up at TamLis, his blue eyes shining, and in them, TamLis saw only love.

Chapter 16

TAMSEN'S FIRST TEST of courage was about to occur.

As happens frequently in combat, the battle exploded with such suddenness that everyone was caught by surprise. Even the most experienced among them were taken completely unaware and many of the dwarves died in those first heartbeats of the attack.

They had been making their way through a small passageway between two larger caverns which they knew from past experience to be a dangerous area. It was layered with huge slabs of dense granite, and was therefore a favorite habitat of granite moles. Now granite moles are not swift, just very large, and possessors of voracious appetites. It is possible to avoid them with proper warning, but the dwarves were given no such opportunity.

The rocks on either side of them suddenly sprouted arms from their undersides and began grabbing the ankles of the dwarves. As the dwarves fell, the rocks lifted up in some mysterious manner, hovered for a heartbeat and then dropped down on top of their startled victims.

Luckily, the rocks landed on lower limbs, thus crushing feet and legs, rather than heads and arms, but even so, several of the dwarves failed to survive the attack.

Chewppa stood in the middle of the corridor, looking around in bewilderment, unable to comprehend what was happening. Then, feeling something touch her ankle, she looked down and saw a hand gripping her left leg.

Now this was something she could understand. Uttering a shrill scream, Chewppa raised the other foot and ripped the hand from its arm with her talons.

The rock monster keened its pain in a strange grating tone, drew in its bleeding stub as well as its other arm and did not move again.

Chewppa's shrill scream only served to disorient the dwarves, but unfortunately seemed to have no effect at all on the rock monsters.

Chewppa stood on top of the rock monster that she had disabled and surveyed the scene, quickly noting the similarity between the rock monsters and mountain abalone.

These were large land-dwelling crustaceans that had left the seas and learned to fasten themselves to the sides of mountains, opening at opportune moments and seizing the unwary bird or small harpy.

These she had learned to pry off the rocks near her Yatil Mountain aerie, after she had lost the taste for red meat.

She pondered the rock monsters for a heartbeat,

then reached down, grabbed the edge of the stone, and flipped it over with a mighty jerk. The underbelly was a surprising arrangement of arms, legs, wildly rolling eyes and row after row of rasping teeth, all of which led to a single central mouth which opened and shut rhythmically, waiting to be fed.

Once on its back the monster proved as helpless as an overturned tortoise. Arms and legs flailed, eyes rolled, teeth snapped and it emitted a constant stream of ugly gurgling growls.

TamSen had also been grabbed by one of the monsters, but had been fortunate enough to fall against another one, rather than flat on the cavern floor.

The rock that had attacked him could not understand what had happened; evidently the creatures were not too bright. It kept tugging on his ankle and hopping up onto what little of his leg it could reach, trying to squash him.

Unfortunately for the monster, TamSen did not have the least desire to be squashed, and having observed Chewppa's actions, he seized the lower edge of the rock and flipped it over on its back.

But the monster still had a firm grip on TamSen's ankle and as it flipped over, it retained its grip on TamSen's ankle, flipping him over as well. As TamSen flew through the air, too surprised to do anything at all, the rock monster took the opportunity to swallow his foot

Over they went, TamSen screaming with the sudden, unexpected pain and the rock monster careening around on its back. As the monster began to settle, TamSen came to his senses and jammed his swallowed foot down hard, hopefully damaging whatever soft tissues line the gullet of a rock monsters' throat, and used his other foot as leverage to pull himself out.

Having learned the trick, TamSen limped to the nearest dwarf, grabbed the rock monster who had succeeded in pinning him, and flipped it over. The dwarf's leg was not a pleasant sight as the rows of rasping teeth had already stripped much of the skin away, but at least the fellow was alive. He flashed the dwarf what he hoped was a smile of encouragement, then rushed off to help the others.

TamSen ran from one monster to another, flipping them over and trying to avoid looking at the horrible carnage beneath them. After a short time, the room took on a truly strange appearance.

Under lit by the torches which had all fallen to the floor, the room seemed to consist of many large stone bowls, rocking back and forth, with arms and legs sticking out of them and waving in all directions. The shadows which they cast on ceiling and floor were strange beyond belief.

Those dwarves who were still able, slowly rose from the floor, careful not to be caught by the grasping hands, which would surely attempt to pull them over the edge and into the gaping maws.

As the dwarves recovered their senses, they took out their swords and began to slice off all the protruding arms and then the legs for good measure. After this was done, they turned to aid their fallen comrades. By the time it was completely done, fully a fourth of their number had died, and another fourth would never walk again without the aid of a staff.

After seeing to his men, Giebort approached Tam-

Sen, doffing his cap as he came. "You have our thanks, sir," he said somberly.

"Our losses would have been much higher had you not come to our aid. Never before have we met such as these, but the caverns are dark and deep and one never knows what to expect."

"Chewppa showed me what to do," TamSen said, feeling his face go red.

"Aye, that is as it may be," said Giebort, "but it was you who saved us and this we will tell to the Wizard Korlim. It will win you great respect in his eyes, as well as those of our people."

"I didn't do it for that reason," said TamSen. "I was just trying to help. Anyone would have done the same."

"No," said Giebort, "not everyone. And if I may be so bold as to give you advice, do not refuse the credit for this battle nor shift it to your wizard master. You have earned our respect. Do not insult us with your modesty. We owe you a debt which can never be repaid—except with our lives."

Chapter 17

WITH A FEW EXCEPTIONS, there were no further mishaps on their journey to the place the dwarves called DwarvenHome.

Those exceptions, which the dwarves dismissed as "nothing," were encounters with several nasty creatures who hoped to eat them for dinner. There was also a sudden unexpected encounter with a huge granite mole.

They dispatched the granite mole easily and left it where it fell, burdened as they were with the dead, the lame and the wounded; they hoped that it would be there when they returned, for its meat with its tight, gray grain and delicate flavor was much prized by their people.

After what had seemed like weeks of endless travels through corridors and chambers that all looked the same, they entered a large room whose roof was hung with sparkling, glistening stalactites of every size and length.

These incredible structures were matched on the

ground below by stalagmites which rose to meet the ceiling above. The torches reflected off the gleaming surfaces, turning the amazing chamber into a fairyland of beauty and light. It was easily the most beautiful sight that either TamSen or Chewppa had ever seen and they lagged behind the tolerant dwarves, stunned by the beauty displayed around them.

Now, even the dour dwarves became noticeably cheery. It was a cheeriness that proclaimed the nearness of home. And now their footsteps slowed to match those of Chewppa and TamSen; they began to look around them for the tiniest hint of movement and they listened for even the faintest whisper of sound, as though expecting something to leap out from behind a rock and get them.

Giebort spoke very quietly to two of his people, who then disappeared into the darkness beyond the light of their torches.

Then, having grown more comfortable with addressing Chewppa directly, he turned to her and said, "The entrance to our home is located on the far side of this chamber. Our presence draws many creatures here where they wait among the rocks, hoping to catch us unaware."

"Our scouts have just gone to search out the ground ahead and report whether all is clear. If so, we must run for the safety of our home keeping as fast a pace as we are able. If it is not clear, we must fight our way across."

Chewppa surveyed the large room, and said, "I fly better than scouts walk. I fly up. I see down. If monsters here, I see them first."

Then taking the torch from Giebort's hand, she

spread her wings, and soared high above them, searching out every nook and cranny of the cavern below. They watched in silence as the torch appeared and disappeared behind tall stalagmites.

Once, there was a small commotion and the torch descended at an acute angle, then disappeared behind a large stalagmite. There was a brief flurry of muffled sounds, then silence.

Once again the torch rose into the air and Chewppa continued her circumnavigation of the huge room. After a time, she returned and handed the torch to Giebort as she landed.

"No more monster. We go."

However, the dwarven guards who were watching over the entrance to DwarvenHome had become very alarmed by the sight of a flying monster with fire coming out of its mouth, something that they had never seen before.

As Giebort's party hurried across the cavern, weaving in and out among the stalagmites, following a course they had obviously traveled many times before, they found themselves face-to-face with an entire contingency of armed dwarves.

"Beware, sir, and take cover!" cried the leader of the battalion, "there's a huge monster circling above, breathing fire!"

Much to the guard's amazement, Giebort and all of his men burst into laughter. Clapping the man on the back, Giebort drew him forward into the thick of their party until they came face-to-face with Chewppa and TamSen.

"Here is your monster," he said with a chuckle, "as well as our esteemed guests! They are the harpy

Wizard Chewppa and her assistant TamSen who have saved our lives and are here to consult with the Wizard Korlim. And now, Sergeant, you may lead us home."

And so began the procession into DwarvenHome which soon took on the aspect of a festive parade. The words "wizard" and "harpy" spread through the corridor faster than torchlight. Those who had stepped aside for their incoming comrades suddenly rushed forward to see this strange, new sight.

As Giebort's men passed among them carrying their dead and wounded, they found themselves bombarded with questions about their casualties, the number of monsters they had fought and, of course, the newcomers.

Giebort had been left at the entranceway, still explaining to the captain of the guards about TamSen and Chewppa. Every word he said was overheard by the throng pressing against them and repeated, often incorrectly, from one dwarf to another throughout the long corridor.

As they moved along the passageway, those in the crowd were presented with the grim sight of their returning comrades, few of whom were uninjured, carrying another who was either far more gravely wounded, or dead.

As they drew nearer, each dwarf was first fascinated by TamSen, with his strange clothing and furry skin, then dumbstruck by the sight of Chewppa.

Now, to be honest, TamSen and Chewppa were definitely an odd couple and would probably have attracted attention anywhere, even on the surface of Oerth; but these dwarves had seen nothing and no one but other dwarves and monsters for the past four hundred years.

Then too, many of them were quite young, young that is as dwarves go, being less than three hundred years old. These "youngsters" had been born in the caverns and knew of the many life forms from the world above only through the stories and legends of their elders.

Dwarves have their legends as do humans and they include many a bloody story about harpies. Their first reaction to Chewppa, then, was one of fear.

It only took a fraction of a heartbeat though before they saw blue stone hanging between the harpy's breasts. Seeing the stone, they fell to their knees, for it was immediately obvious to even the smallest of them that this stone was identical to one worn by their Wizard Korlim.

The result of thousands of dwarves falling to their knees in the crowded passage, already rife with rumor and hearsay, was a trail of pandemonium such as had never occurred in DwarvenHome.

Spears tilted at odd angles and banged other dwarves on the head and other less-hard portions of their anatomies. Arrows were spilled from their quivers, cascading down in painful array. Knees were punched into ribs, backsides bumped into chins and no one was able to keep his balance. Had there actually been an enemy at the gates, it could have easily eaten its fill of dwarf meat.

Chapter 18

THE ENTRANCE TO DWARVENHOME was bare rock, but as soon as one entered the passage proper, the walls were intricately carved with what appeared to be dwarven history.

Once through the passage itself and into the cavern that was DwarvenHome, TamSen was startled to discover that they had somehow ascended to the surface and were actually above ground!

This amazing discovery brought him to an abrupt halt, backing up the procession behind him and causing many a bruised nose. Only after careful study were he and Chewppa able to see that they were still underground and what they saw was but an extraordinary illusion.

The cavern was of staggeringly huge dimensions. Looking closely, after Chewppa pointed it out to him, TamSen was able to make out the far wall, but between them there rose a faint haze such as one might see on Oerth on a fine summer's day . . . or was it actually a cloud?

Following Chewppa's excited chitters and pointing finger, TamSen looked up and saw what appeared to be a bright blue sky shining overhead, but in reality it was merely the roof of the cavern. Here and there, if one looked closely, were a number of blue stalactites where one might have expected clouds or birds.

They found themselves standing on a small rise where the passageway actually entered the giant cavern. The entire panorama of the small, crowded city lay before them, a city that glittered with the sparkle of millions upon millions of precious gemstones.

A small rivulet wove its way across the entire length of the cavern, crisscrossed by bridges at numerous locations. One such bridge was located directly below them and appeared to serve as the main entrance to the city.

From where they stood, even TamSen's unpracticed eye was able to identify the bridge as having been carved from a single solid block of emerald. Another bridge was made of sapphire, another of ruby, and still another of gold.

The homes of the dwarves were encrusted with gemstones; windows appeared to be made of some natural crystalline material. Doors were made of ornately carved precious stones and ornamented with knockers and knobs of gold and silver. The streets and open areas were paved with highly polished adventine, giving it the subtle look of green grass.

The base of a huge stalagmite, a hundred feet or more in diameter, and forty or fifty feet high, rose in the exact center of the cavern. Its top had been leveled, and placed in the exact center was a large emerald throne.

The throne faced east onto another passageway which seemed to project a curious shimmering light.

As they gazed upon the peculiar light, TamSen and Chewppa suddenly became aware of the sound of water.

A single house stood isolated on a rise on the far side of the city, entirely separate from the rest of the community. There did not seem to be anything special about this house; it was certainly no palace, being, if anything, far less ornate than other dwarven homes.

Although it was quite distant, it was extremely well-lit and TamSen could see that there was another, smaller building attached to one side. This smaller building seemed to be in a state of shambles, with crumbling walls and rocks scattered all around.

Then, just as they had begun to wonder what they were supposed to do next, Giebort joined them, saying: "Welcome, friends, to DwarvenHome, please allow me to escort you directly to the Wizard Korlim. I'm sure he'll be most anxious to meet you."

As Giebort led them through the streets of DwarvenHome, pointing out some of the more unusual features to those marvels they had already seen, they began to see dwarven women and children for the first time.

TamSen managed to hide his astonishment at the fact that the women, even the tiniest girls, were all bearded. He had heard the stories, of course, but had not believed them until now.

Chewppa, however, was not so adept at concealing her feelings, and gawked openly, never even noticing that the women and children did a fair share of gawking in return.

Taking note of his guests' amazement, Giebort said, "When we came here more than four hundred years ago, we said our farewells to the mountains of the Crystal Mist.

"It was our intent to live and work here for good King Salik, then king of the realm of Dramidja. Dwarves and humans were to live together in harmony.

"We were to keep one-fourth of all the gemstones and minerals, and Dramidja would receive the remainder. Then, after the mines were worked out, we were to receive the mines as our permanent home. That was Salik's promise, thus the name, DwarvenHome.

"We were to be free of the constant struggles over territory, and the threat of wars. We brought our families, our possessions, our hopes, and our dreams. We moved our wives and children into the caverns when there was nothing but drippy ceilings and granite moles and nought to eat but hardship, blindfish and spiders.

"We have kept our portion of the bargain, but alas, how were we to have known that there were such riches? They will never be depleted in a hundred dwarven lifetimes. "This," he said, with a wide wave of his hand, "is the richest mine on Oerth."

Picking up a handful of gravel, he opened his hand and allowed the dust to sift through his fingers. When it was gone, he was left holding ten or twelve sapphires and emeralds.

"These are the riches for which we came in our youth," he said heavily. "And bitter riches they are.

Now they mean no more to us than bits of worthless glass to use as ornaments. Oh some of the smaller gems can be mixed with clay and will make a fairly decent cement, but otherwise, we have little use for them." He tossed the gems back onto the pathway without a second glance.

"As you can see from the bridges," he continued, "large crystals are best for building massive things, but they are so hard to carry from where they are mined that we seldom bother."

"Then what do you do with yourselves?" asked TamSen, bewildered by the sad tale.

"Oh, we still mine," Giebort said with a twisted smile. "That's what dwarves do. But nowadays, most of our mining is for iron and gold. The gold is very malleable, and can be made into plates, tableware and useful things. The iron, of course, is made into hinges, pots, tools and weapons. Gemstones are pretty, but fairly useless for anything practical."

"Useless?" asked TamSen, having a hard time getting used to the thought of gemstones being considered less than desirable.

"Useless," Giebort said firmly. "We find millions of them every time we clear land for a new home or garden. We use the biggest for fences and gateposts, like these over here," he said, gesturing at a stone fence enclosing a small garden. The fence was made entirely of precious gems, none smaller than Tam-Sen's fist. "We dump the smaller stones with the other debris. They're more a bother than anything else."

"But you could buy whole kingdoms with them on the surface!" TamSen exclaimed.

"But we are not on the surface," said Giebort.

"Then why do you stay down here?" asked Tam-Sen. "Why not return to the surface and buy yourself a kingdom?"

"That is a question for the Wizard Korlim," said Giebort. "We will soon be at his home and he will answer all your questions."

TamSen looked up and saw that the path they were following led directly to the rise on the far side of the cavern. The house, while closer than it had been, still appeared to be some miles distant. He realized that the cavern was even larger than he had first thought.

As they continued walking and talking with Chewppa lagging behind, disinterested in their conversation, TamSen could not help but notice that dwarves were streaming toward the house on the rise and that a large crowd had already gathered on the plain below. Once, he thought he glimpsed someone at one of the windows, but then he blinked and they were gone.

As they walked through the dwarven city, eyes peered out at them from windows and doorways. Occasionally, they came upon a child playing, only to have an alarmed parent appear, scoop the child up and disappear hurriedly. A frightened whisper of the word "harpy" was heard more than once.

TamSen had not forgotten the strange dancing light that he had seen from the passageway. He was intrigued by the peculiar quality of the light and wondered about its origin. He asked Giebort, tentatively, wondering if it were yet another question that could only be answered by the Wizard Korlim, but Giebort smiled and immediately veered onto a path that led off to their left.

This street led between rows of houses and described a giant arc around the base of the central stalagmite. A well-trod path led up the side of the stalagmite; this, Giebort took.

The grade was steep but not difficult to climb. The bulk of the huge phenomenon rose between them and the dancing light, holding them in suspense.

At last they reached the top of the plateau and as they emerged, high above the level of the housetops, they were able to look directly into the passageway that held the dancing light.

Not a mile distant, located directly before them and a throne that had been built to face the amazing display, was a corridor hewed out of the rock wall. This corridor was several hundred hands high and had been cut in the shape of an arch. Directly beyond the arch was a waterfall that fell in gossamer plumes to the ground far below and glowed with a strange green light.

As the water made its final descent, it fell onto numerous ledges, creating a wondrous display of water and light. A cloud of mist shimmered with colors refracted from the gemstones and the waterfall itself. It was a fascinating show of colors and it changed constantly, drifting above the cavern in changing shape and form. Chewppa took TamSen's arm and together they watched the shifting panoply of colors, transfixed by the beauty.

"This is the reason we chose to live in this cavern, above all the others," Giebort said quietly. "The waterfall brings us fresh water from the surface and light as well. The water has fish. Those are the true riches when you live in the underworld; fresh water, light, and food."

Overcome by awe, it took a few heartbeats for TamSen to realize what Giebort had said. When the words sunk in, he turned around abruptly and said, "This water comes from the surface?"

"Yes," replied Giebort. "Somewhere up above us lies a body of water that is clear enough and calm enough to allow sunlight to filter through, nearly ten full hours each day."

"How far we are down?" asked Chewppa.

"Almost three miles," Giebort replied. "But the water has taken on a color of its own that indicates a heavy concentration of emeralds along its passage."

Chewppa looked to TamSen and asked, "Almost three miles? I not know 'almost three miles.' How high is this?"

TamSen thought for a moment and then answered, "A very, very tall mountaintop is, perhaps, a mile above the sea. We are more than three very, very tall mountains below the sea."

Chewppa's eyes widened visibly as the thought of such a great distance soaked into her mind. She turned to Giebort and asked, "Light come from sun? We go out to sun by water?"

Giebort smiled at her naivete. "No. No one could possibly hold their breath long enough to swim three miles. You can't get out that way. There are many other ways to reach the surface that are much easier and safer."

"Are we still beneath the Island of Dramidja?" asked TamSen.

"Yes," replied Giebort. "Our surveyors tell us that

we are directly below a lake, as do the maps we have from old. Living as we do, maps are an important way of life. Even the smallest child can read a map, for it would be very easy to become lost in the countless passages that honeycomb this underworld."

Chewppa began to lose interest. Maps did not interest her, only the subject of the surface; and since the waterfall would not take her there, she ceased listening.

But TamSen was still interested and asked Giebort about the strange glowing light of the waterfall.

"It is not all that bright," chuckled Giebort. "It only looks bright because you have been in the dark for so long. In reality, the light of the entire waterfall is less than the light of two torches. The light for the city comes from yet another source."

"Another source!" exclaimed TamSen, growing confused. "What's that?"

"Perhaps I'd better take you to the Wizard Korlim now," answered Giebort quickly, indicating that TamSen would not be getting an answer to that question either, until he met with the wizard.

At long last, the small party reached the rise on the far side of the cavern. A multitude of steps led to the small house perched on the ledge above them.

It was necessary to make their way through a vast crowd of people, most of the inhabitants of the city, TamSen guessed. As they reached the foot of the steps several people could be seen peering over the ledge above them as though waiting and watching for their arrival. Seeing Chewppa, they disappeared with many an alarmed squeak of fear.

As Giebort led TamSen and Chewppa up the staircase, TamSen saw that hundreds and hundreds of glittering gemstones had been embedded in each step. The stones were of a quality and quantity for which oerth people would gladly kill their best friends.

Noticing TamSen's startled expression, Giebort explained that they had been placed there after the Wizard took a nasty tumble, in an effort to provide him with more stable footing.

As they reached the last step, TamSen turned and took Chewppa's hand. She looked into his eyes and smiled.

As they approached the house, still hand-in-hand, the few brave dwarves who had not fled backed away, taking care to keep a good distance between them.

Then, a young dwarf appeared in the doorway of the house dressed in a fine linen garment that had been woven with strands of gold thread and garnished with the most precious of stones. He carried a golden sceptor which had a magnificent emerald handpiece, carved in the shape of a walking dwarf.

The magnificently garbed dwarf stepped out of the door, all but tripping on the hem of his gown, held up the staff and waited for them to approach.

When they were but a few paces away, he opened his mouth as though to speak, but then caught sight of the stone that hung between Chewppa's breasts and all but swallowed his tongue. He started to kneel, thought better of it and jerked himself upright, then reconsidered again and all but spun into a kneeling position before her.

When he finally spoke, it was in a very quiet, deep voice that sounded more like an oerthquake than the voice of a man.

"The Wizard Korlim is preparing to see you. He has asked that you be made comfortable, and that you excuse the condition of his workshop."

Even if the man had not made mention of the ruins, it would have taken a blind person to overlook the great clutter of stones and debris that was evidently all that remained of the workshop.

"The Wizard Korlim," he continued, "has been resting quietly this day, after the, uh, the accident, and has just learned of your presence."

The spokesman threw a stern glance at Giebort and added, "Perhaps in the excitement no runner was sent ahead to give notice of your arrival."

TamSen caught the insinuation that Giebort was negligent in his leadership, and quickly came to his defense, "Giebort was seeing to the safety of his men. There was no one who could be spared."

The spokesman jumped as though he had been beaten with a whip. He backed up and bowed low before the trio, and quickly assured TamSen that the Wizard Korlim would surely understand and approve. He then excused himself, scooting backward into the doorway of the house. Chewppa chuckled to herself at the young man's obvious discomfort.

Giebort had turned his back to the house to prevent anyone there from seeing the smile he couldn't suppress. Finally gaining his composure, Giebort turned back, once more wearing his usual grim expression.

There was a small flurry of activity at the foot of the stairs, accompanied by agitated whispers and various squeaks. Finally, several very frightened young male dwarves appeared at the top of the stairs, each trying to hide behind the other, eyes wide with excitement and fear. They carried a table and four chairs. Several bearded female dwarves followed in their wake, bearing food and drink.

Table, chairs, food and drink were all in place within heartbeats and all but one of the dwarven women beat a hasty retreat down the stairs, nearly falling over each other in their haste to be gone.

The single exception was a short, chubby woman, with a dark curly beard, dressed in gaily colored clothes. She wore a scarf of woven gold around her shoulders, fastened with an emerald brooch at the neck. She dropped a curtsy to TamSen and Chewppa then smiled warmly at Giebort.

"TamSen, Wizard Chewppa, my wifemate Gaieliah," Giebort said proudly, moving to the woman's side and encircling her ample waist with his arm.

The chubby Gaieliah curtsied again and then moved to the table and began filling glasses from a tall crystal pitcher. She seemed to radiate warmth and confidence, yet TamSen noticed that her hand shook slightly and that she took care to place the table between herself and Chewppa.

TamSen thanked her for the drink, and she smiled warmly, again giving a short, quick curtsy. Chewppa, following his lead, thanked her as well.

As the harpy addressed her, Gaieliah stiffened and almost spilled the contents of the pitcher on her dress. She quickly masked her alarm, then looked to Giebort who was again forced to suppress his desire to laugh aloud. She blushed a deep shade of crimson, then made herself smile and curtsy to Chewppa before hurrying away.

Giebort offered chairs to TamSen and Chewppa, and all three arranged themselves around the table. The chairs had been made to fit dwarves and were approximately the size of human children's chairs, which left TamSen and Chewppa looking and feeling both uncomfortable and foolish.

Less than a heartbeat later, the wizard's assistant appeared at the door and announced in a loud voice, "THE WIZARD KORLIM." Having uttered this pronouncement, he stepped to one side and made a bold flourish as though presenting a king.

They turned to the door expectantly, but no one appeared. TamSen looked at Chewppa, Chewppa looked at TamSen who shrugged. Finally, after even Giebort had begun to fidget, a small, bent figure struggled into sight, holding onto the doorsill as though in danger of falling without its support.

After the finery worn by his assistant, TamSen was totally unprepared for the sight of this small, unassuming little man. He was dressed in a drab, brown tunic and pants, his hair was long and silver, and looked as though it had gone many moons without the touch of comb or brush.

He was frail and bent and shuffled toward them painfully, his fingers gnarled with illness and great age. But his single dominating feature was the brilliant red stone that hung from his neck in a magnificently worked gold breastplate which seemed too great a burden for his small frame.

The ancient, old dwarf seated himself in the chair that Giebort held out for him, wheezing and sighing wearily as though he had traveled a great distance; then he raised his eyes and blinked rapidly as though attempting to see them more clearly. He smiled at them dimly, then turned to his assistant and whispered in a tone that could easily be heard, "Who did you say they were?"

There was a brief interchange of information between the aged wizard and his assistant, but no matter what was said, the wizard looked puzzled and said "ehh?" until all of them were thoroughly frustrated.

"THE WIZARD CHEWPPA! SHE IS A WIZARD! HER NAME IS CHEWPPA! SHE IS A . . . A HARPY!" screamed the assistant, losing all control.

"Eh??? Yes. Yes. Well, I'm happy to see them, too!" replied the wizard, nodding and smiling cheerfully.

"So you're a wizard," he said politely, turning to TamSen.

"No, sir," answered TamSen, as he struggled to free himself from the confines of the tiny chair. When TamSen finally rose to bow to Korlim, the wizard's eyes followed him up and up and up, until his eyes were as wide as his mouth, gaping in amazement.

"This lady is the Wizard Chewppa," TamSen said politely, gesturing toward Chewppa. Korlim then squinted at Chewppa and the sight of her wings brought him up sharply, half rising in his chair.

"It—it's a . . . A . . . A HARPY!" he stammered excitedly, as his hands fluttered up and down at his sides. His gyrations came to an abrupt halt as he noticed the brilliant blue stone glittering at the end of her necklet.

Then, as though this were something that happened often, he quickly sobered and smiled broadly.

"So nice to meet you, my dear," he said in suave tones. "Welcome to DwarvenHome."

Chapter 19

THE DEMON MAELFESH shifted uneasily on his crystal throne. Something was wrong. Something was definitely wrong, although he couldn't quite put his finger on it. He hadn't felt this uneasy since the time he decided to do in his father.

"Those were the days," he reminisced warmly, breaking into vivid red and blue flames, searing the souls imprisoned in the throne beneath him.

"Struggling, conniving, plotting, scheming, the smell of blood and pestilence." He actually spent a heartbeat or so remembering his father who had taught him everything he knew, including, when the time came, how to overthrow and supplant him in his own sphere of power. The old coot had really put up a satisfying battle. It was one reason why Maelfesh had no children of his own.

The flames flickered and nearly died. Maelfesh looked down in alarm. The fires which constantly bathed his body had lost their brilliant color and taken on a sickening greenish yellow tinge. Something was clearly wrong.

Maelfesh rose from his throne, stroking his chin. He would examine his worlds, find the problem and eliminate it. Already, he was cheered.

The Wizard Korlim called his assistant to his side and whispered, "Have you found my glasses, yet?"

"Yes, master," the assistant replied. "And, as we feared, they were broken. Clatto is making you another pair. They should be ready soon."

Korlim turned his attention back to Chewppa. He sat for a moment, his eyes alternating between a wide stretch and a squint. He fiddled with a bit of crystal in his ear then waved a hand toward her necklet and said casually, "What a lovely stone you have there, my dear, may I see it?"

At the approach of his hand, Chewppa began to chitter loudly and then, remembering herself, shouted a loud and emphatic, "No!"

Korlim quickly withdrew his hand, adjusted the ear crystal with a grimace then smiled, and said, "Ah, so you know of the stone's power. Then, you must be a wizard, after all. Forgive me, I had to see if you were merely a hapless innocent who had somehow come by the stone. You understand, of course. Well, my dear, what can I do for you?"

Chewppa had already asked TamSen to do the talking, as she felt less than confident when speaking with others.

More to the point, she was only here in this place because TamSen wished it. She had no interest in the dwarves or their home. She was only interested in one thing, finding Mika-oba.

"We are searching for a party of people and wolves who were lost in these caverns some twenty years ago," TamSen explained.

"We have been told that they may be imprisoned in something called the Pillar of the Demon Hand. We seek guidance, and offer our friendship in return, and whatever else we might give."

Korlim was clearly astonished by the fact that TamSen, whom he had been told was only the assistant, had answered his question, rather than the wizard herself. He looked back and forth between the two of them.

"Now I understand," he said. "You are the wizard, after all. Is the harpy your assistant, or merely an illusion?"

TamSen was taken aback by the wizard's words and, not knowing what to say, said nothing.

Fortunately, Giebort interjected. "The harpy is no illusion, Master Korlim. We have many wounded who can vouch for that."

In the past few weeks, TamSen had learned just how powerful a tool silence can be. He talked volumes to Chewppa while she often remained silent. But her silence had a curious effect on TamSen, the longer she remained silent, the more he babbled, making dumber and dumber comments.

He wondered whether the tactic would work on the dwarves. It was certainly worth a try and besides, he couldn't think of any other way to bluff his way through and still conceal his ignorance.

Korlim studied TamSen through squinted eyes as TamSen sat in expectant silence. "Am I to take it as a show of trust, then, that you allow your assistant to wear the stone when you meet me, or is it a show of your own power?

Again, TamSen did not know the proper reply, so he said nothing.

"I see." said Korlim. "Of course, the answer is obvious; both statements are correct. Please forgive me. I have grown old in this place, with so little to do except dabble in minor magic and some alchemy." He waved his hand toward the destroyed workshop and smiled ruefully.

There was a long, thoughtful pause. Then Korlim said, "You would have me lead you to the Pillar of the Demon Hand? Why? Do you not know that the power contained in that pillar is much greater than one . . . uh . . . than a stone such as yours can hope to fight against?"

A smile crept across TamSen's face. It was working, the information was beginning to flow. TamSen sat quietly, smiling at Korlim in silence.

Korlim, seeing TamSen's smile, touched his own magic stone and said, "I see. Then you know the power of the two stones together. Tell me, Master, are you here to kill me and take my stone?"

TamSen decided that he shouldn't allow Korlim to imagine an answer to that question, so he broke his silence, saying, "Of course not, sir. We offer you our friendship. All we want is your help."

"Let us be more pleasant one to another, then, sir," replied Korlim, returning TamSen's smile with one of his own. He then began the formalities expectant of one wizard meeting another:

"I am Korlim, wizard of the majestic line of the ancient family of Suloise. I am the firstborn son of the frightening and all-powerful dwarven wizard, Krohler, who was the firstborn son of the mighty Slerotin, Last Mage of Power in the Olden Kingdom, and wizard to King Suloise, himself.

"It was he, my grandfather, whose magic power brought our people through the terrible days of the Rain Of Colorless Fire, and delivered them from the long trek through the Sea of Dust, when there was no water to be found.

"It was he, through his powerful magic, who opened a tunnel through the Mountains of the Crystal Mist, and sealed it behind them with the fiercest of magical monsters. It was he who delivered our people into the land of the Yeomanry, where until this day, they reside.

"I am Korlim, wizard of the house of the Suloisian dwarves. I am come to this place with my people to prepare it for those who would follow in future years.

"This cavern, this DwarvenHome, is to be the single home of the Suloisian dwarves for as long as Oerth shall last.

This mighty fortress is ours by claim and by contract, and by promise of the good King Salik, of the Island Kingdom of Dramidja, on the surface of the Oerth, above.

"It shall be ours, with the doing of one small task and we shall reign in the full power of the house of the Suloisian dwarves, until the end of time."

Having finished his long and impressive oration, Korlim smiled to himself and nodded to TamSen, allowing him to speak.

TamSen smiled back at Korlim and thought to himself, Sure, only one small, unfulfillable obligation, to exhaust the caverns of their riches. Well, there was no way he could escape this one with silence. The formalities had begun.

The wizard's oration had brought back painful memories, causing TamSen to remember the times when he had sat with his grandfather as the old man told him stories of the olden days.

Often had he spoken of the formalities which a king must endure. Then, he had recited his own royal lineage and made TamSen and TamLis recite them as well. The children had learned them, to please the old man, not wishing to hurt his feelings, yet uncertain as to whether or not they believed him.

"One day," his grandfather had said, "you will need to recite your lineage before the kings and queens of Oerth. Do not shame me or yourselves by forgetting. When you know who you came from, you know who you are!"

TamSen had obeyed, but never had be thought he would one day recite it thusly. Drawing himself tall, he stood before Korlim and tried to make himself sound as impressive as possible.

"I am TamSen, heir to the throne of the island Kingdom of Dramidja with my sister TamLis. I am the firstborn son of Princess Julia, bearer of the magic stone of the demon lord, Maelfesh the Unforgiving.

"My grandfather was the firstborn son of King Fret the Caring, who was thirdborn son of King Farlostone the Builder, who was the firstborn son of King Brill the Scholar, who was the only son of King Truelo the Gatherer, son of King Salim the Stern Judge, who was the firstborn son of King Salik the

Miner, who was the firstborn son of King Serikin the Conqueror.

"It was Serikin who wrested the ancient Island of Dramidja from the violent race of Island Trolls, who infested its mountains and shores. They died at the point of Serikin's mighty sword, and were heard of in the land no more.

"I am TamSen, heir to the mighty Kingdom of Dramidja!"

His words had far more effect than he could have hoped for in his wildest dreams. Both Korlim and Giebort sat in their chairs as though turned to stone. What little could be seen of their skin, that part not covered by beard or cloth had gone as pale as hoarfrost. The wizard's eyes had all but turned up in his skull and he clutched the arms of his chair with whitened knuckles.

Four hundred years drag by with nothing more exciting than digging gems and killing monsters, he thought to himself bitterly, and now this. It's not bad enough that a rival wizard and a nightmare harpy drop in unannounced, but the wizard turns out to be the one, single human on Oerth who could recall our contract and take away our home!

Even worse for Korlim, the wizard was the son of a princess who was evidently in leagues with his archenemy, the evil and powerful demon Maelfesh.

All this on the one morning when he'd broken his glasses, couldn't see well enough to dress himself and had just blown half of his home to smithereens. It was just too much!

Chapter 20

MEANWHILE, TAMLIS, the other heir to the "mighty Kingdom of Dramidja," was sitting in a rocking chair in the little cottage she knew as home.

She sat alone in the darkness, remembering once again the many things she had been told on that bright, warm autumn day of Nurse's death.

TamLis had returned to her work in the garden, and Tallo had returned to repairing the thatch. Sometime shortly after, TamLis had looked up to see Nurse smiling peacefully and snoring softly. Then, she had drifted off into a calm, peaceful sleep which was to last forever.

TamLis sighed. It would soon be daylight. She had risen early this cold morning to warm the house. Tallo would soon be there.

She was to prepare him breakfast for the first time and then would walk by the ocean, if the day were sunny. The cold sea wind felt good in her face, for there was something about the sea which called to TamLis, in all its many moods and lightened her heavy burden of grief.

"Tallo," she whispered, savoring the taste of his name on her tongue, feeling the warmth the very saying of his name brought to her heart.

How can I be so lucky? How can such a love be mine? Although, she thought with a bitter smile, such a love is certainly befitting a queen such as I.

She stroked the coarse woolen blanket, made from other people's castoff rags, which often served as a shawl, and smiled at the irony of her life.

Once again her thoughts drifted to the disturbing things that Nurse had said about their lives and the future of Dramidja.

Time and again she had lain awake and pondered them. Could there ever really be a war on Dramidja? Who would want to invade Dramidja?

As for she and TamSen fighting against one another, why that was just too ridiculous to even consider. *If* TamSen were still alive, she would welcome him back with open arms. She could not imagine *anything* that would make her dislike him, much less fight against him with an army.

No, TamLis thought with a mixture of sadness and relief, it had merely been the ranting of a sick, old woman. Poor Nurse.

Still, the thought of fighting against TamSen was most unsettling, and TamLis had been unable to shake an awful feeling about Nurse's predictions.

"TamSen! Are you really alive? TamSen, where are you?" cried TamLis. Then, feeling the tears beginning to trickle down her cheeks, she leaned forward and stirred the fire with the poker, trying to keep the chill of the cold room at bay.

And as she sat in her chair, watching the flickering fire, grief and sadness did battle with the first flickers of resentment. Where was TamSen? If he were still alive, why hadn't he returned to comfort her and help her make her way in the world. Why had he left her alone? Where, she asked herself, was TamSen?

The amenities continued between the two wizards. Korlim had tried to coax TamSen into talking about the affairs of the world above. But TamSen did not want to be too open, nor reveal too much, so he said little, always bringing the subject back to DwarvenHome.

At long last, Korlim said, "Enough fencing! Before I can speak further and more openly, I must know more of the stone worn by your assistant. It is, of course, a female stone. Is it the same stone that was worn by your mother? Is it the stone of the demon lord Maelfesh?"

"I don't know," replied TamSen. "It may well be the same stone."

"Do you, then, not know Maelfesh?" asked Korlim.

"I only know the name from the lineage which my grandfather, the last king, taught me as a prince of the kingdom," TamSen replied truthfully.

TamSen felt uneasy about giving facts too freely, but he knew that if he were to learn anything in return, he had to give Korlim some small bits of information.

"You are not, then, in the service of the demon lord Maelfesh, yourself?" asked Korlim.

"No, of course not! TamSen replied. That one was

answered easily enough. "I serve no one. My sister and I are the heirs to the kingdom, and the Kingdom of Dramidja is free. We serve no demon lord, this Maelfesh or otherwise."

A glance of relief passed between Korlim and Giebort, and the conversation suddenly seemed to be free of some hidden tension. As though on cue, a runner approached, delivering Korlim's new glasses.

The glasses appeared to have been made of polished quartz, or some other clear crystalline stone. Korlim placed them on his nose, squinched his face this way and that, shifted the glasses from side to side, then closed first one eye and then the other, while looking at the waterfall. The results of the strange gyrations seemed to meet with his approval.

"Good!" Korlim declared with a happy smile. TamSen was uncertain whether he meant that the glasses were all right, or that it was good that he was not in the service of the demon lord.

"Yes, very good indeed!" Korlim repeated. "In that case, I may tell you that it is the demon lord Maelfesh who has kept us trapped in these caverns for so long.

"Oh, it's far from torture being here, mind you. We have made a very decent home for ourselves and our families. But we have not been able to make this the true home of the Suloisian Dwarves, as had been our intent.

"Soon after we arrived we came upon a small vein which held these special stones. Several were mined and sent to the king. It was soon discovered that they held powerful magical properties.

"Then, the demon Maelfesh found us and descended upon us like a flock of fire-rainers, appearing out of nowhere and nothingness. He stood as tall as the cavern and blazed with the fires of a million cities that grew brighter with his every move. The very sight of him almost blinded me. I have had to wear these glasses ever since."

Korlim pointed up to the roof of the cavern. "Do you see that layer of turquoise which forms the ceiling of our city?" he asked. TamSen nodded.

"The bottom level of that layer marks a barrier which we cannot rise above. All cavern floors which we enter must be lower than that level. Anyone who ventures above that mark, anywhere in the caves, dies.

"Maelfesh trapped us here for all eternity. You see, Maelfesh does not kill. That would be too quick and painless. Maelfesh punishes, maims, tortures, traps, imprisons, that is his way. We have been down here almost four hundred years.

I'm now almost five hundred and twenty years old. I have long since given up hope of seeing the rest of our people join us here in DwarvenHome. I've watched the end of my lineage draw near in this prison. I thought that I had failed. I had lost all hope . . . until now.

"There is a large vein of gold that lies just above the band of turquoise. Embedded in this vein of gold are the magic stones, brothers to these worn by myself and your assistant, which would give us the power to break free of Maelfesh's curse. Yet, we cannot reach them.

"We can go into the cavern where they are found and look at them, wishing . . . hoping, but they are forever out of our reach. Aside from the stone which I have here, and the stone which your assistant wears, we can reach no others.

"We must join forces, you and I," cried Korlim, his glasses all but falling off his nose. "We must fight the demon Maelfesh. Surely, with our two stones together, and the joining of your magic powers with mine, we could defeat him."

"I have no fight with demons!" TamSen said quickly. He had no intention of being drawn into any such conflict. All he wanted to do was find this Mika-oba and find a safe way out of the caverns, back into who-knows-what kind of trouble. But whatever it was, that trouble would be a thousand times more welcome than fighting a demon.

Unaware of TamSen's thoughts, Korlim turned from TamSen to look at Chewppa. There was a look of pure lust in his eyes which ignored her bare breasts completely and stared straight at the blue stone which hung between them.

Once again, Maelfesh felt a twinge of unease that he could not identify. Maelfesh hated to feel bad, but more than that, he hated to feel bad and not take it out on someone. He called Brog, an aspiring demi-demon, before the throne.

"You have incurred my wrath!" he bellowed.

"My Lord, I do not understand!" groveled Brog. "I would never knowingly offend you! Please forgive me! I will repair the damage! I will serve you better! I will do whatever you want!"

"Then do this . . ." stormed Maelfesh as he waved his hand sideways, watching with glee as a sheet of fire sliced across the room. Brog's head popped off its body and bounced across the floor.

"Carry your head in your arms until you have made your amends! Now pick it up and get out of my sight!"

Maelfesh settled back on his throne and watched Brog's body as it felt around frantically for the head which lay gasping in silence and pain.

Maelfesh still felt that faint, unidentifiable unease, but all in all, he did feel better.

Chapter 21

"STONE NOT BELONG to demon!" Chewppa said suddenly. "Stone belong to Mika-oba. Mika-oba my father! Mika-oba great wizard! Mika-oba best wizard on Oerth! Stone belong to Mika-oba not demon. Mika-oba not demon!"

Korlim's eyebrows raised so high as to nearly vanish into his hairline. He raised his eyes to those of Chewppa's, which were now glowing a dangerous shade of gold.

"Your harpy assistant is the daughter of a wizard?" he said, "Hmmm, tell me more of this Mika-oba, my dear."

TamSen tried to hush Chewppa, sending her signals with frantic wiggles of his eyebrows and alarmed looks, but she averted her eyes from his and the words seemed to spill from her lips faster than TamSen had ever heard her speak.

"Mika-oba can find every losted child, do many miracles. Mika-oba finded my sister, Mika-oba falled from high mountain and not die. Mika-oba destroyed city of bad humans. Mika-oba best wizard on Oerth."

The more Chewppa talked about Mika-oba, the more excited she became. She began jumping up and down like a small child having a tantrum, shouting, "We go find Mika-oba now! We go find him, NOW!"

Long before TamSen could get Chewppa quieted down, Korlim and Giebort were all but lying on the ground, holding their ears and grimacing with pain. Chewppa's voice, loud by any standards, was painful in the extreme to the poor dwarves.

At one point, Korlim, nearly overcome with the pain, almost silenced her with a spell. But he held back, realizing that it was not the proper way to treat the daughter of a wizard, even if she were a harpy.

In the hours of discussion that followed, Korlim proved himself to be totally honest with Chewppa and TamSen. Well, *almost* totally honest. Never once did he mention the one requirement needed to complete the contract before the dwarves could call the caverns their own. But TamSen could understand the dwarves' silence on that painful subject and did not probe.

Korlim tried every way he could to get Chewppa's stone away from her, but Chewppa refused to take it off and even refused to allow Korlim to touch it.

Failing to achieve that goal, Korlim next tried to persuade them to join forces with him against Maelfesh. In this, both TamSen and Chewppa were agreed; they wanted nothing to do with fighting a demon.

Korlim sighed deeply and began a long doleful la-

ment about his people, using anything and everything that might elicit even the slightest bit of sympathy.

He told of trying to shoot the magic gemstones out
of the ceiling with bow and arrows and of the many
other ploys they had tried, all of which had failed.
Over and over he repeated the need for a second
magic gem. The tirade went on forever.

"Stone is in ceiling?" Chewppa said at last, long
since tired of hearing the old man talk.

"Yes, of course," said Korlim.

"You stop talking, I fly up and get them," said
Chewppa. "It easy."

A light seemed to glow out of Korlim's eyes. He
was completely still for a heartbeat and then yelled,
"Of course, you can fly!"

"No!" shouted TamSen.

"Why?" asked Chewppa.

"WHY?" Korlim cried in terror, his newfound joy
sinking within his breast.

"How do we know that the curse won't kill
Chewppa if she flies above the line?" asked TamSen.
"What exactly was the curse?"

"Uh . . . uh . . . uh," stammered Korlim.

"I was there. I heard it plainly," said Giebort who
had been sitting quietly, holding his silence. "The
curse applies to dwarves only. "Once, we caught a
baby cavernquatch and tried to train it to jump high
enough, hoping that it would be able to pluck some of
the gems out of the ceiling. But, alas, cavernquatch
are not trainable, nor," he said with a shudder, "can
they be housebroken.

"We tried many other monsters over the years,

most do not grow tall enough, others are either too stupid or too wild as in the case of the giant cave bats. We lost more than fifty of our people to that venture."

"I have been working of late with explosives which would shake the stones loose from the ceiling," offered Korlim. "Alas, the best I have been able to do is blow up my own workshop."

"Well, if you are certain that there will be no harm to Chewppa, I will allow it," TamSen said. "But if anything happens to her . . ."

There was a long pause before Korlim answered.

"It will serve us nothing to lose her. It would be as much of a loss to us as it would be to you. When the fight comes against Maelfesh, we will need all the help we can get. The fighting power of a harpy is legendary. Besides, just wearing the stone puts her in great danger. Maelfesh will certainly not allow one wizard to have two stones. Malefesh will punish her for wearing just the one. Your grandfather called Maelfesh the Unforgiving. He is most certainly that.

"No, my friends, I'm afraid that like it or not, you are in this as well as we. When the fight comes, as it will, it will not be our fight alone, but yours as well."

And so, Korlim had finally learned the truth about his visitors. TamSen was the heir to the throne of Dramidja and not a wizard after all. Chewppa was the daughter of a wizard and not a wizard herself. The real wizard it seemed, was locked inside the Pillar of the Demon Hand.

This Mika-oba could surely be counted on to be a friend to the dwarves since it was undoubtedly Maelfesh who had trapped him in the pillar.

Thus, the plan was devised to journey first to the

room of the magic stones where Chewppa would fly to the ceiling and pluck out the magic gems. She would obtain one blue stone for Korlim and a red one for this Mika-oba fellow, giving each wizard a complete set of stones.

"In fact," said Korlim, "since harpies are, by nature, magical beasts, maybe you should have a set of stones, too."

After retrieving the stones, they would then try to find some way of freeing Mika-oba from the pillar so that he might aid them in their fight against Maelfesh. Korlim was certain that once Chewppa retrieved the stones, Maelfesh would not be far behind.

Chewppa was not very excited about having to get more stones. All she really wanted to do was go to Mika-oba. But it had been her suggestion that had given rise to the plan and after listening to Korlim, even she had to agree that it was the only way to free her father.

Eyes bright with excitement, Korlim excused himself. Since he would have to accompany them to the Pillar of the Demon Hand, there was much to be done! Plans to be made! Provisions gathered! Spells prepared!

Giebort proposed that they be accompanied by at least a thousand fighting dwarves, since Maelfesh would undoubtedly call down all manner of demons of his own. He knew they would need all the help they could get.

TamSen and Chewppa were left to their own devices as magician and fighter rushed off to begin their preparations for the long-awaited day.

Finding themselves alone was a welcome relief.

Hand in hand, they wandered through the city. Wherever they went, they were gawked at with a mixture of curiosity and fear. But whenever they stopped to wonder over some structure or natural phenomenon, they found a dwarf at their elbow, ready and anxious to answer their questions. They were offered food and drink at every turn.

The emerald throne, they learned, had been prepared for the dwarven king for the time when they were joined at last by the rest of their people. It had never been used and was considered sacred. No one else was allowed to sit in the throne; to do so would be considered an act of treachery.

They met many dwarves who seemed to speak in a complicated gibberish of which they understood very little. Chewppa pressed one of them to find out whether or not the waterfall could be used for a way out. He launched into a long, complex speech accompanied by sketches drawn on the side of a building which lasted a very long time. Finally, losing interest, Chewppa turned to TamSen and said, "I think he say 'No.'"

They did however, learn that the waterfall was comprised of ground water, and did not come from a hole in the actual bottom of the lake. The light, according to the dwarf, filtered down through a gigantic quartz crystal which had to extend for some distance, its point most probably penetrating the bottom of the lake and forming a "light pipe."

Through this information, TamSen realized that the lake could be none other than Pyramid Lake, which was located on the far side of Dramidja.

Tales held that the lake was bottomless. Old legends told of King Salik the Miner, swimming down deep and returning with a tale of a huge crystal pyramid sitting on the bottom of the lake bed.

Out of deference to the king, who had been but a boy at the time, the lake was called Pyramid Lake. From that point on, so the story went, Salik had been extremely interested in mining the riches of the oerth. TamSen had never believed the tale, believing it to be but a folk tale, but realized now that it was true.

As they walked around the city, one very young boy tugged at the feathers on Chewppa's leg. She looked down to see a pair of huge, round eyes staring up at her in wonder.

"Can you weally fwy?"

"Yes," replied Chewppa. "I fly good."

"I wish I could fwy!" the young boy said, his eyes gazing inward as though at some hidden dream.

"You can," said Chewppa as she picked him up and leaped into the air. They flew in a large circle around the city. At first, the child was stiff with fright, but soon, the long-dreamed fantasy had become a reality. He began shouting in his high-pitched child's voice, "I can fwy! I can fwy! Wook at me! I can fwy!"

Chewppa returned to TamSen's side to find that the child's mother had arrived and had fainted dead away. She deposited the child on the ground carefully. All but overwhelmed with the joy of a dream come true, the child hugged Chewppa on the leg before he rushed off to tell his friends.

Within heartbeats, a crowd of children had gathered around Chewppa begging her to "fly" them.

She turned to TamSen as they plucked at her with their sticky little fingers, and she couldn't help but smile. Throughout the rest of the long day, Chewppa flew children on aerial tours of their city, listening to their squeals of fear and joy. There seemed to be an endless supply of them. After several hours she was exhausted, her stomach sore from being kicked, her arms aching from the weight of them. The trips became shorter and then shorter still, but no dwarf child was refused.

Afterward, they passed a house where a blind girl sat singing. The sound of her voice drew Chewppa like a magnet. The song was very similar to one she had heard the farmers sing. She listened carefully and learned the melody and began to sing along with the girl. The girl stopped and listened, but Chewppa continued on, caught up in the song.

How long had it been since she had sung? How long had it been since she had felt like singing? Chewppa felt the beauty of song surge through her, and she gave herself up to it. The farmer's song finished, she slipped into a song that harpies sometimes sing on the highest peaks of the mountaintops, a song for singing when weather is warm and stomachs are full, unmindful that the song of a harpy hypnotizes all those who hear it.

Then, for a time, the only movement in the cavern of DwarvenHome was that of pots boiling over on the fires. Even Korlim, with all his magical power, was stopped in his tracks by the song of ultimate joy. Even the children were stilled by the beautiful music and, closing their eyes, they drifted off to sleep

Slowly, regretfully, Chewppa finished her song,

noticing for the first time, that all those around her appeared to be frozen. Shaking TamSen's arm, she brought him out of his stupor and together they returned to Korlim's dwelling, drawing shy, sleepy smiles from all they met.

Chapter 22

THERE WAS NO NIGHT in DwarvenHome. Upon returning to the house on the rise, Korlim explained that a magic torch had been found lying beside the Pillar of the Demon Hand many years ago. This torch had been placed high at the peak of the turquoise ceiling where it would light the city forever.

But they knew from their weary bodies when night had come and were grateful to learn that a house had been provided for them. There was no question in anyone's mind but that they should stay together—they were a pair.

This was the first night they had spent together with any degree of privacy or comfort since they first huddled together in the darkness on the stairs.

They lay on a soft pallet, not the usual small dwarven bed. Awkwardness and sheer inexperience led to several surprises and ample embarrassment, but they learned and it was all they had dreamed of and more.

They lay back on the pallet, entwined in each other's arms, thinking their own private thoughts.

As far as Chewppa was concerned, she had never been closer to anyone in her entire life, including her mother and sister. She was happy with TamSen, he had become her whole life; she did not want to think of being without him. As far as she understood the word, and to the best of her ability, Chewppa loved TamSen.

As far as TamSen was concerned, there were no human women who had ever cared for him, other than Nurse and TamLis, so it really didn't matter that Chewppa was not entirely human. She was everything he had ever wanted and that was enough. He loved her with all his heart.

TamSen thought about his sister and Nurse briefly, wondering how they had made out in his absence, wondering if they even missed him. Then Chewppa sighed softly in her sleep and TamSen was brought swiftly back to the present moment. He leaned over and studied Chewppa's beloved profile in the dim light, then kissed her gently, unwilling to rouse her. Within heartbeats, he was asleep as well.

After a time, the city began to stir. Dwarven males began to gather at the foot of the waterfall. Giebort appeared at the door of the little house and after a good deal of foot scraping and throat clearing, knocked on the door and entered, greeting them heartily.

"Good morrow to you! Did you sleep well?"

They smiled at each other, having slept little, but well. Making themselves ready, they returned to Giebort's house and ate a large repast.

Attempting to be polite, TamSen sat in the small chair that was offered him, suffering greatly; but

Chewppa stood. She had barely learned to use knife and fork and could not concentrate on using the strange implements while cramped in the tiny chair and standing was hardly better.

Gaieliah, seeing her discomfort, called to her and led her to the high kitchen worktable. There they ate together, standing up, and slowly, they began to talk.

While Giebort and TamSen discussed the logistics of the coming day's journey, Gaieliah and Chewppa lapsed into the common talk of women everywhere, no matter what their backgrounds.

This type of camaraderie was new to Chewppa and, much to her surprise, she found that she loved it. Gaieliah told her funny things about Giebort, and Chewppa shyly shared a few comments about Tam-Sen. They laughed together and became friends.

Then, standing up and stretching, Giebort drained the remainder of his cup, pulled on his boots and began to gather his weapons, acting as though this were merely a day like any other.

Far be it for a dwarf to show fear, thought TamSen as he watched Giebort with admiration. Here we are about to go do battle with a demon who has more power than any magician or wizard, and he acts as though it is nothing. Well, then, so will I, and he rose from the table and stretched, easing the pain in his aching back while calling to Chewppa.

As Giebort and TamSen turned to leave, Gaieliah clung to Chewppa's arm, holding her back. Chewppa saw tears welling up in Gaieliah's eyes.

"They say that you are a fierce fighter, more fierce than any ten of our menfolk. Please watch out for Giebort, Chewppa, don't let him die . . . please."

Chewppa hugged Gaieliah and reassured her as best she could that she would watch out for Giebort, knowing well that in the heat of battle, it might not be possible.

She pondered this new implication of love as she followed the men. What if something were to happen to TamSen? TamSen had been very protective of her. What if he were to die? Did she feel the same way about TamSen as Gaieliah felt about Giebort? The answer came strongly and swiftly. Yes.

It was a good feeling, and Chewppa swore to herself that any demon who came near TamSen would die long before regretting the mistake.

At long last, the entire mass of dwarves was organized and made its way out of the passageway that led from DwarvenHome to the outer caverns.

Small bands of dwarves were forced to steal silently through the caves, keeping their presence secret from the monsters who would attack them. Large numbers could move loudly, making their presence known, scaring the monsters away.

As DwarvenHome faded behind them, knowing well that some of them might never see it again, the leader sang a cadence song that lifted their spirits, and promised their victorious return. Each line was repeated by those in the ranks:

"A dwarven band marched out one day.
A dwarven band marched out one day.
They kissed their wives and went away.
They kissed their wives and went away.
They killed the monsters one by one.
They killed the monsters one by one.

And came back home when day was done.
And came back home when day was done.
Keep in step.
One, two.
Keep it up,   *Three, four.*
Carry on.
One, two, three, four.
One, two . . . three, four!"

However, once they had put a safe distance behind them, and they were certain that the sound would no longer carry back to their families, the songs changed somewhat. There was one song that Chewppa particularly enjoyed. She learned the words to the chorus, and sang along with the marching dwarves, blasting the words out with great vigor.

> *"We roamed across the Sea of Dust,*
> *Our throats were dry and gritty,*
> *An' we outrun the damn Balklun,*
> *An' came to the Forgotten City*
> > *When the winds were high,*
> > *The dust was dry.*
> > *Oh me, oh my! And so was I!*
> > *But I, my love, did often plyyyyyyyyyy*
> > *In the Forgotten City!*

> *"Oh, I met a girl with a mighty bust*
> *And she did love her drinkin'*
> *We had delight 'most every night;*
> *We spent our nights a'dinkin'!*
> > *When the winds were high,*
> > *The dust was dry.*

213

Oh me, oh my! And so was I!
But I, my love, did often plyyyyyyyyyy
In the Forgotten City!

"Her hair was like a fresh bouquet,
Her body firm an' pretty.
Her husband, though, walked in one day
As I played upon her . . . elbow!
  When the winds were high,
  The dust was dry.
Oh me, oh my! And so was I!
But I, my love, did often plyyyyyyyyyy
An' weren't it just a pity!

"The Forgotten City was so hot!
In summer it got hotter.
I gladly paid th' handsome maid.
Each night, you bet, I bought 'er!
  When the winds were high,
  The dust was dry.
Oh me, oh my! And so was I!
But I, my love, did often plyyyyyyyyyy
An' then I quick forgot 'er!"

The countless raucous verses ate away at the miles and the hours. Chewppa's spirits soared higher and higher. The aerie had never been like this. I like peoples, she thought. I like dwarves and I like fight demons. This fun!

But fun, like many other things in life, can often be of a fleeting nature. Chewppa noticed briefly that TamSen seemed to be worried about something, but when she asked him, he turned away, saying only,

"Nothing." Chewppa smiled to herself, thinking that he was worried about her.

But TamSen continued to look unhappy and she grew alarmed. The more she queried him, the more he denied that anything was wrong. In reality, he didn't know the cause of the vague uneasiness within him. It was nervousness of sorts. The presence of the dwarves had begun to grate on him and he wished that he could be away from everyone for a while; to be alone.

Chapter 23

THE STALWART BAND reached its objective after only a day's travel. There had been no encounters with monsters, nor had they expected to have them, a band that size was seldom bothered by anything that wished to live.

Two strong dwarves had carried Korlim in a small sedan chair, for he was unable to travel in any other manner due to his advanced age. Korlim could have cast a spell of floating on the sedan chair, but to do so would have deprived his men of the honor they derived from being at his service.

At Korlim's command, the entire company came to a halt. The dwarves placed the sedan chair down in front of a barren stretch of the cavern wall.

Korlim stepped down from the chair with Giebort's assistance and, chanting a spell below his breath, he gestured toward the wall. Suddenly, a doorway appeared out of nowhere, seeming to melt through the rock before their eyes.

Korlim gestured for Chewppa and TamSen to

come forward, for it had been decided that only the three of them were to enter the chamber where the magical stones were to be found and mined.

It had further been decided that no one of them were to have both colored stones in their possession until all the stones were secured.

Chewppa was to leave her blue stone with Tam-Sen. She would then fly up to the ceiling and bring down another blue stone. This stone would also go to TamSen. She would then bring a red stone to Korlim, a blue one to TamSen, and a second red stone to Korlim.

In this way, TamSen would always have a number of stones equal to, or greater than Korlim's. This plan had been devised as a final precaution in the hope that Maelfesh would not be alerted by the possession of two different stones.

Korlim knew that there was power enough in the possession of both colors to threaten Maelfesh, but beyond that, everything was a gamble.

Each of them took a torch from Giebort and entered the chamber. At first, everything went according to plan. Chewppa flew up to the roof of the chamber with a dwarven pick and dislodged the stones in the agreed sequence. They encountered no unexpected problems and Maelfesh did not appear.

It was this very ease of the mission that caused Chewppa to reason that TamSen should have a set of stones of his own. Korlim could not prevent her from doing so, although he became very alarmed and had to sit down.

Chewppa made the two extra trips with no complications, despite Korlim's fears. It was only after she had completed her final flight and TamSen was taking possession of the last two stones, that disaster struck.

Now, as one might imagine, Chewppa was not an experienced miner. In dislodging the crystals, she had also weakened a section of the roof. As they were making the final transaction, a piece of rock fell from the roof and struck Chewppa on the wing. She cried out in pain and dropped one of the crystals which skittered across the rough floor and came to rest near the dwarven wizard.

Without thinking, Korlim leaned over and picked it up.

Those who remained in DwarvenHome heard a voice cry out, "THE THRONE!" Looking up, they saw a huge, fiery demon sitting on the throne, engulfing it in flames. Spills of flames licked around his feet and gobbets of fire dripped from his fingers, flowing over the edge of the plateau; they were soon curling round the walls of the nearest houses sending the inhabitants fleeing in terror.

"WHERE IS KORLIM?" the demon shouted, his voice so loud and reverberating so deeply that it shot cracks through buildings and loosened stalactites, causing them to drop onto the amassed dwarves below, causing numerous deaths.

His question unanswered, Maelfesh stretched out his hand and flames shot out in a great arc, wrapping themselves around a fleeing female dwarf. The dwarf was drawn up into the air and dangled in front of the horrible apparition.

Maelfesh stared into her eyes for a heartbeat, then

realizing that he would have no answer from her, flicked his fingers outward, sending the female flying across the breadth of the city where she landed with a sickening crunch against the far wall of the cavern.

Time and again he selected a hapless victim and tried to extract the information he sought in various inventive ways.

At long last, he found what he searched for, a dwarf who feared for his own life more than those of his fellows. He sputtered out the information between gasps, all the while begging for his life.

Maelfesh grinned, a most terrible thing to see, and setting the dwarf down gently, touched him on the very top of his head, setting him afire like a candle.

Accompanied by the agonized screams of the dying dwarf, Maelfesh sat back in the throne and smiled to himself, nodding happily.

So it had come at last. Well, it was time. He was ready for a fight. Maelfesh enjoyed fights. Especially when there was absolutely no doubt as to who would be the victor.

Chapter 24

TALLO HAD TOLD his parents of Nurse's strange prophecies. He recounted her every word, but his mother shrugged the whole thing off, saying that it was but the ranting of a dying woman.

His father, however, who was one of the island's leading merchants, took the story far more seriously and with a good deal of concern.

What if they *were* to come under attack? They had been without any form of government for twenty years now, and everyone had gotten along just fine. But what if . . .

Growing more and more alarmed at the thought, Tallo's father called a meeting of the leading citizens, relaying Nurse's comments. They did not laugh either, quickly seeing the danger implied.

It was decided that they should place the sole remaining member of Dramidja royalty in a position of responsibility. Not real authority, of course, just responsibility.

And as far as authority was concerned, there

should be a council of, what would they call themselves? Advisors! Yes! There should be a council of advisors appointed from among the island's leading people, all of whom just happened to be gathered there at that moment.

These advisors would guide their new monarch in all matters, and see to it that things remained under control.

Votes were taken to see who would become a royal advisor. Strangely enough, all present were fortunate to be voted the title.

Next came the formation and staffing of all important official offices. After that was done, one man stood up and said, "Uh, shouldn't we tell TamLis what has been decided? Somebody ought to tell her, I suppose."

They quickly appointed another delegation, charged with enlightening the last living member of the royal house.

"Wait," said the newly declared minister of finance, a portly fellow who had buried three wives before their time. "She's nought but a mere girl. We can't allow a *girl* to sit on the throne, even if she has got all of us to advise her. What she needs is a husband! And children!"

This thought found much favor among them, even from those who were married, for many of them had sons whom they thought would make the perfect king.

Therefore, the council's first bit of advice was to themselves: say nothing to anyone until they themselves or their sons had an opportunity to woo the future queen.

It was true that none of them were of royal blood, but they were island born and that ought to stand for something. And after all, having a king for a son surely couldn't hurt business.

Meanwhile, the once and future queen was having a hard time of it. Upon Nurse's death, Dame Quotar had offered her a job as housekeeper and maid.

On this particular day, TamLis sat in a rocking chair in the front room of Quotar's cottage. A huge pile of clothing lay on each side of the chair. She had darned, patched, or sewn the items in the left-hand pile. The right-hand pile was still to be done.

As she rocked, she hummed a tune and drifted in thought, wondering how Shmerk always managed to be there when it came time to leave. TamLis despised Shmerk and was constantly fending off his advances.

He didn't care for her in the same way that Tallo did. He only wanted to kiss and fondle her and then boast about his prowess to his equally disgusting comrades. She had heard his lewd boasting many times.

Fortunately, Shmerk was out this day, mending fences with his father. All was quiet in the house, or at least would be until Dame Quotar arrived with more for her to do. Although life could be better, it could certainly also be worse.

Toward afternoon, there was a loud commotion outside as a number of horses thundered into the small courtyard. Their riders leaped to the ground and pounded on the door with their fists.

TamLis leaped to her feet in alarm. There were very few horses on Dramidja and those were only ridden on the most important of occasions—weddings, funerals, and the annual festivals.

What could have brought them to Quotar's house on this cold winter's day? Something terrible must have happened! TamLis rushed to call Dame Quotar then returned to answer the door.

Four well-dressed men were standing beside the door, looking down at TamLis. Still clutching her darning, TamLis told the men that Quotar was out mending fences, but that Dame Quotar would be down any minute.

But it seemed that the men were not interested in the Quotars, any of them. Dropping to his knees, one of the men, he who seemed the most preeminent, took her hand, placed it to his lips and kissed it. The touch of her down on his lips made him wish that he had been a little less formal and he was grateful that she could not see his expression.

"My queen!" he said in a heartfelt tone, and the others bowed low as well.

The next few days were an amazement to TamLis. It was explained to her by her new panel of advisors that they had realized at long last how wrongly they had treated her. She was publicly acknowledged as the royal princess and as soon as she chose a consort, she would reign as queen.

Strange as the situation was, TamLis soon became accustomed to being treated as royalty. And perhaps not so strangely, a resentment began to grow inside her for all the years of hardship that she and Nurse and TamSen had endured.

Activity swirled around her as arrangements were made to crown her as TamLis the First. Her Royal Highness, Queen of the Island Kingdom of

Dramidja.

Announcements were sent out to the Caliphate of Ekbir and the Sultanate of Zeif, as well as to Tusmit, Ull and Ket.

Zeif was neutral toward Dramidja. The Sultinate had only one city that could be considered a port. That was Zeif, the capital. Very little trade went there from Dramidja. Most of its income was derived from business with Ekbir and Tusmit, and across the Plains of the Paynims, from Ull. Zeif would have little to lose from the formation of a new kingdom on Dramidja.

Ekbir had received almost all of Dramidja's trade, once the old kingdom had collapsed. It was certainly cause for concern that a new kingdom was being formed.

But the Caliph of Ekbir and TamLis's grandfather had been the best of friends since childhood; and the Caliph, now an old man with more riches than he could possibly spend in the few remaining years of his life, decided that some things were more important than money.

Ekbir had remained friendly toward Dramidja throughout its time of trouble. In fact, it was the Caliph's continued friendship that had allowed Dramidja to remain free. That, and the fact that no one really wanted to own it. As a gesture of binding friendship, the Caliph was asked to perform the actual coronation.

A date was set for the following spring. There was no longer a castle, but a small kingdom like Dramidja would not need one immediately. A house would do for the moment, and besides, thought the disgruntled

Minister of Finance, who had found no favor in TamLis' eyes, it would be cheaper.

Logs were cut from the wintry woods, and construction began. Meanwhile, many gifts from those on the island, as well as from abroad, began to arrive. There were hens and geese and cows and sheep as well as some exotic songbirds that were eaten, sadly, by a cat who was not the least impressed by their place of origin.

Couches and chairs arrived by ship, constructed of fragrant woods and inlaid with precious gems. Clothes cut from the finest fragile silk that clung to her body like webs of gossamer were mounded inside chests of ebony and gold.

Jewelry fit for the queen that she would soon become, necklets and bracelets, rings and diadems set with rubies and emeralds, diamonds and sapphires, garnets and gold and silver twinkled up at her out of platinum caskets. Strands of pearls looped over the backs of chairs and hung from doorknobs, and loose gems escaped their coffers and rolled along the floors.

TamLis was overwhelmed, as were her countless suitors who plied her with even more gifts, and though she treated all the suitors kindly, there was never any thought in her mind of choosing anyone besides Tallo.

It was he who had loved her when there was nothing to gain but the jeers of his companions. It was he who had remained at her side through the days of grief following Nurse's death, and he who had courted her quietly and helped keep Shmerk at arm's length. It was he whom she loved and would wed.

Unable to persuade TamLis to consider any of

their own sons, her advisors told her that her only job was to "keep herself pretty" until the coronation. But TamLis was not so dumb that she did not realize that meetings were being scheduled by the newly formed Council of Royal Advisors.

"The meetings will be dull, boring and long, Your Majesty, we are sorry," said the advisors when she asked for the schedule of meetings. And this was their intent, to make the meetings as dull and boring as possible so that TamLis would lose all interest in the actual running of the government.

"That's all right," TamLis replied calmly. "I'll be there, anyhow." It would be worth it, no matter how boring, TamLis thought, for she was to be the queen. Anything was worth enduring if you were queen. No more poverty. No more loneliness. No more laughter or taunts. No more pain. She was to be queen.

Chapter 25

THE VERY INSTANT Korlim touched the blue stone while still holding the red stones, he realized what he had done and dropped it. His heart hammered inside his chest and he was overcome with terror, expecting to see the demon materialize before him. Had Maelfesh been alerted? He crouched low, his hand hovering over the blue stone, ready to grab it again if the demon appeared, ready to combine their power to protect himself. But nothing happened. Absolutely nothing. Slowly, wondering what was wrong, wondering if they had been held in thrall all those long years for nothing, Korlim crawled to his feet.

Chewppa was somewhat bruised by the falling rock, but her wing did not appear to be broken. Regrouping, the odd trio gathered the precious gems and left the chamber, rejoining the waiting troops.

Korlim held up the red stones for all to see. He motioned for Chewppa to do the same with the blue. A cheer rose up, shaking the very walls. The dream of DwarvenHome was now within their grasp.

The journey to the Pillar of the Demon Hand was still more than a day's journey. Korlim tried to tell himself that it was not such a long time to wait for one who had waited nearly four hundred and fifty years.

It was decided that the stones would remain separate until they reached their goal; only when they reached the Pillar of the Demon Hand would the magic-users receive their own sets of stones. As much as Korlim longed to hold them in his hands, even he had to admit that it was not yet safe to do so.

Korlim's hatred for Maelfesh boiled within him and then he smiled. Having the power to fight Maelfesh would be almost as satisfying as setting his people free. And having a powerful wizard help him was more than he had ever dreamed possible.

He pondered the value of pressing on without a night's rest. If they continued, they could reach the pillar sooner. However, they had driven themselves at a hard pace so as to reach this spot as soon as possible, and the men were tired.

Once Maelfesh learned about the stones, he would be on their trail and they would need all of their strength to face him. It would surely be the worst fight they had ever had, and quite possibly the last fight for many. Since it did not appear that the demon had become aware of their presence yet, a good night's rest seemed to be in order.

"Thank goodness my mistake was not serious," Korlim muttered to himself, unmindful of just how great a cost it would prove to be.

The group marched through the caverns and passageways in the highest of spirits. The eldest dwarves had arrived more than four hundred years ago only to see their dreams turn into ashes, thanks to Maelfesh. Now, the score was about to be evened.

The younger dwarves were equally pleased. They had been born here, and knew the old country of Yeomanry through stories alone. They had never lived under the rule of the dwarven king. Nor had they ever seen the surface of Oerth. For them, sunlight was the soft glow of the waterfall, and nothing more. Yet, the elders dream of overthrowing Maelfesh was their dream as well.

Korlim was happy, for he was finally going to get his revenge. And Chewppa was ecstatic; she was going to rescue her father, at last.

Only TamSen was unhappy. Try as he might, he couldn't understand why. If this group in the pillar were those whom his grandfather had told him about, he would soon find his mother, the Princess Julia. She would then become queen and restore the Kingdom of Dramidja to its former glory. Once that happened, being the heir to the throne would bring him the respect he had always desired.

TamSen told himself that he should be happy because Chewppa was happy. He should be happy because his friends, the dwarves, were happy. He should be happy simply because he should be happy. So why, then, did he feel so awful? Why was he so nervous and irritable? He hadn't felt this way in a long time, not since, since the night before the sheep were killed. . . . Oh, no! he thought with alarm. By all the Gods, not again!

TamSen stayed to himself most of the day. He kept away from Chewppa, Korlim and Giebort as well as the rest of the dwarves, skirting the edges of the caverns in a sort of self-imposed exile.

When the band stopped for the evening, TamSen paced back and forth, feeling like a caged animal. A shudder ran through him as he pictured himself as a wolf in a cage. The darkness and the walls of the caverns suddenly felt oppressively close.

He wandered to and fro among the dwarves, who were settling in for the evening. Finally, he reached the perimeter of the encampment and still he continued on. Suddenly, there was a bright flash of light shining full in his face. Then a voice, rough as gravel, shouted, "Halt!" and he found the tip of a spear touching the end of his nose.

TamSen's eyes all but crossed as they followed the shank of the spear down until he saw a dwarf looking up at him.

"Halt and identify yourself!" the guard said as he looked TamSen as straight in the eye as their unequal heights would allow. His voice held a definite threat.

"What?" said TamSen, stifling a smile, almost unable to believe what he was hearing.

"Identify yourself!"

TamSen looked down at himself. He was easily twice the height of the tallest dwarf. He was certainly the only human this dwarf had ever seen in his entire life.

He looked over at the dwarf encampment. As far as he could tell, he was the only one there with tall pointed ears and downy covering. In his present mood, TamSen really didn't feel like dealing with this type of stupidity.

"Who on Oerth do you think I am?" he asked the guard.

"You must identify yourself properly, Master Tam-Sen!" the guard replied.

"Why?" asked TamSen.

"Because that's the way it's done, sir. It's regulations."

"Wha? Oh, rats! I am TamSen, heir to the Kingdom of Dramidja, with my sister Tam . . . Listen. I don't have to go through all this for you! You already know who I am!"

"State your business, sir!" the guard said gruffly, ignoring TamSen's comment.

"Well . . ." muttered TamSen. He really didn't have any business, he was just wandering aimlessly. "I'm just wandering around, that's all."

"Passage beyond the perimeter is forbidden without a pass, sir." said the guard in a serious tone.

"A pass?" TamSen said in amazement.

"Yes, sir. A pass."

"But I just want to walk around without stepping on people" TamSen said.

"Passage beyond the perimeter is forbidden without a pass, sir."

Now TamSen was beginning to get irritable. "Well, where do I get this pass thing?"

"No passes are being issued at this time, sir."

"Well, if passes *were* being issued, sir, where would I get one?" snarled TamSen.

"I don't know, sir, I've never gotten one."

Well, what in the name of all the gods do they look like?" TamSen asked. He was becoming very upset and his voice could be heard for a goodly distance.

"I don't know, sir. I've never seen one. They're never issued in the outer caverns," said the dwarf, cursing his luck and wondering why TamSen had chosen his post among all the others.

"Well, whom are they never issued by?" TamSen asked sarcastically.

"I don't know, sir, maybe by Commander Giebort."

"*COMMANDER* Giebort?" TamSen asked. Hearing Giebort called by a high-ranking military title grated on TamSen's nerves. But then, everything seemed to grate on TamSen's nerves tonight.

TamSen turned and stomped away from the guard, much to the guard's relief, searching for Giebort. Of the army of one thousand, perhaps one hundred lay between the guard and Giebort, and TamSen stepped on or tripped over at least ninety-nine of them.

At one point, he brushed his leg against the point of a lance. In his anger, he turned and kicked at the lance. Thankfully, he did not hurt himself, but a neat slice was taken out of the front of his shoe, and his toe now stuck out of the hole. By the time he found Giebort, sitting with his back against a wall, eating slices of blue mold cheese, he had worked himself into a finc fury.

"Why in hades do I need a pass, and how do I get one, and what on Oerth is a pass, anyway?" he shouted at Giebort.

Giebort had seen TamSen tripping and cursing his way through the crowd, and had sat patiently waiting for him to arrive. Now he set aside his cheese and his knife and took out his pipe and began the long process required to start it.

He pulled a pinch of dried fungus tobacco out of a

granite moleskin pouch and stuffed it into the bowl of the pipe as TamSen fumed. Then, as TamSen's face started to grow mottled, he tamped the tobacco down with his thumb and struck a flint, drawing the spark down into the pipe with loud wet sucking sounds.

The pipe glowing cheerfully, Giebort, puffing his pipe slowly, looked up at TamSen, and did not answer for the longest time. Once again, TamSen was to learn the power of silence.

As TamSen stood there, waiting for an answer, he began to realize how ridiculous he must look. His back began to itch and turning halfway around, his hand raised, he saw the entire company of dwarves staring at him. His face turned bright crimson till even his ears felt like they were glowing and he felt himself a complete and total fool. He lowered his arm and sat down quickly. In a low tone he muttered, "I just wanted to go for a walk."

Giebort took the pipe from his mouth and dug into the bowl with a tiny tool. Without looking up he said, "There are monsters out there. Do you want to face them alone?"

Now TamSen had yet another reason for feeling foolish. He hadn't even thought of the danger, that was really stupid.

"Look, I need to talk to you . . . alone," he said, looking around at the other dwarves.

"I wondered when this time would come," Giebort said, and waved his hand at the company dwarves. They smiled and returned to their own activities. "Come," said Giebort. "Let's walk for a while."

Giebort rose, placed his pipe in his mouth, and the two men began walking toward the forward perimeter in silence. At long last, they had put some space between themselves and the main group of dwarves, entering the area between the camp and the perimeter guard. Giebort sat down on a rock and motioned for TamSen to do likewise.

"I have a problem," TamSen mumbled, "and I'm afraid it may affect some of you here."

"That's not the way I would have started this little talk," Giebort replied, "but go on. One start is as good as another."

This was the second time Giebort had made a reference to "this little talk." TamSen didn't understand what he was referring to but didn't feel like pursuing the point, having too much else on his mind.

"I guess you know, I'm a human," he said, "but I'm a wolf, too. And, uh, you see, up on the surface, on Oerth, there's a thing called the moon, and once each month it gets 'full,' which is to say, it is at its brightest."

"I know that," Giebort returned, "You forget that I lived on Oerth in my youth."

Forgetting Giebort's history made TamSen feel foolish and feeling foolish made him even more irritated, if such a thing were possible.

"Yeah. Well. Each month during the full moon, something happens to me. I don't know exactly what it is, because I never can remember what happens. But sometimes I wake up the next day and find that I've done really terrible things. And I seem to do them as a wolf, not as a human.

"I don't want to hurt any of your people. I also don't want them to mistake me for a monster and hurt me. I'm sure that you see now that I have to get away for a while."

Giebort sat up straight, his eyes open wide in surprise. "Well, this is certainly not the little talk I expected to have!" he said. "Of course, I understand now. How could I not have known, you're a werewolf!"

TamSen had never heard the word before. "A what!?" Then, realizing what Giebort had said, he said, "You mean, there are others like me?"

"I've only heard of them in tales and legends," Giebort replied. "Never did I believe that they were real! Goodness! That really does pose a problem. We must talk to Korlim, right away!"

Giebort started to rise, but TamSen reached out in the darkness and caught his arm, motioning for him to stay. "There's something else I'd like to talk about, too," he said, somewhat sheepishly.

"Ah!" replied Giebort, "Now comes the little talk."

Only then did TamSen realize that Giebort already knew what was on his mind. He sighed, hoping that the conversation would be easier than he had imagined.

"You love her a lot, don't you," said Giebort, hoping to ease the way.

"Yes, but I don't know . . . well, I don't know a lot of things. See, I've never . . . well, I've never even had a girlfriend before, and well . . . uh . . ."

"I haven't seen any trouble between you two," Giebort said.

"No, there's no trouble, but well . . . I never had a father, and uh . . ."

"Listen. You're no different than anyone else,

man or dwarf. Hell! Even the monsters out there in the darkness probably have the same problems.

"A human father could give you the answers he learned over, say, thirty years of living. An' believe me . . . that still won't be enough! Why, I'm still trying to learn the questions after four hundred years of marriage!"

"Well, I'm only twenty years old, and I don't know *any* of it," said TamSen.

"Look, lad. I could give you lots of advice, lots of hints, and lots of instructions," Giebort said, "but what it all boils down to is this: You've gotta love her. You've gotta love everything about her, or don't even try to love her at all. Love what you like . . . that's easy. Then, learn to love what you don't like . . . that's hard.

"It's funny," mused the dwarf. "A woman gets raised in the same city, with the same upbringing, the same religion; you court 'em for years, then marry 'em and find out that they're completely different from the person you thought you knew. But no matter, you've gotta love 'em, anyway.

"Now, your woman has a *lot* of differences to love. But they probably aren't all that different.

"So she has talons instead of toes. Her feet can't be much colder'n Gaieliah's. And the toenails can't be much sharper, either." Giebort chuckled and glanced over at TamSen only to discover that the boy was not sharing his humor.

"Well, that's my advice boy. Just love her. All of her if you want the love to last forever.

"Don't ever let yourself get used to her. Don't ever start treatin' her as something ordinary. Come to think of it, you might have an easier time with that one than most folks do.

"Now, as for the particulars about women . . ." Giebort began. Then he stopped and placed his head over to one side, listening.

TamSen listened too. He had been aware of the sound for some time. It was almost like the murmur of wind, a wind that was blowing through the caverns and was only now reaching them.

The sound had been hovering just below the threshold of hearing, but now rising to a pitch that had seized everyone's attention.

All conversation came to an abrupt halt as the sound suddenly changed from that of wind to the bellow and screams of hundreds upon thousands of massed monsters, echoing in the darkness. All around them, dwarves scrambled to their feet, grabbing for their weapons.

The rising sound was coming from beyond their rear perimeter. Lancemen immediately dropped to the ground at the edge of the perimeter, facing the direction from which the attack would come. They set their lances firmly and prepared for the onslaught as bowmen took up their positions directly behind them.

The sound grew and grew and grew until it became one loud concentrated howl that rang in their ears without abating. At first, there was only the noise and the empty darkness and then, suddenly they were upon them.

The monsters poured out of the darkness, paying them no heed, rushing headlong into their midst. They did not pause to choose their paths but crushed stalagmites, stalactites, dwarves and each other in their blind run, flattening whatever did not give way before them.

When an obstacle did not move, they crashed into it, and were themselves crushed in turn by the press of monsters behind them. The monsters tripped and fell over the larger stalagmites, over their own feet, and the pile of fallen monsters lying in their path.

Once within bow range, the monsters became moving targets for the dwarven arrows. The dwarves slew hundreds of them, large and small. And as the monsters appeared and fell to their arrows, the others surged forward over their dead bodies.

Slime snakes slithered between the lancemen and around the feet and ankles of the bowmen. A solid swarm of eight-legged stalag-mites, the size of a human hand, came next, covering the dwarves completely.

The tiny, darting, pinlike feet were everywhere. The mites were in too big a hurry to bite, but that was small mercy for those whose bodies were covered by the awful creatures.

They fought frantically to throw off the thousands of legs that crept over their faces and arms, down the back of their tunics and pants and up their legs.

The thundering herd of monsters was now within a hundred yards of the dwarves. The pile of dead bodies grew taller and taller as the arrows sought out new targets as the monsters climbed over those who had fallen before them. Within heartbeats, the pile grew taller and taller, towering above them in the darkness. And still the monsters came.

As the full force of the attack reached the line of

spearmen, the leading monsters impaled themselves on the dwarven spears and fell. But those behind pushed them forward and many of the dwarves were crushed beneath the very creatures they had killed.

Every monster and dwarf who fell was immediately covered by crawling and slithering things. There were thousands upon thousands of tiny creatures swarming over the walls, floors, and roof of the chamber.

The leathery sound of cave bats muffled all other sounds overhead. Huge spiders fell on the dwarves, but not in attack, for they wasted no time as they hurried away, following their larger and more frightening companions.

Three of the largest granite moles the dwarves had even seen plowed through the embankment of dead monsters and headed directly into the thickest gathering of dwarves. They were shot with arrows and speared from all directions, but took no note of their injuries and continued to run at a frantic pace. The largest mole trampled at least fifty dwarves before it fell to the floor and died.

Since the attack had come from the rear, Giebort had a short time to assess the situation. He quickly ascertained that the monsters were not attacking the dwarves themselves, but were retreating from something else.

Giebort soon saw that it was both foolish and futile to try to stem the flood of monsters and ordered his men to retreat to the walls of the cavern.

But saying and doing were two different things. Many dwarves were crushed by the monsters before they could get out of the way, but the bulwarks formed by the bodies of the dead slowed the monsters' advance considerably, giving the dwarves a slight edge.

Most of the dwarves were able to reach the sides of the cavern where they stood and watched in awe as the frenzied mass of monsters poured past them in the flickering light of the torches.

No one could even begin to guess what had caused the giant exodus, it was beyond anything they had ever seen or ever imagined.

"What on Oerth could have made them so afraid?" Giebort shouted.

Chewppa stood in a deep crevice in the side wall, her wings spread protectively over Korlim.

Korlim peered out between the bottom fringe of feathers, watching the rout in horror. He was all too afraid that he knew what had caused the frantic flight. Something so fierce as to send monsters running in fear of their lives. He groaned and sank back against the rock, clutching his head and moaning softly to himself, "By all the gods who are holy, I'm leading a thousand of my men to their deaths."

Chapter 26

THE FLOOD OF MONSTERS, reptiles, insects and unidentifiable "things," continued unabated for a very long time. The dwarves pressed themselves against the cavern walls and clung for their very lives to crevices and protruberances.

They tried as best they could to bear the constant waves of spiders, mites, roaches, cavern crabs, slime snakes, and the variety of other wriggling and crawling creatures that swarmed over them. Every inch of exposed skin teemed with the onslaught.

One dwarf had been caught while bathing in a cavern pool. Soon, the creeping, crawling things became too much for him and he fell from the wall, screaming and slapping at the blanket of living things that covered his body. He was soon trampled by a passing giant ant lion which was, itself, covered with insects and spiders.

Many of the creatures that died emptied their stomachs and bowels in their last spasms of life. Others merely bled from numerous wounds. The smell of their blood was fetid and rank. The horrible sounds, the stench of the dead and dying, and the awful smells now mingled with the dust disturbed by their passage.

The air became all but unbreathable. Dwarves fell from the wall, gasping for breath and scraping at their noses, mouths and ears to free them from the things that had crawled inside.

At last the torrent began to slack. More and more they took note that many of the larger creatures who rushed past them were maimed and brutally disfigured. Some were missing huge chunks of flesh; others had been luckier and merely displayed long deep slashes in their flesh. They trailed dark streams of blood, and one was seen dragging its own entrails. The creatures' piteous cries and their screams of agony and fear only served to heighten the horror of the terrible procession, and the grievous tumult actually roused pity in the hearts of the dwarves, their ancient enemies.

After the last of the monsters had passed, the floors and walls were still covered with the smaller, slower moving creatures.

As the nightmarish sounds began to fade in the distance, the dwarves slowly separated themselves from the walls. They were badly shaken and jumped up and down and beat their bodies in an attempt to rid themselves of the last of the crawling bugs. Sanity returned slowly.

Yet even while they were still hopping around the cavern floor, Giebort began shouting commands. He passed back and forth among them yelling orders and pushing dwarves around, as though they were children who had misbehaved, rather than fighters under seige.

"PICK IT UP! GET THAT GEAR IN ORDER! WHAT'S THE MATTER WITH YOU? GET THAT % + &*&?###!!! THING ON RIGHT! MOVE! MOVE! MOVE!"

Within heartbeats, an extremely miserable band of slightly less than nine hundred dwarves stood at attention in a rough formation. Their bodies were still covered with crawling, biting things.

Giebort passed up and down their ranks, slapping both dwarves and gear into their proper positions. He approached the front of the formation and stood there for a moment, so all could see him. He, like the others, was covered with crawling insects, yet he stood perfectly still. He then began to yell at them in a voice louder than TamSen and Chewppa had ever heard him use.

"Listen up, you dwarves! Whatever scared those monsters is MEAN! But that doesn't mean it can scare US! DOES IT!!!"

The nine hundred dwarves joined in unison, mumbling an incoherent jumble of vague grunts.

"I SAID, IT DOESN'T SCARE US! DOES IT!!!" Giebort yelled.

The chorus of mumbling was a little louder this time, but still incoherent.

"WHAT ARE YOU? A BUNCH OF BARE-FACED, SKINNY CHILDREN? SOME KIND OF MEWLING BLINDFISH? I SAID, IT DOESN'T SCARE US . . . DOES IT!!!"

Again, there was a low mumble, barely discernable as: "No . . . no . . . no . . . sir. No sir . . . sir . . .

sir . . ."

"WHAAAAAAAAAAT?????"

"No, Sir!" came the reply and this time it was clearly distinguishable.

"AW' RIGHT! NOW! LISTEN UP!"

It startled TamSen and Chewppa to see the normally mild Giebort acting this way. However, within a short span of time, he had managed to whip nearly nine hundred scraggly and disorganized troops into a coherent and orderly group.

Within heartbeats, he had raised some nine hundred odd demoralized spirits to where they would at least try to survive. By pushing, shoving, and yelling at them so ruthlessly, he had probably saved their lives, and they all knew it. They were behind him and believed in themselves once more.

Now I see why he's a commander! TamSen thought.

Giebort's next objective was to get the entire company moving as quickly as possible. Any delay would only permit morale and purpose to lapse.

Many of the dwarves had not been able to pick up their possessions before Giebort forced them into formation. The last rank was ordered to remain behind and retrieve all the weapons and gear it could find. Torch-bearers were positioned to the front and rear ranks. The formation was now surrounded by light, and the order was given to march.

There was no question as to who was in charge. Whatever Giebort commanded the dwarves to do, the three "wizards" did as well, without asking questions or offering advice.

Giebort passed among them, seeking out his most

capable men and reassigning them to the rear of the formation. He knew his men well, knew their individual abilities and talents, and he picked his lieutenants carefully.

He wanted his best fighters positioned where the danger would be. He knew that he could not afford to allow the formation to hesitate, much less stop. Strict order and unity had to be kept at all costs. Under Giebort's expert leadership, the marching formation changed character from roughly-organized to finely tuned.

There were no further incidents; nor did Giebort allow them to rest for more than a few heartbeats even though there were no signs of pursuit. Every time they stopped, Korlim directed his sedan bearers to Giebort's side and harassed him to continue on:

"Maelfesh's demons!" he repeated over and over again. "Maelfesh was alerted, I tell you. He has brought his demons. They are here, doing their evil work! I can feel their presence! We must get to the pillar! We must hurry."

A demon lord is not unlike the commander of an army himself, and Maelfesh had been carrying out his own inspection and selection of men, or rather, demi-demons. He had a large variety to choose from, but in the end, not wishing to deprive other worlds of his handiwork, he chose only twenty of his very worst demi-demons.

These particular demi-demons had been cast into his very special Pit of Undying Hatred centuries before and had languished there growing more and more hateful with every passing decade.

As Korlim suspected, Maelfesh had indeed sent his demi-demons in to the caverns, knowing they would slaughter anything and everything in their sight. He selected them not only for their hatred and cruelty, but because they hated him, Maelfesh, most of all.

Maelfesh knew that these particular demi-demons would much rather attack him than the dwarves. Therefore, he had placed the demi-demons on the opposite side of the dwarves from where he would make his own attack. The demi-demons could reach Maelfesh only by fighting their way through the dwarves, killing everything in their path.

They were truly frightening, to tell the truth, which Maelfesh made a point of never doing, they even frightened him a little. But he was in no danger; for long before they reached him, he would pluck them and send them back to the Pit of Undying Hatred. It was chancey, but that was the fun of it.

"Ah!" murmured Maelfesh. "Strategy, tactics, chance . . . I love it. I've missed it so. I shall have to war with these puny mortals more often!"

The demi-demons were hideous things, capable of frightening lesser beings to death by their mere visage.

Their original features were long since obliterated by their long immersion in hatred. One could no longer say that this one had been a man or that one a monster, or even that this one had begun its life as a demi-demon. Their origins were no longer of any importance. It was what they had become that was the issue.

They were a horrifying collection of cruel, leering mouths, jagged teeth, slitted eyes and claws and talons that could shred and tear. They were dark, black in color, for that is the color of hatred.

The demi-demons had already slaughtered every living thing that they had been able to catch, and were now fighting with each other over the carcasses. Several of them were busy simply destroying the walls and roof of the cavern.

Hatred welled out of them for anything that enjoyed actual physical existence, and they were content, for the time being at least, smashing rocks. Soon, though, they would tire of things that could not fight back and go in search of live entertainment.

Chapter 27

GIEBORT HAD CONTINUED to hurry his men toward the Pillar of the Demon Hand. Korlim had used his energy as best he was able, entering trances and using his far vision to keep close watch on the progress of the demons. As yet, he had seen none, but he knew that their luck would not hold.

Now and then, as he came out of a trance, Korlim would grab one of his many books of spells, frantically flip through the pages till he found what he was searching for, then memorize the spell and turn down the page corners for reference.

TamSen and Chewppa merely marched along in silence, holding hands, but not speaking.

At long last, the company of dwarves approached a division of passageways. One corridor angled off to the left and another to the right. Giebort hesitated not at all, but marched his men into the left branch and then brought them to a halt.

After several heartbeats, he approached Korlim's sedan chair and waited. When Korlim failed to notice him, Giebort reached over and shook the old man gently on one frail shoulder.

"Master Korlim," he said, "We have arrived at the fork."

Korlim looked up at him as though in a daze. It was apparent that he was just emerging from yet another trance. He saw Giebort standing beside him, saw that they had stopped, and he grasped the situation immediately. "Are we there?" he asked. Giebort nodded.

Korlim climbed down from the sedan chair with Giebort's assistance and faced the rear of the company. He raised his hands, closed his eyes, and began to mumble something that no one, not even those closest to him, could understand. Several of the older dwarves recognized the words as those of the olden tongue, but none beside Korlim knew what the words meant.

For a heartbeat, nothing happened. Then slowly those in the rear began to stir and mutter excitedly among themselves. TamSen and Chewppa who had been positioned somewhat near the front of the column, pushed their way back and found that the passageway no longer existed, it was sealed with solid rock.

"It wouldn't normally be a real wall, you understand," Korlim said to Chewppa. "But the demons that follow us have magical abilities of their own and would detect an illusionary wall and run right through it.

"Normally, an illusion would serve the purpose of deterring whatever follows as well as allowing us to escape through it," said Korlim. "But this one is quite real. Stone. Rocks. We are trapped inside, just as they have been held outside. But I prefer being trapped by a wall than being caught by the demons."

And no one cared to disagree.

Korlim held onto Chewppa's arm as he climbed back into the sedan chair. When he was seated, he continued to cling to her arm, indicating his need to talk. He called TamSen over and drew him close on the opposite side so that he might hear what was being said.

"Harpies are, by their very nature, magical creatures. So are werewolves. But then, so are demi-demons. Any abilities which you have naturally, the demons will possess, as well. Any strength you possess, they possess. You are accustomed to preying on helpless animals. Do not make the mistake of thinking of these demi-demons as helpless. They are by far, other than MacIfesh himself, the most dangerous creatures you will ever face.

"Chewppa, you are able to mesmerize your prey with your song; they have the ability to mesmerize with a single glance. Your talons can claw through many thicknesses; theirs can rip and shred.

"More importantly, they possess two things that you do not, experience and evil cunning. But you have something with which to defeat them; you have the stones!"

Korlim looked Chewppa directly in the eye and said quietly, "Now is the time, give me your necklace."

Chewppa pulled back against the wizard's arm. Despite everything she knew, she was reluctant to part with her necklace. She had never even considered giving to to TamSen and she loved him. She certainly didn't love Korlim.

Then, seemingly against her will, her hands began edging toward the necklace. Was it the situation or the old wizard's command? It didn't matter, she was driven by some inner compulsion to do as he asked. She removed the necklace from round her neck and handed it to him.

Korlim took one of the red stones in one hand and held up the blue stone of the necklace in the other. "When this is done," he said, "know that Maelfesh will not rest until we are dead."

Then, hesitating not a heartbeat, he brought his hands together and joined the stones in a brilliant flash of light. Centered in the necklace was a stone that was at once both red and blue. Both colors seemed to be in the same place at the same time without mingling.

"That does it," said Korlim, "we're in for it now!" He handed the necklace back to her and said "Quickly, give me another blue stone!"

Chewppa handed a second blue stone to Korlim which he clasped to the red stone embedded in his own golden breastpiece. Bright shafts of light radiated between his fingers and from the edges of his hand. His stones had joined, as well.

"Now *he's* in for it!" Korlim grinned. "Finally! I have the power to fight against Maelfesh! Now, hurry, give me another stone for TamSen!"

After TamSen's stone was joined, Korlim pulled a necklace out of one of his copious pockets and fastened TamSen's stone to it, after removing an innocuous gemstone that dangled from the end of the chain.

"I must try my powers," he said to TamSen, "just to see if they work!" He spoke a quiet spell over the necklace and TamSen's brilliant stone disappeared, replaced by the original dull stone. Korlim wriggled happily like a child who has just been given a puppy.

"I put a spell of disguise on it," Korlim explained hurriedly, seeing the angry expressions on TamSen's and Chewppa's faces. "I have done this for a reason.

"Werewolves do not possess strong magic except at the time of the full moon, so it follows that you will have the least power among us. Since we do not have the luxury of knowing when Maelfesh will attack, I have hidden your stone so that he will not see you as a threat. He will attack us first. The stone will give you power but hopefully he will not understand why."

Korlim handed TamSen the necklace and instructed him to place it in his pocket. Nor was he to put it on, until it became necessary. This was the stone that would be given into the hands of the great wizard, Mika-oba.

"Listen closely," Korlim said, "for I am going to try to teach you in the short time we have remaining to us, all that an apprentice learns in years. Very simply, I am going to tell you how to use the magic that you have within you.

"Magic, you see, is not just the sole property of learned men like myself. It is not merely in these spell books or in potions or brews. Magic is the gods' given gift that lies within each of us, to some extent or another.

"The real question is not, 'Am I magic?' but rather, 'How do I get to my magic when I want it, and how do I control it?' Well, I will try to show you.

"When you want to do something, imagine it already done. The more real it becomes in your mind, the more real it truly becomes. The magic of making things happen is no harder than deciding in your own mind that that is the way it will be."

"That sounds easy enough," said Korlim, "but it is very hard to do. Chewppa, if you go into this battle with Maelfesh worried that either you or TamSen may die, then one or both of you may well die. But, if you enter into it with the absolute belief that there is no way you will allow anything to happen to either of you, then nothing will.

"But remember, Maelfesh will be going into battle equally confident that he will defeat us all. The question is, then, who can be the most certain that their way is the truth? Who has the firmest resolve?

"The real magical property of these stones is not that they enhance some value mystical power. They simply allow their bearer to see the truth clearly. Whatever you decide things are, then they *are*. This must be clear and firm in your mind at all times.

"Do not go into battle hoping to win. Go to battle having already won . . . that is how you use the stones.

"You see, all the magic of all the wizards and mages, all the warlocks and demons who ever lived, is nothing more than the magic of the world which the gods have made for us.

"When you battle Maelfesh, you must know that his defeat is but a single step in freeing your father. Just a minor inconvenience that must be dealt with before you can leave this place.

"If you have any doubt, you will make that doubt into a reality. From this moment forth, you must believe that Maelfesh has already been beaten. I know it in my heart and it is true."

Well, thought TamSen, now if we could only convince Maelfesh of it, too.

"There is one more thing that must be said," Korlim continued. "As you recall, according to the history which you recounted, your ancestor, good King Serikin, who originally conquered the island, slew the Island Trolls, 'and they were seen in the land no more' . . . Well, that is not completely correct.

"I'm sorry to say that King Serikin was not really the hero you think. The trolls got into a dispute with Maelfesh over a trivial matter and he condemned them to the caverns, forever, just as he did your Mika-oba.

"King Serikin and his armies merely arrived at an opportune moment, just in time to take credit for ridding the land of the trolls.

"Are—are you trying to tell us that, that . . ."

"Yes," Korlim said with a sigh. "Maelfesh imprisoned the island trolls down here in the same vicinity as the Pillar of the Demon Hand. The entire area has become a vast prison, filled with all manner of dwarves, demons, dark elves, island trolls—in short, all those who have ever displeased Maelfesh.

"It is quite likely that any disruption of the spell that binds Mika-oba will free the Island Trolls, as well. If that happens, they will not hesitate to serve Maelfesh, hoping to gain their freedom by winning his favor. They too, will join in the battle against us."

Chapter 28

BEFORE TAMSEN AND CHEWPPA could even grasp the full scope of this awful news, Giebort suddenly brought the entire company to a halt. A forward scout had just returned, bringing him news that seemed to have shaken him badly.

Their objective lay just beyond the next turn in the passage. However, the scout had returned to report the presence of a huge monster that filled the passage from top to bottom, side to side and dripped with blue fire.

Never having seen Maelfesh himself and discounting the scout's terror, Giebort incorrectly assumed the thing to be one of Maelfesh's minions. He therefore brought his best fighters to the fore, lined the men in battle formation and advanced slowly.

As they rounded the turn, they saw a creature made entirely of fire standing against the far wall. Blue flames dripped from his extremities as though they were melting, dropping flaming gobbets on the floor.

The horrible spectre stood at least thirty feet tall and lit up the entire cavern with the sickly glow of dead meat fluorescing in darkness.

"*Well, Korlim, so you have a little stone,*" said the vision. "*Do you think you can fight me with its power? What will you do, throw it at me?*"

The evil spectre roared with laughter and the waves of heat singed their skin and shriveled their beards.

It bent forward, a single blazing hand on its fiery hips and pointed at the dwarves. The pointman of the formation began to scream, grabbed his helmet and ripped it off his head. His hair was on fire and his scalp could be seen to bubble with the intense heat. His face and arms were covered with blisters that sloughed off, revealing the cooked flesh beneath them. His screams turned to a sickening gurgle and the unfortunate dwarf dropped to the ground, dead.

His spear remained upright for a long heartbeat, then slowly melted and oozed to the ground beside its former owner. This awful sight was viewed with horror by all those who had stood behind him.

"Remember," Korlim whispered to Chewppa and TamSen, "He's already lost. We don't have a thing to worry about! The battle is won!"

But TamSen and Chewppa, like all those who had witnessed the horrible spectacle, were frozen with fear. They stood staring wide-eyed with open mouths at the huge fire demon and did not reply.

Korlim slowly climbed down from his sedan chair, pretending cool nonchalance. He dusted his tunic and straightened his pants. At long last, he looked up at the fiery, glowing demon as though he had only just noticed that it was there.

"Maelfesh, I do believe you're putting on weight!"

The image of evil that towered above them all grinned. "*You no longer cower before me?*" it boomed, "*Excellent! I do so enjoy destroying those who fail to show me proper respect! There are so many snivelers these days!*" The echoes of Maelfesh's voice rumbled thoughout the passageway.

"You're in our way, fat one," Korlim continued, as though they were merely discussing the weather. "If you will move aside now, we promise not to hurt you."

Maelfesh's uproarious laughter nearly deafened everyone in the cavern. This upstart of a dwarf wizard! This mere mortal! Hurt the mighty Maelfesh? Oh, this was going to be excellent fun!

The booming laughter not only hurt their ears, but was also spreading the heat of the demon's body. The lead troops were forced to fall back in order to keep from being roasted alive.

Finally, Maelfesh's short sense of humor ended. The monstrous image replied, "*If this weren't even better than I had hoped, I would kill you all right now. You're doing fine, little wizard, keep it up!*"

"Very well," said Korlim, just as nonchalantly as before. "You make a nice, showy display, but I see that you are afraid to meet us as you really are. Obviously, you know that if you did show your real self, we could easily push you aside like the demi-demon baby that you are. You seem to want to hide behind illusions, Maelfesh. What are you really? Some kind of sickly human?"

The grin remained on the demon's face but the aura of blue flames that framed his body began shooting sparks at the very edges. The image swelled and rose to even greater dimensions. *"Very well! I will meet you as I really am. But you will regret it!"*

The flaming blue monster began to shrink, and as it shrank, it grew brighter and brighter. At last its brightness culminated in a blinding flash. There before them, in seeming darkness, stood the figure of Maelfesh, only slightly larger than human in size. His body was still covered with flames, which licked and curled around the rocks and stalagmites nearby.

A seething hiss came from the demon, as though a wet finger had been touched to hot iron. The fire that issued from this smaller version of Maelfesh leapt into the air with a life of its own. A plume of yellowish smoke rose from his body and began filling the air with the choking stench of sulfur.

A few of the dwarves peered over the edge of their shields to see what was happening. Maelfesh waved his hand and sent a sheet of flame rolling over them, catching a few full in the face. Screams of agony rent the air as they burned alive and others vomited where they stood.

Korlim ignored the death and mayhem and strolled over to Maelfesh. A look of surprise appeared on the demon's face. Maelfesh aimed a finger at the ground and it turned to molten lava. Korlim continued walking as though it were a fine summer's day.

Maelfesh flicked his fingers and the lava began to bubble and pop, spattering Korlim's pant legs. Korlim paid it no mind and it fell back harmlessly, causing not the least bit of damage.

Korlim stood directly before Maelfesh, smiling. The demon, who was by this time, in a full rage, raised his hands over the dwarf wizard's head. Korlim was engulfed in a solid sheet of blinding flame, which showered down on him with all the violence of a torrential downpour.

The dwarven band had risen to its feet and was ready to rally forth to protect its beloved wizard. Yet nothing appeared to be happening to Korlim. He simply stood in the wash of searing flames, smiling impishly at Maelfesh.

Maelfesh exploded with anger. He pointed directly overhead, causing the ceiling to melt. Molten stone poured down onto Korlim, covering him completely. A sigh went up from the dwarves.

When the flow of lava ended, a new stalagmite had formed on the floor of the cavern with Korlim at its core. Only then did Maelfesh lower his arm, giving a snort of satisfaction at the results of his handiwork.

His satisfaction was short-lived, however, for much to his amazement, the red, glowing lava that had formed around Korlim began to glow even more brightly. It continued to glow until it melted away and flowed to the floor where it created a steaming puddle around Korlim's feet.

"Ah, refreshing," Korlim said with a smile, "Somewhat like taking a hot shower." Then, growing stern, he said, "you disappoint me, Maelfesh. I had really thought that you could do better than that. It was simple. Any first level magician could do as well.

"Did you really think so little of me as to use the same trick twice and not expect me to figure it out? Really, it meant no more to me than . . . this!"

Korlim raised his arm, extended his palm upward and made a small lifting motion. There was a rushing sound that began somewhere behind the dwarves and then a huge, round ball of water floated over their heads and flung itself at the fiery demon.

Maelfesh's eyes widened as the water flew toward him. He pointed at it quickly and flames shot out of his fingertips and arced toward the ball of water. Without the slightest of sizzles, the water parted as though flowing around a rock in midstream and continued on toward the demon.

As the torrent reached its goal, Maelfesh vanished, leaving Korlim to be drenched. There was nothing illusionary about the water, it was quite real and as it formed puddles of its own, Korlim stood dripping and shivering in the cold cavern air.

The old dwarven wizard turned to TamSen and Chewppa and motioned them to his side.

"Come! Come!" he urged. "Those were just the opening formalities. He'll be back in full force, soon. We must hurry and free the wizard, Mika-oba. We will need his help!"

As TamSen and Chewppa stood waiting for further direction, Korlim turned to Giebort and said, "Well, it is upon us now, old friend. Best prepare your troops for the worst. It will be here soon."

"Which direction will it come from?" said Giebort, looking around him and trying to decide where to make his stand.

"From any side! From all sides!" replied Korlim. "Just be ready and expect anything!"

Giebort placed his best fighters in a half-circle at

the rear and formed another half-circle in front of the formation. He moved the archers into the center of the circle and placed the pikemen along the inner edges of the semi-circles. Now he was prepared for an attack whether fore or aft.

Chewppa and TamSen followed Korlim as he turned to one side and entered a small crevice in the side of the cavern, which they had seen but to which they had attached no importance. This crevice soon opened onto a second chamber far smaller than the one they had left.

It was quite dark and their torches barely illuminated the deep gloom. Then, as they advanced into the room, they saw it, the Pillar of the Demon Hand. It was everything they had ever dreamed it to be, a huge column, wider around than twenty men could circle with clasped hands. It glowed and shimmered in the light, radiating beams of red and blue light, not unlike their own magic gems. Indeed, it seemed as though the pillar, which ran from floor to ceiling, was composed entirely of the magic stones.

Shadowy forms could be seen vaguely in its depths and there, to the left, farthest from them, was the demon hand, a horrible, ugly, green scaly thing tipped with long, curved talons that seemed to twitch under their gaze.

Chewppa cried out and leaned forward as though to hurry to her father's side, but Korlim's hand shot out and grabbed her firmly by the shoulder.

"Stop!" he cried. "Has your desire blinded you to everything other than that which you wish to see? Wake up, child! Look around you and beware, or you will jeopardize us all!"

Shaken from her vision, which had indeed been channeled toward Mika alone, Chewppa noticed for the first time that lying between them and the pillar was a huge mass of grayish-pink flesh.

This awful apparition was segmented into large round sections, much like those of a caterpillar. Each section was equipped with legs that ended in curved, pointed pincers. Each pincer glistened with green fluid. The floor beneath the horrible thing was scored as though with acid, where the fluid had dripped. Even now, the pincers dug into the rock and tiny wisps of red-orange smoke drifted into the air. The monster was more than twenty feet long and barred the way from one side of the small chamber to the other.

Korlim held his torch on high, illuminating the monster further. With this movement, one end of the monster swung toward them, revealing, huge bulbous eyes, like those of a fly, as well as an immense pair of steel-gray pincers that protruded from the sides of its gaping mouth.

"What on Oerth is it!" TamSen cried.

"A present from Maelfesh," Korlim replied in a softer voice. He made a motion with his hands, urging them to remain both quiet and still. "It is the larva of the jade-eating moth. As adults, they are harmless; however, in their larval form, they will devour anything they can catch. Their appetites are insatiable."

"How do we get around it?" asked TamSen.

"I'm afraid we don't," said Korlim. "Even if we were to kill it, its blood is like acid and would dissolve our bodies on contact. Its body is covered with fine hairs like tiny pins. One touch and you are paralyzed. It is too large for us to pass or lure aside."

"Can't you use your magic?" TamSen asked.

"Yes," replied Korlim. "But this is no illusion or magic image. It is real and killing it would take much of my power, rendering me useless for the fight to come. Maelfesh is very clever, I fear. He has set me a task that I must perform to defeat him, but performing the task will defeat me instead."

"I fly over monster," said Chewppa and she flapped her wings as though to demonstrate her ability as well as her desire.

"It might work," Korlim muttered as the larva twisted its huge head toward them. As it began creeping forward, its mandibles ground together and green fluid dripped from its mouth spattering and hissing on the ground below, in anticipation of the meal to come.

"Quick, give me the last blue stone," shouted Korlim. And as Chewppa complied, he pressed it against the last red stone. Once again, there was the now-familiar blinding flash and the stones were joined.

Korlim shoved the stone into Chewppa's hand then threw a torch under the larva's head. As the larva pounced down on the flaming torch, Korlim yelled, "Fly! Fly! Put the stone into the demon hand! QUICK!"

Chewppa leaped into the air and glided over the larva with precious little room to spare.

By the light emanating from it, Chewppa was able to land safely beside the pillar. As she looked into its depths, hoping to catch a glimpse of her father,

Chewppa saw another pair of eyes looking out at her. It was an unsettling sight. Unable to see much besides vague, shadowy forms, she walked around the pillar until she came to the ugly demon hand.

Then, just as she was about to place the stone in the horrible hand, it lunged toward her, grabbing desperately at the stone.

Only her quick reflexes allowed her to pull back, and as she did so, the pillar wavered and then turned into a demon before her eyes.

She fell backward, as much from terror as from surprise and as she fell, she felt the stone being wrenched from her hand by some invisible force behind her. She tried to pull back, to release the stone, but neither was possible. The force grew stronger and stronger and then, unable to resist it any longer, Chewppa screamed helplessly as she was pulled into what appeared to be thin air, and was gone.

Korlim and TamSen stared in disbelief at the space where Chewppa had vanished, stunned by what had transpired.

"*Did you like that any better?*" asked a voice. Turning, Korlim saw Maelfesh leaning against the wall beside him.

Korlim was still too shocked to reply.

"*What I did was make the real pillar invisible, then placed an illusionary pillar in front of it with a demi-demon, loyal to me, of course, inside of it. Your flying apprentice just handed the demi-demon the stone.*"

"Admit it, wizard," said Maelfesh, as his voice grew harsh once more. "*I have bested you. There will be no stone to give to the wolf-wizard, unless you choose to give him your own. I have beaten y—!*"

Maelfesh's boast was cut short, interrupted by a series of peculiar sounds from the far side of the chamber.

The first noise was followed by the sound of a heavy body falling to the ground.

Korlim and Maelfesh looked at each other to see which one of them had created the trick, but both seemed to be at a loss, and the trick went unclaimed.

Next came a deep grunt, as though someone had run into something in the dark. This was followed by a woman's voice, loud and quite deep, most unwomanly as a matter of fact, bellowing, "You little twerp! Keep your hands to yourself! I'm a lady and don't you forget it! Now where's that bungling fool who got us into this mess! MIKAAAAAA!"

The language that followed can, unfortunately, not be repeated here. Suffice it to say that the string of exclamations and expletives brought an expression of rapt attention to Maelfesh's fiery face.

Hornsbuck had always claimed that Lotus Blossom's language was foul enough to make the devil himself blush. It was evidently true.

The demi-demon standing beside the illusionary pillar had never heard such a dazzling display of splenetic virtuosity. Not once had a word been duplicated. The startling statements, filled with all - but - impossible physical suggestions, gave the demi-demon new insights, and distracted it from its proper task.

The demi-demon listed with increasing awe and drew nearer to the invisible pillar which had swallowed Chewppa, trying in vain to see the creature who was the source of the wonderful words. Within heartbeats he had located the source of the swearing. Or to be more exact, he had located the hand of the swearer, the hand which was, at that very moment, squeezing his neck and ending the misery that he had mistaken for life.

Maelfesh's demi-demon, loyal though it was, died, crumpled in the hands of its invisible assailant. The head was soon separated from its body and bounced across the floor, spewing thick, black blood in its wake.

Chapter 29

NOW, MIKA HAD BEEN STANDING on one foot for twenty years. When the magic of the spell was broken and the pillar collapsed, his leg failed him, seized by muscle spasms of the worst sort, and he tumbled forward and fell flat on his face.

As the headless body of the demi-demon bounced past him, Mika rolled across the floor, out of its path and a spell leaped to his lips with an ease that he had never known before. He could not have explained it, even if he had had the time, nor did it matter, for there was a bright flash of light and the demi-demon's body burst into flames and was consumed before the ashes landed on the ground.

Maelfesh and Korlim were transfixed, not knowing what was happening. Then, by the flare of the demi-demon's blazing body, they saw a shock of wild hair appear over the top of the larva body. The hair was soon followed by a gigantic arm waving a sword in a most serious manner.

Hornsbuck stormed over the body of the worm,

bellowing out the anger and frustration that had been bottled inside him for the last twenty years, looking for someone on whom he could vent his rage. He had his choice of a frail, bent old dwarf, or Maelfesh, the source of all their trouble.

Maelfesh raised his hand to throw a sheet of flame, but unexpectedly, Korlim leaped to block his attack.

Quick as his reaction had been, Korlim was not fully prepared for the full impact of the blast of fire. He was not killed outright, but his powers were very badly drained.

The fire struck the stone on Korlim's breastplate and was absorbed. But the radiance of the flash shone in all directions, bathing everyone and everything in the chamber with a deep purple light. This purple light cast no shadows, for it penetrated and shone through everything it touched. And in the wake of the purple flare was peace, for when its brilliance faded, Maelfesh was gone.

Chapter 30

MAELFESH FOUND HIMSELF lying flat on his flaming backside at the base of his crystal throne. He had been beaten. Never before had such a thing happened, but it had now.

Maelfesh rose to his feet and bellowed in rage, almost beside himself with fury. All thought of sport was gone from his mind. His next attack would not be done for fun in the hopes of reliving his youth. This was no longer fun; it had become serious.

"I will call all the forces of evil to aid me," he screamed. "I will kill them all! I will defeat those accursed mortals even if I lose my own essence in the doing!"

"He will be back," said Korlim. "I know him and I can promise you that he'll be back and when he does, he'll not be content with robbing me of my power or my stone. He'll come back to maim, to torture and to destroy. He'll come back for our souls. We must be prepared! We must hurry!" And forgetting all thoughts of conserving his strength, Korlim threw a spell on the giant worm that put it to sleep.

But few of those gathered were listening to his words of advice. Hornsbuck and Lotus Blossom were standing above Mika's prostrate form, cursing him with every foul word in their combined vocabularies. Even Tam, RedTail, and the princess were growling, giving voice to their displeasure over the years of confinement for which they all blamed Mika.

The moment for which Mika had prayed had finally arrived; and now that it was here, his closest friends in the world, the only ones who really cared for him, seemed ready to kill him. Mika buried his face in his hands and groaned.

But Mika was not the only one who was being abused. Strangely, the mild-mannered Korlim had begun to yell at someone or something, too.

"So there you are, you idiot!" he fumed. "WHAT did you think you were doing? I *told* you not to try to get them out, but *no*, you had to do it your way! You never listen! Didn't you stop to think that you could have been caught in there forever! Why, I have a good mind to stick you back in there for a few centuries, just to teach you a lesson!"

As TamSen and Chewppa stared, a small dwarf emerged from the pillar where the Wolf Nomads and the wolves had been trapped, and leaped over the slumbering worm. The small dwarf rushed to Korlim with widespread arms ignoring his angry words completely. Never had they heard Korlim speak in such tones, nor lose his calm so completely. Not even the demon Maelfesh had angered him so. Who was this small dwarf and what had he done to so anger the magician?

Far from being overwhelmed by this great display of hostility, the dwarf flung his arms around the frail old man, hugged him tightly and whirled him around in a circle, causing the wizard's beard and his robes to wrap around them both. "Glad to see you too, pops," said the stranger. "So what took you so long to get us out?"

Korlim's acerbic comments finally slowed and then stopped altogether; and he threw his own arms around the stranger and hugged him in return.

Finally the young dwarf put Korlim down on the ground; and walking forward, arm in arm, they joined TamSen and Chewppa.

"This," Korlim said proudly, with tears shining in his eyes, "is my brave but impulsive son, Bijel. I might never have gotten him out without the Wizard Mika's help." And only then did he notice the tempest that was taking place at the foot of the now-vanished pillar.

The curses and growls had not ceased, but had grown even more fierce. Mika was huddled into himself, seeing little future in arguing with his "friends."

Korlim approached the angry party and began to speak. "I do not know the reason for this extraordinary outburst," he said, "but judging from my own reactions, I suggest that the emotion might possibly be misplaced.

"You are free of the pillar and alive, for the moment at least. If you wish to remain free and alive, I suggest that we ready ourselves—for Maelfesh will soon return."

His words cut through the babble of voices and the

nomads turned to look at him, allowing Mika to scramble to his feet, his leg cramp all but forgotten a a beautiful young harpy, far more attractive than the one he had consorted with so many years ago, slipped under his arm and helped support his weight. Mika grinned at her as feelings other than cramps returned in a rush, and he allowed his hand to casually dangle over her chest.

"There is not time to introduce ourselves formally at the moment, but Wizard Mika-oba, I must express our gladness at your presence and your powers I must also say that it has been a privilege knowing your daughter. Her aid has been as welcome to us in our battle with the demon as yours will be."

The harpy smiled up at Mika, a dazzling, winsome smile that stunned him; then his brain turned to ice a the meaning of Korlim's words penetrated his brain His DAUGHTER! Mika's hand all but leaped of Chewppa's shoulder; and losing his balance, Mika almost toppled to the floor. Only the harpy's quick re flexes, aided by the strong arm of the strange hairy fellow with the wet nose who seemed to be her com panion, broke his fall; and they set him back on his feet as though he were old and doddering.

Mika stared at the harpy with an open mouth, his mind racing. His daughter. Could it really be? There *was* that incident in the sky over the mountains out side of Exag, but he had never thought . . . still, the act *had* been consumated. Mika stared at the smiling harpy more closely, differently this time, searching her features for something familiar.

Hmmm, the girl *did* have intelligent eyes, and her nose and mouth were well-formed and rather noble now that he actually studied them. And her chin, yes, he could see hints of courage and strength in the cut of her jawline. As to her other attributes, Mika cleared his throat and quickly returned his eyes to her face. It wouldn't do to think about that part just yet.

A father! Ah, well, it would take some getting used to, and if he had ever thought of it at all, he had always assumed that his children would be male, but he supposed that there could be worse things to happen to a man than learning he had a daughter. Smiling awkwardly, Mika took Chewppa in his arms and embraced her.

Seeing that Chewppa and TamSen were going to be all right, TamSen had turned to the trio of wolves and knelt before them, his heart pumping hard, wondering which of the three of them was his mother.

He reached out tentatively and stroked them on their muzzles. He knew from his grandfather's stories that one of them must be his mother and one, his father, but which was which he could not say. He had never even seen a real wolf before. Nor could he tell the difference between male and female.

While TamSen was struggling with his dilemma and Mika and Chewppa were smiling at each other, Hornsbuck had wasted few words, merely stalked over to Lotus Blossom, grabbed her around the waist and dragged her into the shadows, his intentions obvious.

TamSen rose to his feet, crossed to Mika's side, introduced himself quietly and asked which of the wolves were his parents.

This bit of news from the hairy young fellow was almost as big a shock to Mika as learning that he had a daughter. He studied the fellow, taking note of his features—which were quite nice if you could ignore the wet nose and the big ears—but of course not as pleasant as those of his daughter.

TamSen repeated the question and Mika, startled from his reverie, gestured toward the princess and TamTur, both of which were staring at TamSen with great interest. RedTail was nowhere to be seen, having followed Lotus Blossom and Hornsbuck into the darkness.

TamSen sank to his knees and was immediately bathed by the hot tongues of his parents.

The scene was tender, with everyone meeting everyone else, renewing vows, and so on, but Korlim knew that the moment must be postponed if they were to survive. Maelfesh would delight in catching them napping, he entertained no notions of chivalry and fair play; dead meat was dead meat, any way you sliced it.

Finally, with the exception of Hornsbuck, Lotus Blossom and RedTail, who had still not returned, Korlim ushered the entire party out of the chamber, through the passageway and into the waiting throng.

At the sight of them, the army of dwarves burst into cheers which echoed throughout the caves. Seeing Bijel, who had been a favorite among them, they began to chant, "BIJ! BIJ! BIJ!" until Giebort put a halt to it with a sharp command. A short conference with Korlim apprised Giebort of the circumstances; and realizing that they had very little time to lose, the dwarven commander readied his meager defenses.

Chapter 31

MAELFESH'S DESIRE FOR BLOOD was about to be realized. The demi-demons whom he had unleashed on the cavern of precious gems had finished demolishing that treasure house and were now loose in the passageways, searching for some new form of entertainment.

Reaching the spot where the dwarves had been overrun by the monsters, they tasted their first drops of dwarven blood. They were off like a pack of hounds, baying after their prey. They were stymied but briefly by the stone wall that Korlim had used to block their passage. They did not bother to use their limited magic on it, contenting themselves with bashing it apart by sheer physical force.

They loped along at full speed. There was no thought of stealth; they cared nothing for silence, and were howling and braying like a pack of banshees. The closer they came, the higher the pitch of hate boiled within them.

Then they came within sight of the dwarves. The

froth bubbled from their mouths and long strings of slaver drooled from their lips and coated their black bodies. They were led by a hideous demi-demon who was missing an ear as well as an arm. His left eye was nothing more than a lump of scar tissue, and the right eye gleamed with the fires of the eternally damned.

The pack of demi-demons charged full force at the army of dwarves. There was no thought for personal safety, there was no cunning, no plan except to obliterate, to kill. They were driven by pure and total hatred for life and the need to destroy all things that lived.

The bowmen needed no urging, no signal, but shot scores upon scores of arrows into the leader who showed no signs of weakening. Then, by some stroke of luck, some help from the gods, an arrow struck the leader in its single eye and it paused, its jaws snapping with futility as it tried to remove the arrow.

Sensing its weakness instantly, its companions fell upon it and ripped it limb from limb, scarcely caring that heartbeats earlier, it had been one of their own. Death, any death, was all that they desired.

Only one of the demi-demons had not deviated from its intended target and continued on toward the dwarves. The dwarves fired salvo after salvo of arrows at the horrible thing. By the time it reached the front ranks, it looked more like a huge deformed porcupine than a demon; but still, it did not stop.

As it ran into and through the pikemen, its body was pierced and shredded by the razor-sharp blades. Still it was not slowed and was, if anything, further enraged by their attack.

Its gigantic clawed fists slammed in one direction,

crushing dwarves beneath its force, then swung back, impaling the fallen bodies on its cruelly curved talons.

It scooped one dwarf after another into its mouth, biting them in two and spitting out the pieces. The dwarves rallied to their fallen comrades and the demi-demon was soon covered with more dwarves than arrows. The swarm of dwarves would have appeared to the casual observer, had there been such an unlikely person, to be much like a colony of ants covering a fallen grasshopper.

Slowly, the mass of beings fell to the ground. The demi-demon had been cut into scores of bloody bits. But the gore was comprised of equal amounts of dwarven blood.

At the first outcry, Chewppa had flown high above the scene and now commanded a ledge above the demons who were busy devouring their fallen leader. She directed a loud screech toward them, intending to mesmerize them and render them helpless, fair game for the dwarves. The screech was powerful, one of her very best and would have served to still any normal creature.

But the demons were far from normal creatures and responded to only one emotion, hatred. One of them heard her and responded only by throwing a bloody, half-gnawed limb at her. As the grisly bit of meat struck the wall beside her, splattering her with gray-green blood, she fell silent.

Once their fallen leader had been reduced to a mere grease spot on the ground, the remaining demi-demons surged forward once again. The front ranks of the dwarves suffered heavy losses as the demi-demons thrust through them. One by one the demons fell, but tens by tens they took the heroic dwarves with them into death.

Chewppa, undeterred by the failure of her scream, sank her talons deep into the neck of one of the demons and rose into the air, suspending the demon above the dwarves' heads. As the monster struggled to free itself, it was stabbed and slashed from all sides until it died.

Korlim attacked another demon with a sheet of cutting fire; but though it was sliced in two, each half quickly rose and fought its way forward, claws and teeth reaching out for Korlim. It took a long, long time before the thing was finally dead.

At the end of this great onslaught, several demi-demons were left alive behind dwarven lines, standing back to back completely ringed by dwarves. The demons were so exhausted that even their endless supply of hatred was not enough to enable them to continue fighting. Exhausted they might be, but they were far from defeated. Giebort used this short period of grace to order a regrouping of the troops.

It was at this very moment, as all but the front and rear lines were milling about, that Maelfesh struck in full force. Giebort had placed his strongest and best fighters at the front and in the rear and this logical but mortal strategy nearly proved their downfall.

The wall of the cavern against their near side began to sag like a broken jar of warm jelly. And as it collapsed, slowly dissolving and leaving large gaps between top and bottom, it revealed a formation of Island Trolls standing behind it who had been entombed in its mass since that day, long centuries before when King Seriken "conquered" the Island of Dramidja.

As they stepped free of the wall that had been their prison for so long, Maelfesh's voice boomed out: *"Fight for me or return to your prison forever! You can win your freedom this day by serving me! Kill the dwarves! Kill them all!"*

Faced with the awful alternative, the Island Trolls surged forward into the side of the disorganized dwarven formation, slashing out with their long claws and biting with their terrible pointed teeth.

The dwarves fell back, aghast, from this new, unexpected enemy, for they knew all too well that trolls cannot be killed; no matter what portion of their hideous gray-green flesh is struck from their bodies, trolls continue to live, to reform and to fight on forever.

The trolls had been imprisoned in the wall more than seven hundred years earlier following the great battle with Serikin. They were groggy and few of them had weapons. More than half their numbers were women and children, but even the weakest Island Troll is a force to be reckoned with.

The dwarves fought valiantly, slaying trolls by the hundreds only to see them reform. Korlim's fire was necessary to incinerate the awful creatures and to burn every last bit and piece of them into nothingness. But their horde seemed infinite, while the dwarves lost numbers steadily.

The Island Trolls, determined to remain free, took a gruesome toll. And their very presence served to encourage the demi-demons, who renewed their attack. The dwarves were beseiged from without as well as within and many fell, never to see their home again.

The Island Trolls surged forward through the breach of the dwarven formation, into the very center of their midst, only to find themselves face to face with a band of demi-demons.

The demi-demons did not care who they killed; death was death to them and the weakened Island Trolls proved easy prey. They slashed and chewed their way through the trolls and soon found their way to the opening in the cavern wall where they waited with open mouths and twitching claws for the next troll victim. If such a thing were possible, their hatred reached unknown levels of rapture.

This unexpected reprieve offered the hard-pressed dwarves the smallest flickering of hope. The flow of Island Trolls had increased, emerging from the wall by the hundreds along the entire length of the wall. If the trolls could be funneled between the dwarves and the demi-demons, the demi-demons could be used as unwitting allies. Giebort's leadership was tested to the limits that day and not found to be wanting. He swung a column of troops around, pressing the demi-demons into the advance of the trolls. It was bloody mayhem.

Outraged at the unforseen demise of his plan, Maelfesh appeared in the air above the chaos of skirmishing trolls, demons and dwarves. He pointed his flaming fingers and sheets of fire rained down into the middle of the dwarven band. Actually, he cared little for the demise of the dwarves themselves, but he wanted to punish Korlim once and for all. He did not want to kill Korlim, of course, he wanted him to suffer horribly and interminably.

Chewppa saw Maelfesh and soared into the air to do battle with him. As she rose, a bolt of fire lanced down at her, only to be deflected by another bolt from the ground below.

"Get away!" cried Korlim, the light of the fires turning his glasses to bright shiny orbs. "He's mine! I've waited a long time for this moment!"

With a schoolboy cackle, Maelfesh hurled yet another firestorm, and then, ever the strategist, he disappeared again. Korlim searched overhead in vain for the target for his wrath.

Chapter 32

MIKA, HIS LEG STILL SEIZED with cramps, hobbled about on the edges of the action. Whenever and wherever he saw an opportunity, he cast a spell that took one more opponent out of the battle. TamTur and the princess fought at his side, taking out the anger of their imprisonment on whomever and whatever ventured within reach of their snapping jaws. Unfortunately, they could not always distinguish allies from enemies; not a few dwarves bore the marks of their displeasure long after the battle was done.

TamSen fought beside them as well, his heart swelling with pride at the sight of his parents, strange though the sight was. Then, at the very height of the battle, a terrible aching anxiety came over TamSen, all but immobilizing him. He searched his mind but could not identify the source of the horrible feeling. All he knew was that he was in great danger.

TamSen grabbed the necklace that Korlim had given him, the necklace that contained the magic gem, its power masked behind the facade of a worthless stone. All he knew was that he had to protect himself from whatever was about to happen. As he fell to his knees, all but overcome, he slipped the necklace over his head and then fell to the ground, enveloped in a sheath of blinding pain.

Heartbeats later, a long, mournful howl echoed throughout the cavern, all but drowning out the sounds of battle. Dwarves and trolls who had fallen in battle, knowing themselves near death, heard the dread sound and thought that it must be the Hound of the Dead come to carry them away.

How close they were to being correct! A gigantic wolf rose up from the place where TamSen had fallen. It was more than eight feet in length and its head was as high as a human's. Around its neck was a gold necklace, hung with a dull, plain stone.

The wolf looked around him and then, without hesitation, darted forward through the press of dwarves into the area dominated by the Island Trolls. The wolf seized a troll and shook it from side to side at lightning speed until it resembled nothing as much as a pile of limp rags. TamSen tossed the troll up into the air with a quick backward flip of his head and the troll was neatly finished off by a bolt of Korlim's fire.

Again and again he seized the advancing trolls. His fangs clicked and his growls echoed with such ferocity that the trolls began to fall back. He chased after them, entering their ranks and snatching first one, then another. His powerful jaws snapped bones and his fangs shredded their flesh.

Trolls fell over one another in an attempt to escape the awful beast. And as they fell back, a way opened before TamSen and he suddenly found himself looking directly into the glowing eyes of several demi-demons. The demi-demons towered over him like a wall of black hatred. For the first time, TamSen paused.

One of the demi-demons brought its gigantic fists up into the air above TamSen's head. It reared backward, ready to bring its fists down when it abruptly froze in mid-motion. The demon leaned forward and squinted its eyes at a fiery scene taking place across the cavern. Maelfesh! Maelfesh was once again hovering above the action!

The demon opened its arms wide, shook both fists in the air and howled a sound of pure, unadulterated hatred, unmindful of the arrows striking its body, the spears bouncing off its thick hide, never mind the huge werewolf biting at its leg. None of that mattered now.

The demon began to stride across the cavern, its eyes fixed on its fiery goal. It waded through the masses of trolls and dwarves locked in mortal combat, dragging the werewolf at every step.

Its howl of hatred attracted the remaining demi-demons and they too saw Maelfesh and began fighting their way toward him. Aside from the demi-demons, Maelfesh was having other problems as well. Dealing with Korlim had not turned out to be the simple matter he had assumed it would be; with the added power of both magic gems, the dwarven wizard was very nearly his equal. They were engaged in an incredible duel of fire and magic.

What made matters even worse was the addition of the young dwarf at Korlim's side, the one who had been swallowed by the pillar years before in an abortive attempt to rescue those trapped within its depths. This dwarf was a nuisance, no more than a gnat really, a bother, a distraction. But every time Maelfesh attempted to swat him out of the way, Korlim used the opportunity to attack. Now the upstart was throwing rocks at him! Of all the indignities!

Bijel continued his furious assault, adding a tirade of insults and taunts. He threw more rocks. He scooped up water from the cavern floor and spewed it at Maelfesh. He even jumped up and down and made faces. Then, he pointed at Maelfesh and laughed out loud, making obscene comments about the temperature of his private parts. Strangely enough, even though Bijel could not actually hurt the demon, his antics were taking their toll on Maelfesh's concentration. It was this very lack of concentration that was to prove his downfall.

As strong as Korlim had become, he was still no match for Maelfesh's experience and cunning. But Korlim had created a universe in his mind wherein Maelfesh would be defeated; and this served him in good stead. Maelfesh was now so intent on his battle with Korlim and the annoying gnat that he was totally unaware of the approach of the pack of remaining demi-demons from behind.

The demi-demons hated everything that lived, but above all else, they hated Maelfesh. It was Maelfesh who had put them in the Pit of Undying Hatred. It was he who had left them there for centuries. It was he who had turned their hatred against all of existence. It was he for whom their hatred burned the brightest.

With a suddenness that took even Korlim by surprise, the demi-demons grabbed Maelfesh from behind, whirled him around to face them and then began to tear at him.

His flames twisted around them, searing their skin and licking around their limbs. Their skin burned, then bubbled and melted, revealing the flesh and corded muscle beneath. But still they clung to him and tore at his head and his arms, his legs and his torso. Maelfesh lashed out at them with flames of greater intensity, but no matter what he did, their hatred drove them on. They would not release him to save themselves.

Korlim, afraid that the flames would overwhelm them before they were able to cause him some real damage, called forth a sheet of never-ending water and directed it at Maelfesh.

Maelfesh, genuinely worried for the first time in centuries, struggled to break free long enough to say the spell that would send the demi-demons back to the Pit of Undying Hatred. He pulled his head loose and spat out the words to half of the spell. A demi-demon, its mouth bared in a black grimace of unquenched hatred, jammed its fist in Maelfesh's fiery mouth just as Maelfesh uttered the final words. Then the curtain of falling water struck.

Suddenly the demi-demons were gone, banished once more to their bottomless pit. Maelfesh lay on the ground in a pool of water, his flames extinguished by the continuing stream of water. For the first time, he could be seen as he really was. He was ugly! His skin hung from him in folds, gray and sickly. His features were that of an old, old man who had lived long past his time. His mouth hung slack and his chin was all but non-existent. He attempted to cover his spindly shanks and the loose flap of chin that hung down from his pot belly with thin withered hands, to protect them from the continuous fall of water.

Korlim raised his hand again, but then, the dwarf wizard sagged and crumpled to the ground, his energy all but drained away at last by the demands of the great battle.

The flow of water ceased. Maelfesh struggled up onto one elbow, his lips pulled back in a grin to reveal toothless gums. He slowly raised a bony hand, pointed it at Korlim and began to chant.

He never finished the words. A streak of gray flew through the air, landed on top of the old man that was Maelfesh and seized his throat with gleaming fangs. Maelfesh's hand rose weakly as he realized too late what had happened; then, it was done. His hand fell back upon the ground and the great wolf rose with the demon's throat clutched in his bloody jaws. He turned and glared at those who stood watching him in dazed horror, growling as though daring them to touch his trophy. Then, TamSen turned and skulked off into the darkness.

Two or three heartbeats passed in total silence before anyone stirred. No one wanted to fight any more. The battle was over. Suddenly, there was a sound of giggling and two large disheveled figures appeared in the passageway that led to the side room that had contained the Pillar of the Demon Hand.

"What's all the racket?" asked Hornsbuck and suddenly, much to Hornsbuck and Lotus's amazement, everyone, dwarves, humans, harpies, wizards and trolls alike, burst into laughter.

Chapter 33

ISLAND TROLLS ARE NOT REALLY what you would call stupid, just very, very slow. Given enough time, they can comprehend almost anything. So when several of the more dense trolls tried to resume their slaughter of the dwarves, Giebort ordered the dwarves to protect themselves but to break off the attack. One and all began to chant, "Maelfesh is dead!" over and over. Slowly, the Island Trolls realized that there was no longer a need for war.

An uneasy truce encompassed troll and dwarf as the clean-up began. Slowly regaining his strength, Korlim placed a sedative spell over all to prevent further hostilities. Next, he tottered over to the grisly remains of Maelfesh's body and using a platoon of Giebort's men, directed that the body be cut into a hundred different bits and each of the body fragments buried long distances from the others with a holy relic pressed deep into the flesh. He knew that Maelfesh was not really *dead*, for demons do not die so easily. But he was gone from the Oerth and had been banished to a lowly plane of existence where hopefully it would take many, many centuries of effort before he rose to a position high enough to cause them any problems again.

As the dwarves and trolls moved among the survivors, they counted the dead, and only then did the full extent of their losses become apparent. Of the ten thousand Island Trolls, less than a thousand remained alive. Of the nine hundred dwarves, 453 were alive and only a handful had escaped without any form of injury.

There were many problems to be faced in the near future, but for now, there were the wounded and the dead to be cared for.

Mika was having problems of his own. Now that the battle was done, he was faced with one angry she-wolf, one that had no intention of being put off even as much as one heartbeat longer.

"So, is this the fabled magical stone then?" Hornsbuck asked in a deep rumble, looking at the stone that Mika still clasped in his hand. Strangely enough, with the passage of the demon, Mika's hand had not returned to normal but retained its demon form.

"Yes, it must be," replied Mika, looking into its red-blue depths. "And I know it's time." And without even thinking, the correct spell just popped into his mind with a simplicity and ease that embarrassed him. I can't let it look this easy, he thought to himself. She'll never believe that I couldn't have done it long before. She'll think that I kept her a wolf on purpose. She'll kill me!" Thinking quickly, he decided that it was necessary to stage a big production to convince the princess of the spell's difficulty.

Mika took three stones and placed them in a triangle around the princess. She ceased growling and began to take an interest in what he was doing. She wanted to help. She would do anything to return to human form.

"Stay right there," said Mika and then he directed the others to follow him as he began to walk around the princess in a clockwise direction. He made some motions with his hands that made no sense to anyone including Korlim who was looking on with a bemused expression on his face. Mika then touched his magic stone to the princess's forehead, hoping that the theatrics had been sufficient as he uttered the words to the ridiculously simple spell. The last word of the spell was followed by a soft "poof," and a dazzlingly beautiful human woman stood inside the circle of stones.

Everyone cheered. Mika had finally succeeded! And then, all eyes turned to gawk at the princess. An embarrassed hush fell and their eyes swiveled away, searching for somewhere else to look, for the princess was quite naked.

The princess looked down at her hands, her human hands. She looked down at her arms, her human arms. Then she looked down at her naked body, her naked human body, and then up at the circle of embarrassed onlookers. She was naked! Naked in front of them all! Her fury began to rise and she all but flung herself at Mika, ready to kill him once more.

Lotus Blossom laughed, a boisterous, good-natured guffaw, and reached over and grabbed the princess by her arm. She dragged her back into the passageway, chuckling. "Don't you pay them men no mind, lady. It don't matter none. If the gods had wanted women to keep everything covered, he woulda' borned them with three hands. C'mon with me. Hornsbuck won't never no mind ifn' I shed some of these here clothes. We'll go back here an divy up what I'm wearin'."

TamTur watched them go, crying low and soft in his throat, but Hornsbuck gave a decidedly Wolf-Nomadic snort and grin, and elbowed Mika hard enough to knock him off balance. "You sure know how to pick 'em," he said. "Feisty wench, too." Hornsbuck pointed to Chewppa then, who continued hovering in wide-eyed admiration over her father, the great wizard. "That un's just as pretty as the other. Well, from the waist up, that is!"

Chewppa was still all but overwhelmed by what she had just witnessed. As she watched the princess walk off with Lotus Blossom, a look of stubborn resolve came over her features. She turned to Mika and grabbed him by the arm, all but spinning him around to face her.

"Me too!" she cried. "Change me! Make me so I never harpy again! Make me beautiful woman for TamSen!"

"Yeah, Mika!" added Hornsbuck with a leer. "Do it again! Change her too! I want to see that trick a second time!"

"No, Chewppa!" cried a voice from out of the darkness; and Mika was spared the decision. TamSen emerged from the shadows, himself once more, the specter of the wolf gone for yet another turning of the moon.

"TamSen! I want be beautiful for you!" Chewppa cried. "I want you love me forevers!"

"Chewppa, I will always love you. I love you now, just the way you are and I don't want you to change. Please, please stay the way you are." And Chewppa saw the love in his eyes and knew that he spoke the truth. Their arms circled each other and Chewppa's wings rose up around them as they embraced and shielded them from the eyes of others.

Korlim had recovered to some small degree and, although he was still weak, he was addressing himself to the problems of his people. Carried on a litter by two dwarves, he cast healing spells on those dwarves and trolls who could be saved. And in the instances where a healing spell would be of no use, he cast a spell of sleep so the fighter could die in peace.

After the battlefield had been brought to order, Korlim directed the litter to the place where the humans stood. He was introduced to Mika-oba formally, following the elaborate procedure required between two fellow wizards.

Korlim explained all that had gone before to Mika and Hornsbuck, about how the magical blue and red gems worked when combined, enhancing one's abilities and were capable of turning even the most normal of men into people of power.

Mika interrupted to ask about the effects on a man if he used a blue or female stone. Wouldn't it turn him into a woman? Korlim looked at Mika in disbelief, wondering if he were perhaps jesting. But Mika remained serious, worried about the great length of time he had used the blue stone and its possible effects on his manhood.

"There is no truth to the matter at all," replied Korlim, seeing that Mika was indeed troubled by the matter. "One stone is as effective as the other and will in no way affect you adversely."

Mika looked down at the magic gem, thinking back on all the times of worry caused by that night in Jayne's bar when first he had heard that tale. Now he wondered at the source of that disquieting gossip and knew that Maelfesh was behind it in some unknown manner. Anger vied with relief and relief won.

Only one thing was left out of Korlim's telling, the story of TamSen's stone. When TamSen would have spoken, Korlim signaled him to silence. For the time being, it would remain their secret.

In the time that followed, as they made their way back to DwarvenHome, all of those who had been imprisoned in the pillar found it in their hearts to forgive Mika. After all, he had merely been in the lead on that fateful day. In truth, Mika had not forced them to follow him, they had done so of their own volition and so, they had to accept a fair portion of the blame themselves.

The Princess Julia, newly draped in one of Lotus Blossom's blouses, which covered her like sackcloth down to her knees, had gone so far as to be pleasant to Mika, although she still seemed to prefer the company of TamTur, the father of her children. TamSen had found favor in her eyes, although the idea of having a son her own age took some getting used to. TamSen had no such problems and was happier than he had ever been with a mother and a father (albeit a wolf) as well as a woman of his own (albeit a harpy) to love and love him in return.

302

Not to be outdone, Mika and Chewppa grew very close. Mika developed such an overwhelmingly strong sense of fatherly pride, pointing out every single thing she did to Hornsbuck and Lotus, that they soon learned to avoid him when he was in this mood. And thanks to the magic stone, he was able to uphold Chewppa's image of him as the world's most fantastical, wonderful wizard.

Chapter 34

UPON THEIR RETURN to DwarvenHome, Gaieliah gave Giebort a hero's welcome that kept him out of sight for days. Other families were unable to share her joy and mourned the loss of loved ones, but each slain fighter was given the highest honors of the Suloisian dwarves. They had died to free their people from the oppression of evil; they had not died in vain.

During the journey home, Korlim had spoken to Princess Julia about the contract on DwarvenHome. A pact was quickly formed. Upon her coronation as Queen of Dramidja, the contract would be rewritten.

It was decided that no more gemstones would be mined, except for the dwarves' and the Queen's own use. To empty the mine of its precious gems would be to render them as common and without value on Oerth, even as had happened in DwarvenHome.

It was now winter in the world above and the princess had much to learn about the events of the past twenty years. It was decided they would remain in DwarvenHome until the following equinox to prepare for the journey above-ground. By then the princess would have a full understanding of the world above and other plans could be made as well.

There was still much to be done in DwarvenHome which was, after all, part of her kingdom. There was still the matter of the Island Trolls to be resolved; something had to be done to ensure that there would be no more fighting between dwarf and troll.

Trolls were known to be fierce, unintelligent killing machines. But these trolls had lived on their island in isolation and peace for so long that they had developed separately and were unlike trolls elsewhere. Their history had been one of peace before the Oerth king descended upon them and slaughtered them in great numbers; and before they had been sealed up in the walls of the cavern.

Long conversations with the trolls revealed the startling fact that they preferred to live in peace. They spoke of their fascination with the beautiful cavern and voiced a wish that they could be allowed to live underground in harmony with the dwarves. Korlim and Julia gave them their permission, and dwarves and trolls set about constructing homes in the cavern, which the trolls named "NewHome."

At a victory celebration, Korlim announced that he would no longer be their wizard. It was his intent to spend his remaining years teaching all his knowledge to his son, Bijel. No one was happier to hear of this decision than Malklun, Korlim's assistant. The job had been thrust on him once Bij had disappeared into the pillar. He was delighted to return the post to Korlim's son and heir.

Bij was overjoyed. Now he could swashbuckle

through the world on grand adventures! And so began the colorful life of the Mage Bij, the wildest wizard in the history of Oerth. But that is a story for another day.

And now, only one matter remained unresolved, of those matters that Korlim had any intention of speaking of: the matter of the lineage of dwarves.

"We are the educated ones," he confided to the princess. "The ones who have risen above the common dwarf. Forgive an old man if he sounds snobbish, my dear, but the dwarves of the Yeomanry are generally an unruly lot. They tend toward lawlessness and drink. That was, of course, more than four hundred years ago. However, I seriously doubt that much has changed. We may even have a new king, of whom we know nothing. We must send someone to Yeomanry to learn the situation. I fear what the future would be if thousands of dwarves were to suddenly appear in DwarvenHome and learn of our riches. Besides, the emerald throne was destroyed by Maelfesh and it may take years for us to cut another . . . if you know what I mean."

The princess knew exactly what he meant. If the world were to learn of the riches that lay buried beneath her small kingdom, her empire would soon be overrun with every cutthroat and thief on Oerth. She and Korlim smiled at each other, their understanding complete.

Chapter 35

THEIR FAREWELLS SAID, the long journey to the surface was begun, accompanied by Giebort and a full complement of his men heavily loaded with provisions.

The Princess Julia allowed no magic gemstones to be taken out of DwarvenHome other than those worn by Mika and Chewppa, and the dull, drab stone that Korlim had given TamSen.

The journey itself was long and uneventful, and it was with great joy when at last they found themselves standing on the stairs at the base of the throne. Giebort followed Korlim's instructions, and as the base rumbled aside, he and his men fell back into the shadows, whispered their farewells, and were gone, back into the darkness from which they had come.

TamSen had wondered at the fact that none but Korlim and Bijel had chosen to come with them, but Korlim explained that it was the consensus of most of the dwarves that they actually preferred living underground. The fact that they had been *forbidden* to return to the surface had played heavily on their minds. Julia and Korlim decided that the dwarves' part of the story would be completely excluded from any tales told. The fewer people who knew of their presence, and that of the gems, the better.

Quotar's son, Shmerk was standing in his pasture tending sheep, when the ancient throne began to move backward. He stared in open-mouthed amazement as a pair of wolves emerged from the black hole. Next came TamSen, who did not look the least bit dead. Hard on TamSen's heels came a whole crowd of people whom Shmerk did not recognize, with the single exception of the harpy.

Shmerk soon recovered his wits and ran down the hill bleating out his news. In no time at all, they were surrounded by crowds of people, exclaiming over the amazing return of TamSen and the long-missing princess.

Before long, the news had spread throughout the town, even to the home where TamLis lived while waiting for the new castle to be built. At first, TamLis could not believe what she was being told but then she followed the crowds and saw that indeed it was true.

TamSen hugged TamLis and half-heartedly apologized for his absence, not really understanding the pain that he had caused her. His joy was so obvious, his love for Chewppa so apparent, as was the fact that he had not really missed her at all, that TamLis's heart clenched itself into a hard knot.

Nor did Chewppa improve matters between the twins. It mattered not to Chewppa that TamLis was TamSen's sister. She was a woman and she had thrown her arms around him and held him tight.

That was enough for Chewppa. As TamSen introduced the two women to each other, they smiled coldly under his unseeing eyes, and silently declared their enmity.

TamLis was all but forgotten by everyone, with the exception of the loyal and loving Tallo.

The princess took control of the city within hours of entering its boundaries and was soon busy with plans to restore it to its former power.

The festivities for crowning TamLis continued and expanded, becoming even more grand. The only difference being that it was Julia who was to be crowned, rather than TamLis.

This, as well as the fact that Julia had wrinkled her nose at TamLis and given her but the most perfunctory of greetings, did not sit well with TamLis. She had tried to understand, but a lifetime of deprivation had risen up and stuck in her throat, making it all but impossible to bend her knee and suddenly give over her loyalty and love to this young woman who was singlehandedly destroying her life.

The merchants were unhappy, as well. They soon learned that they would never be able to control the Princess Julia, who was quicker by far than they and twice as sly. She abolished their council and reduced their own sense of importance to dust. Needless to say, they took every opportunity to whisper their support to TamLis.

On the day before the coronation was to occur, TamSen received a note from TamLis. It read:

Dear brother,

Forgive me, but I cannot bear to step aside and watch what was to be my throne taken from me by my mother. You and I are the heirs to the throne, not our mother. She did not age a single day while she was trapped in the pillar. She is no older than we and will live as long. We will never have the throne, even if we wait our entire lives.

It is not fair, TamSen. Where was she all those long, lonely years when we needed her? She does not love us, nor will she ever. She is no mother to me, but a stranger, and I do not accept her claim to my heart any more than I accept her claim to the throne.

Tallo and I have gone in search of allies who will support our cause. We will return, and when we do, the throne will be ours!

Your ever-loving sister,

TamLis

It was many years before TamLis and Tallo were heard from again.

Julia became Queen of the Island of Dramidja. She ruled wisely and well and loved her son and his wife with all her heart.

Hornsbuck and Lotus Blossom were amply rewarded for their part in her rescue and decided, after some soul-searching, to settle down in Dramidja and open a waterfront pub that specialized in spirits and victuals. It suited them well and they prospered.

Korlim, Chewppa and, for a time, Mika, formed the historic Great Circle of Wizards, which became legendary in the history of Oerth. Bij attended the circle as well, for he would one day inherit his father's stone. TamSen was included also, for it was discovered that he had great powers of his own, although the reasons for this would not be learned for many years.

Mika's hand had, for some unknown reason, retained its demon form. For a time, he considered changing it, with his newly developed powers, back into a human hand. But he had become strangely fond of it, hideous as it was. He could count on it to draw attention in any circle. Men bought him drinks in order to hear the tale, and he won every arm wrestling contest that he entered, even besting the powerful Lotus Blossom.

He could always depend on the hand to grab a beautiful woman on some portion of her anatomy that normal manners forbade. Such outrageous behavior never failed to serve as an introduction and his apologetic manner as he told his sad tale, all the while squeezing and caressing, usually gained him a sympathetic listener, who generally fell under his charms.

Aside from these little pleasantries, Mika was offered the position of Grand Wizard by the queen, who was forced to acknowledge her debt to him and wished to settle it once and for all. But it was a strange relationship, one that still crackled with the tension between them. This was coupled with the strangeness that TamTur felt, seeing she who had been his mate returned to her human form. All in all, it was an untenable situation, and one sunny summer day, TamTur and Mika left the Island of Dramidja with full purses and heavy hearts, having said their goodbyes to those whom they loved.

The dwarves and the trolls continued to live in peace and anonymity beneath the island for years to come until the day that TamLis and Tallo returned with an army of Yeomanry dwarves and began the Oerik-TamLian Wars. But that, as they say, is a story for another time, about another age, in the history of the land of Greyhawk.

ABOUT THE AUTHOR

ROSE ESTES has lived in Chicago, Houston, Mexico, and Canada, in a driftwood house on an island, a log cabin in the mountains, and a broken Volkswagon van under a viaduct.

At present she is sharing her life with an eccentric game designer/cartoonist, three children, one slightly demented dog, and a pride of occasionally domestic cats.

Other books written by Ms. Estes include nine of TSR, Inc.'s ENDLESS QUEST® series of books, as well as *Children of the Dragon* and *The Turkish Tattoo* published by Random House, and *Blood of the Tiger* from Bantam.

She began her GREYHAWK™ trilogy of Mika-oba, Shaman of the Wolf Nomads, with the best-selling *Master Wolf*, and continued with *Price of Power* and *The Demon Hand*, all from TSR, Inc.

New From the Creators of the DRAGONLANCE® Saga in 1988

THE  NOVELS!

THE CRYSTAL SHARD
by R.A. Salvatore

Second in the series of fantastical FORGOTTEN REALMS™ novels, *The Crystal Shard*, written by R.A. Salvatore, tells the saga of the people of Ten-Towns, led by the mighty warrior Wulfgar, and their epic struggle, in a harsh and pitiless land, against the relentless invasion of barbarian hordes.

On sale now!

BLACK WIZARDS
by Douglas Niles

The sequel to Douglas Niles's thrilling *Darkwalker On Moonshae*, which placed on The New York Times best-seller list, *Black Wizards* picks up the story of the troubled heir to the legacy of the High Kings, Tristan Kendrick, and Robyn, his druid-companion. When the Prince of Corwell departs on a blood quest, his journey is interrupted by the vision of a long-dead queen who rises mysteriously from the sea, challenging Tristan with an obscure prophecy that tells of his destiny. Meanwhile, back on the Moonshae Isles, the Black Wizards plot Tristan's downfall, and once again threaten the peace of the Ffolk . . .

On sale in May!

FROM THE CREATORS OF
THE DRAGONLANCE® SAGA

LEAVES FROM THE INN OF THE LAST HOME

Compiled by Tika and Caramon Majere, Proprietors

"The Complete Krynn Source Book," as edited by
DRAGONLANCE authors Margaret Weis and Tracy Hickman, brings together for the first time all the poetry, songs,
recipes, maps, journals, legends, lost manuscripts, scholarly
essays, time-line chronology, herbalism, numerology, runology, and artifacts of Krynn, in one loving and lavish catalogue that is a must for devoted readers of the
DRAGONLANCE saga.
Available now!

THE ART OF THE DRAGONLANCE® SAGA

Edited by Mary Kirchoff

Collector's edition of new and previously published
sketches and full-color paintings of the DRAGONLANCE
saga as depicted by TSR's well-known staff of artists and
other superb illustrators. Interviews with the series authors,
Margaret Weis and Tracy Hickman, and the TSR artists,
illuminate the creative process behind the magnificent visual
interpretation of this fantasy classic.
Available now!

THE ATLAS OF THE DRAGONLANCE® SAGA

by Karen Wynn Fonstad

A complete atlas by a noted cartographer detailing the
lands and places of the DRAGONLANCE® novel and game
saga. Including extensive maps and descriptions of the world
of Krynn, as created by Margaret Weis and Tracy Hickman.
A unique and comprehensive gift book for serious fans of the
DRAGONLANCE® fantasy series.
Available now!

FROM THE CREATORS OF
THE DRAGONLANCE® SAGA

DRAGONLANCE TALES, VOL. I:
THE MAGIC OF KRYNN

First in the series of short-story collections set in the popular world of the DRAGONLANCE® saga, as edited by Margaret Weis and Tracy Hickman. Seven weeks on The New York Times' list of paperback best-sellers, this volume boasts sea monsters, dark elves, ice bears, hideous, hydra-headed serpents, loathsome draconian troops, and all the familiar companions. The acclaimed new novella by Weis and Hickman gazes into the future of Caramon and his mage son, and into the dark nether-past of Raistlin.

Available now!

DRAGONLANCE TALES, VOL. II:
KENDER, GULLY DWARVES, AND GNOMES

Second in the series of short story collections, as edited by Margaret Weis and Tracy Hickman, spotlights the fascinating other-worldly creatures of Krynn—with untold tales about the irrepressible kender, gully dwarves, gnomes, and other minor races. Includes short story contributions by some of America's finest young fantasy writers and a fascinating new novella by Weis and Hickman chronicling the new generation of heroes!

Available now!

DRAGONLANCE TALES, VOL. III:
LOVE AND WAR

Third in the series of short story collections, as edited by Margaret Weis and Tracy Hickman, recounting DRAGONLANCE® tales of heroism and romance, of noble sacrifice and doomed friendship, of conquest and endearment. This volume of fresh Krynn lore by a group of TSR writers will be capped by "Raistlin's Daughter," a powerful new novella that will open yet another chapter in the life of the series' most complex and extraordinary character, Raistlin, the sickly mage-scholar.

Available now!